"Lord Lacey, I have a proposal to make."

"What sort of proposal?"

"A marriage proposal."

"Miss Monteith, do you know what they call me? Wicked Nic. Do you understand *why* they call me that?"

"I believe because you are a rake, my lord. That is immaterial."

He stood up, looming over her so that she had to stretch back her neck to meet his eyes.

"It is not immaterial. Women like you do not marry men like me."

"I didn't think you were such a prude," Lucy said.

"There are some rules that even I prefer not to tamper with."

SARA BENNETT

Led Astray By A Rake

THE HUSBAND HUNTERS CLUB

AVON

An Imprint of HarperCollinsPublishers

AVON BOOKS
An Imprint of HarperCollins*Publishers*
10 East 53rd Street
New York, New York 10022-5299

Copyright © 2009 by Sara Bennett
ISBN 978-0-06-133691-1
www.avonromance.com

First Avon Books paperback printing: June 2009

Avon Trademark Reg. U.S. Pat. Off. and in Other Countries, Marca Registrada, Hecho en U.S.A.
HarperCollins® is a registered trademark of HarperCollins Publishers.

Printed in the U.S.A.

10 9 8 7 6 5 4 3 2 1

This book comes with a thank-you to my friends, writing and nonwriting, who keep me sane when times are tough, and who put up with long silences on my part while I'm writing. This one is for you!

Led Astray By A Rake

Prologue

Miss Debenham's Finishing School
Graduating Ball of 1837

The ballroom was a kaleidoscope of color. Young girls and their families and friends, the staff of the finishing school and its supporters, and a sprinkling of local dignitaries, all in their finery and vying for attention. The girls in particular were dressed to be admired, because these were Miss Debenham's latest crop of respectable and refined young ladies, ready to be set, like jewels, before the country's eligible bachelors in the hope that those gentlemen would be dazzled into proposing marriage to them.

That was the object of the exercise, after all. That was why the families had spent good money to send their daughters to Miss Debenham's Finishing School: to procure a good marriage. The school was renowned for it, and Miss Debenham was known to trot out the names of some of the highest in the land and claim them as her own successes.

Miss Olivia Monteith knew very well what was meant by "a good marriage." Financial security, respectability, maybe even a title and the chance to raise herself and her family into the aristocracy. Marriage was like any other legally binding contract, written in language that was cold and precise. But nowhere in those close written lines was there any mention of the heart. Of love. Of happiness. Of desire.

"Miss Monteith, how do you do?"

Olivia smiled and replied to the greeting in her usual calm, cool manner, never for a moment betraying her inner agitation.

"I was speaking with your mother, Miss Monteith. She told me you will not long be a miss. Should I congratulate you?"

"No, please don't, nothing is settled . . ."

"If you say so." The smile was arch and disbelieving.

Olivia moved away, followed by the usual murmurs and stares. She was aware she had the kind of beauty that was currently much admired— fair hair and blue eyes and a porcelain complexion. Combined with English reserve and natural restraint, this caused others to believe she was devoid of emotion, almost cold.

Unfortunately for Olivia, this was very far from the truth. Beneath her cool and calm beauty beat a warm, passionate heart. In reality she was a woman who longed to seize life with both hands and live it to the full, with all its ups and downs. She wanted a husband who could share such a life with her, a man she could love wholeheartedly, and who would love her. She didn't expect perfection, she wasn't a fool, but better to be unhappy sometimes than to feel nothing. When she contemplated the future her parents planned for her she felt like a frightened child, because if she was to marry and live without emotion, then she truly would become the ice queen.

Olivia moved on through the crowded ballroom, smiling and bowing her head in acknowledgment to those who claimed her acquaintance, and all the time she was moving ever closer to her real goal. Escape. As she drew nearer to the side door, her heart began to beat harder and she found it difficult to breathe, although no one who did not know her well would ever have guessed her feelings from her demeanor.

She reached the door and slid out into the shadowy corridor, closing it softly behind her. At once the noise was muffled, and the air was blessedly cool against her flushed cheeks. For a moment she stood, simply enjoying being alone, and then with a laugh she picked up her white tulle skirts and began to run swiftly along the passageway in her satin slippers. One of her carefully arranged curls tumbled to her shoulder, another bounced over her eyes. She didn't stop, climbing a set of narrow stairs toward the very top of the building, and a place where only a very few of Miss Debenham's girls ever ventured.

The door at the end of a final short flight of steps was closed, but Olivia did not hesitate in opening it and entering the little room with its sloping ceiling and single small window. A candelabra covered the scene in soft light, picking out the figures seated in a circle on the floor, their beautiful dresses folded about them, their expectant faces turned to hers.

"Olivia! At last! Now we can begin."

Olivia knelt down in the space they had left for her, arranging the yards of her expensive dress about her, tucking her truant curls behind her ears. "I couldn't get away," she said, and took a deep breath, pressing a hand to her tight stays. "I had to run."

While most of Olivia's acquaintances would refuse to accept that she would ever move faster than a ladylike stroll, these were her friends, and they understood. Fondly she looked about her, knowing that here she could be herself.

Miss Clementina Smythe—Tina to her friends— loyal and sweet; Lady Averil Martindale, selfless and good; Miss Eugenie Belmont, daughter of a rackety family; and Miss Marissa Rotherhild, a bluestocking with a wicked smile. They were all of them different, but their dreams and hopes were the same.

Marissa leaned forward, her dark eyes bright. "I bring this meeting of the Husband Hunters Club to order. Who wants to state our aims? Olivia?"

"Very well." Olivia became serious. "Everyone knows a young lady must marry and marry well, but why shouldn't the young lady have a say in the matter? We five have sworn to take our fate in our own hands, and to marry the men of our choice. That is what the Husband Hunters Club is all about."

"What is our motto?" Marissa declared.

Five voices answered. "The only husband worth having is the husband you hunt yourself."

"What is our quest?"

"To find the perfect husband and to pursue him with all the feminine weapons at our disposal."

There was laughter and excitement, until Olivia's words cut through the froth like a knife. "This is our last night at Miss Debenham's."

Silence fell as the girls remembered that the time had finally come for them to leave this safe nest and put their stated plans into action.

"The rest of our lives begins now, and if we don't want to end up like poor Barbara Jones-Holt, we must fight for our future happiness," Olivia urged.

There was a silence while they all remembered Barbara Jones-Holt, another of Miss Debenham's debutantes, who had made a brilliant marriage to a duke, a man old enough to be her father. Barbara came to visit before the wedding, and her eyes were the saddest they had ever seen. Like a trapped bird that knows it has no hope of escape from its cage.

Olivia shuddered now at the memory. "Win or lose," she said, "we have to try."

From the heartfelt murmurs of agreement it was clear the others were also remembering poor Barbara.

And then Marissa gave a laugh and the atmosphere lightened. "This is the night we vowed that each of us would name our quarry," she reminded them with a wicked smile. "The names will be written down in the club book, and when we meet again in one year's time we will see who has caught the husband of her choice." She looked about her. "Who will go first? Olivia?"

Olivia leaned forward, her blue eyes shining as she met her friends' expectant gazes. "Yes, I will go first."

"Oh Olivia, tell us do, who is your perfect mate?" Tina whispered, holding in a nervous giggle.

Olivia hesitated, wondering if she dared speak aloud the dream she was carrying with her.

But Marissa was having none of it. "Tell us who it is!" she declared impatiently.

Olivia knew now was not the time to be coy, and yet the name on her lips felt dangerous and risqué, and her cheeks grew hot again as she spoke: "I want to marry Lord Dominic Lacey."

"Wicked Nic?" Tina squeaked loudly, while the reactions of the others ranged from amazement to dismay. Of course, they had all heard of Wicked Nic Lacey.

"He is very handsome," unshockable Marissa said thoughtfully, "but then most rakes are. It goes with the nature of the beast." She tilted her head to one side as she observed Olivia. "But I think there must be more to your wanting to marry him than his face."

"Yes. There is." Her cool demeanor was disturbed, as if a ripple passed over her surface, giving a glimpse of the passion within. The real Olivia Monteith. She smiled, her eyes gleaming with humor and the ability to find something amusing in even dire circumstances, a trait she took great care to keep hidden from all but her closest friends. English society did not appreciate levity in its young ladies.

"When I was ten years old Lord Lacey promised to marry me, and since then I've never met another man I liked half as much."

Appreciative laughter, and Lady Averil gave a mischievous grin. "If anyone can tame Wicked Nic, then I believe it is you, Olivia."

"And after all, a promise is a promise," agreed Tina, "even if you were only ten."

Eugenie produced a bottle of champagne with a flourish. "Compliments of Miss Debenham's!" Eagerly glasses were held out as she poured the sparkling liquid. "Let us make a toast," she said.

"To the Husband Hunters Club!"

Their voices lifted with their glasses, while below in the ballroom the graduation went on, the guests and families all innocently unaware that their worlds were about to be turned topsy-turvy.

Chapter 1

Two weeks later, in Hampshire

Olivia held her hands tightly folded at her waist, refusing to fidget. She was not a fidgeting sort of girl, but right now she would have loved to straighten her sleeves or pat at her hair or twitch her skirts. The walk to Castle Lacey, rather than calming her, had only given her more time to worry.

What if he rejected her?

She'd known Lord Lacey all her life, and had called him a friend for most of those years, albeit a secret friend. Until three years ago they'd met now and again to chat—a habit that was formed when Olivia's sister died—and he'd seemed to genuinely care about her. Yes, he'd thought of her as a child, and if he noticed the stars in her eyes when she looked at him, he pretended he didn't. The very fact of the secrecy—innocent though their meetings were—made their meetings more special, and knowing that her parents would have been horrified if they knew what she was doing gave them an extra deliciously dangerous quality.

The Monteiths and the Laceys had lived in the same village for centuries, but that did not make them socially compatible. The wealthy Monteiths had risen from humble country folk to country gentry, and were keen to rise further. The Laceys were aristocrats, blue bloods, and aloof—although what they had to be so proud about Olivia had never been able to fathom. Yes, they did live in a castle, but it was large and drafty and reputedly cost them a fortune. Yes, their name was tangled up with kings and queens and the more important dates in British history, but being mentioned in history books meant they were cunning enough to be on the winning side, not that they were brave or particularly loyal.

Setting aside Wicked Nic's reputation, and apart from the social differences, the match would be a good one. Entirely suitable. Perfect in fact. With the Monteith fortune and new blood, and the Lacey lands and old blood, the two families would combine forces.

Not, she reminded herself, that the suitability or otherwise of the alliance of their families was what had brought her to Castle Lacey this morning. Not directly, anyway. The Laceys would mean nothing to her if it wasn't for the identity of the current heir. Rake and wastrel, the sort of man respectable mothers warned their daughters about, and respectable men secretly envied. The sort of man women sighed over and longed to tame, even knowing they'd more than likely end up brokenhearted.

Lord Dominic Lacey was known far and wide as Wicked Nic for good reason.

But the respectable Miss Olivia Monteith didn't entirely agree. Over the years she'd seen a very different Wicked Nic, a man capable of great kindness, a man who would make a good husband, and she was determined to have and hold him, from this day forward, till death did them part.

Lord Dominic Lacey dipped his pen into the ink pot and tried to pretend his leg wasn't hurting like the devil. Usually that grinding ache meant a change in the weather, but outside his windows the sky was a cheerful blue and the birds were singing maniacally.

He paused to admire the walled garden, reaching down to try to rub some of the pain away. The broken bone had never healed properly—he hadn't sought treatment until it was too late, and this had been the result. He supposed his mother would say he'd had his just deserts for all the chaos he'd caused; a self-inflicted punishment. He knew that in his heart he believed her to be right.

The tap on the door turned his thoughts away from a past he preferred to forget, and gratefully he looked up as it opened. Abbot, his manservant, valet, and—although neither of them would admit it or overstep the social boundaries—his friend, stood watching him with keen gray eyes.

"My lord. There is a visitor come to see you."

"A visitor? What sort of visitor?" Nic threw down his pen, the estate books forgotten.

"A very attractive young lady visitor," Abbot replied, with a smile that creased the lines about his eyes. Although he was only ten years Nic's senior, Abbot's hair was almost entirely gray.

Nic was genuinely surprised. "Surely she's not here alone? No attractive young lady would dare come visiting me alone. I might lose control and ravish them."

Abbot snorted.

"At least, that is what they think."

"Or hope," Abbot said wryly. "What will I do with her? Send her away?"

"No, don't do that. I want to see this brave and attractive young lady. Show her into the parlor. Do you think tea . . . ? Or something stronger?"

"Tea, my lord, definitely tea."

Nic nodded. "Tea it is then. Oh, and Abbot, does this brave and beautiful young lady have a name?"

But Abbot, by error or design, had already closed the door.

Olivia sat straight-backed on the very edge of the chair. Her bonnet was set at a jaunty angle, the feather curled just so, and her dark blue dress flattered her, and was perfectly suited to a morning visit. She felt confident, which was just as well because she needed all the confidence she could muster. She might appear to be her usual calm self, but beneath her serene exterior was a maelstrom of turbulent emotions.

Her anxious state wasn't just because she was about to put a marriage proposal to Wicked Nic Lacey. There was the additional worry that since she'd come home her parents had been putting increased pressure upon her to marry Mr. Garsed, their choice of a suitable husband. Try as she might to hold firm against them, they were beginning to wear her down.

Mr. Garsed was handsome and rich, and if he was vain about his appearance, there were worse faults in a man. He would look after her and spoil her, basking in her beauty and good taste and her suitability as his wife. And—the main reason for her parents' eagerness for the match—his home was on the other side of the village, which meant that apart from occasional visits to London, it would be as if she had never left them. Her life would hardly change.

She loved her parents dearly and she understood their anxiety to have her close, but such a tame, mundane existence wasn't what Olivia wanted at all.

Where were the passion and the excitement? Where were the racing pulse and pounding heart and desperate longing? Mr. Garsed inspired none of these things in her, and she knew he never would. If Olivia married him she would wither away within the year, and become a shell of the vibrant girl she was now. She must fight to prevent it; she must find the courage to reach out for what she wanted.

The door opened and a gentleman entered.

Tall, broad-shouldered, his dark hair a little shaggy, his features saturnine, and his dark eyes deep-set, he was staring back at her boldly, rudely, and when he didn't speak she was obliged to stand up and hold out her gloved hand.

"Lord Lacey, how do you do?" she said politely, showing him how it was done.

"Good God." He took her hand in a hard, warm grip. "It's Miss Monteith."

Well, he remembered her. That was a start.

"What can I do to help you, Miss Monteith?"

He still held her hand, and as he raked his gaze over every inch of her, not restrained by any idea of impoliteness or impropriety, his eyes were lit by a spark deep within. Olivia knew this was one of the reasons she liked him so much. He was so different from everyone else she knew. Wicked Nic said and did exactly as he liked, and the rest be damned. It must be very restful not to feel compelled to mouth meaningless platitudes and offer compliments you didn't mean. It must be very liberating.

"We are neighbors, Lord Lacey. Do I need a reason to call on you?"

His smile made his rather austere face warm and handsome. "Of course you do, Miss Monteith. I'm surprised a woman as beautiful as you is allowed anywhere near a man like me. Do your parents know you're here?"

Her anger only made her seem calmer, her blue eyes cool as a frozen river, but he must have sensed something of her true feelings, because a quizzical frown drew down his thick dark brows.

"We are also friends, Lord Lacey, or at least I used to think so."

"Friends? Well, perhaps. It's been years since we met and spoke, Miss Monteith, and you are no longer a child."

"I am twenty years old, Lord Lacey, and will be of age within twelve months. I can do as I please."

"I like the sound of that but I don't believe it," he retorted. "As you please? A woman like you? You can no longer do as you please, Miss Monteith."

The silence was broken by a loud throat clearing, and a male servant entered with a tea tray. The man, shorter than Nic, and with gray hair, carried the tray to the low table in front of Olivia, and bent to set it down. His gray eyes flicked up to meet Olivia's briefly, curiously, before he straightened and turned to his master.

"Tea, my lord, as requested. Is there anything else you require?"

"No, Abbot, thank you."

The door closed behind Abbot and left them once more alone. Nic gestured at the tea things. "Will you pour?"

Happy to oblige, Olivia busied herself with the

familiar, calming ritual. She could feel him watching her intently as he sat opposite, but she ignored him, refusing to meet his dark gaze until she was ready.

He received his cup and saucer with thanks and proceeded to load the tea with sugar. "You have been away from home," he said, in that direct way she liked.

"I have been attending Miss Debenham's Finishing School in Dorset for the past year."

He smiled, leaning toward her, and she felt herself drawn like a pin to a magnet. "And are you 'finished,' Miss Monteith?"

"Most definitely, Lord Lacey."

He laughed quietly, still watching her. "So, what happens now? Will you be launched into society?" He stirred the sugar into his tea. "A woman as beautiful as you could snare a duke or an earl. A lord, at the very least—"

"A lord like you?"

He stopped stirring his tea. His smile faded. "No, not like me. Women like you do not marry men like me and live happily ever after . . ."

"Humor me. Why don't women like me marry men like you?"

"Very well, I will explain, Miss Monteith. I am a rake and you are an angel. Polite society would be appalled by such a match, and rightly so."

"I didn't realize you were a prude," Olivia said.

"There are some rules that even I prefer not to tamper with."

Olivia felt her hands begin to tremble, and set her cup hastily down on the tray. Briefly she looked away to the fireplace, to gather her words and her courage. Could she do this? Could she really? But then she remembered Mr. Garsed and what a future with him held, and she knew she could do anything in her desperate attempt to secure the marriage and the future she craved.

"Lord Lacey, I have a proposal to make to you. I hope you will listen."

He was watching her, that frown back between his brows and an oddly intent expression on his face. "What sort of proposal?"

"A marriage proposal."

He laughed. After a moment, when she didn't respond, he stopped. She saw he had begun to rub his leg, and wondered if that was the one he had broken all those years ago. When he noticed her interest he stopped, his manner a little less friendly. "I assume you will tell me why you want to marry me, Miss Monteith."

Olivia launched into her speech.

"I have practical reasons. My family is wealthy and we are neighbors. I know we are not titled, but surely in these modern times, where engineering and science and manufacturing are making men great no matter what class they originally came from, such a thing as a title can be overlooked? It is time to set aside old values and enter the new Victorian age. A marriage between us would encapsulate all that is exciting and daring. It would be a breath of fresh air in a world that has grown stale."

He seemed stunned, and it took a moment for him to reply. "Miss Monteith, do you know what they call me? Wicked Nic. Do you understand *why* they call me that?"

"I believe because you are a rake, my lord. That is immaterial."

He stood up, looming over her, so that she had to stretch back her neck to meet his eyes. "It is not immaterial. Modern times or no, society has not changed, and marriage to me would destroy your good name and your reputation. You would be blackened by me, you would be ostracized . . ." Again he frowned. "Or do you think your spotless reputation would make me pure again? Believe me, it wouldn't! You would suffer, and you would regret ever giving such a preposterous idea voice. No, Miss Monteith, I will not marry you, and I find it amazing you would ask. You are no longer a child—you should know better than to imagine there could ever be any sort of future between us."

Olivia, tired of straining her neck, stood up and faced him.

"You made a promise. Are you now breaking your word?"

"I did what?" he all but shouted.

Olivia raised an eyebrow, unshaken by his temper. "You promised to marry me."

"I don't believe you are bringing that up again after all these years."

"Ten years, to be exact. It happened where the stepping stones cross the stream. You said you would marry me when I came of age, and I accepted. I was ten years old and you were twenty-two."

He put a hand up to his eyes and rubbed them. "Good God," he muttered. "The woman is insane."

"I remember it perfectly well and I am not insane. You called me a witch."

He dropped his hand and looked at her again, once more taking in her face and figure, her hair and eyes. "You know I didn't mean it," he murmured. "I was going through a bad patch. I'd probably been drinking my father's brandy—I used to do that when I was home from Cambridge—fell asleep in the soup once or twice."

"Lord Lacey . . ."

"It was afternoon and I went for a walk and you were . . ." His mouth twitched. "You were climbing over the stream on those cursed stones."

"Stepping stones."

"Yes, well, you fell in."

"You startled me by yelling."

"I could see you were going to drown, of course I yelled."

"You frightened me and I fell in and almost did drown, except you saved me. You sat me in the sunshine until I dried and told me it was our secret and not to tell. And I said—"

"You would have to tell unless I married you, and then you would be legally obliged not to tell."

He stared at her and shook his head. "Are you sure you were only ten? No wonder I called you a witch."

"You proposed to me and I accepted."

He limped to the window, favoring his injured leg. "So you did. I was in enough trouble that summer without being accused of drowning you, Miss Monteith."

"When my sister died—" she began.

"Yes." He looked at her over his shoulder, his expression troubled. "I remember your sister."

Sarah was her older sister, her only sibling, and she had been away at school. She had caught a chill, and instead of recovering she grew weaker and sicker, and died. Nic had come upon Olivia wandering desultorily along the lane. He walked with her, leading his horse, and his soft, kind way of speaking, his generosity, were all good memories during that dreadful period of sadness. He might try and play it down, but to Olivia it meant a great deal.

"You were very kind to me."

"Kindness is a simple matter, Miss Monteith. It means nothing."

"We began to meet by the stepping stones and talk. You made me laugh. There has not been much laughter at home since my sister died, and our meetings were something I looked forward to."

He rubbed a hand over his face. "It was all perfectly innocent, but imagine what it would do to my reputation if it became known I was playing big brother to you?"

Olivia shook her head decisively. "I never thought of you as a brother."

His eyes narrowed. "I know you didn't, Miss Monteith. I was aware you had a girlish fascination for me but I chose to ignore it. "

She felt her cheeks heat up. He knew she was in love with him all these years and he "chose to ignore it"? "You used to call me Livy."

His shoulders shook with laughter. "Then you can't possibly marry me. 'Livy Lacey'? What self-respecting woman would lumber herself with a name like that?" His smile faded and he grew serious again. "Come now, Miss Monteith, be sensible; you know such a proposal is not binding. You were a child and I a fool. You can't hold me to something like that. You would be a laughingstock if you tried."

"Perhaps, but I still want to marry you. I am quite serious."

Impatiently he pushed his hair out of his dark eyes. "So I see. You are a beautiful woman. You could have your pick of men. I don't understand why you have chosen me."

Because, she thought, *you are everything I want in life.*

"Will you agree?" she insisted.

He hesitated, and she thought for a moment she'd won, and then his gaze slid over her again and he smiled with regret. "You're grown up. And as much as I would like to have the pleasure of your presence in my bed every night, Olivia, I have to say no, I will not marry you."

She thought of arguing, of pleading, but in the end she decided whining would not further her course, and she should leave it there. For now. The matter had been set in train and that must be enough until next time. Leave him guessing. Olivia walked out of the room and did just that.

Out in the hall, Abbot, the manservant, was pretending to straighten a mirror. He turned when he saw her and hurried to open the front door for her.

"Miss Monteith, I do hope you will call again," he declared fervently.

His manner was strange, and she stopped and looked at him. "I don't think Lord Lacey wants me to call again, Abbot."

"Lord Lacey has so few visitors. He is a troubled and lonely man in need of company." He seemed to be trying to tell her something, and when she didn't answer, he spoke even more forthrightly. "Miss Monteith, you are exactly the sort of young lady he needs to have visit him more often."

Well, at least someone appreciated her, Olivia thought, as she began her walk home. But she couldn't help feeling a little down. *Did you really expect him to say yes this soon?* She must prepare herself for a long campaign rather than a swift skirmish. And surely that was the whole point of husband hunting? The more difficult the hunt, the more satisfying the happy ending.

Wicked Nic was a good man—he'd been generous and kind to her during a difficult part of her childhood—but according to his manservant, he was also a lonely man. He'd admitted he found her attractive. Perhaps it was time to bring into play some of her feminine wiles, Olivia thought, with a little smile. If cool, rational argument did not work, then an appeal to the senses might.

And Nic Lacey was a very sensual man.

Nic, shaken, bemused, and enchanted, swallowed his tea without tasting it. Olivia Monteith was a beauty, with the sort of glacial air that spoke of little emotion. Except that Nic had seen a great deal of emotion in her sapphire blue eyes. It bubbled and seethed below the tranquil surface like a volcano that might erupt at any moment.

When he had met her before, she'd been a child—amusing and charming, yes, but a child nonetheless. Three years ago he'd realized she was growing up. It was at one of their innocent little trysts when he'd seen that they must stop. It was the turn of her head that did it, the curve of her cheek, the soft pout of her lips. All of a sudden he'd seen that to continue meeting was to invite the sort of trouble he didn't want. He'd been thinking of her as a child but she was nearly seventeen, and showing promise of the woman she'd become—intriguing, delicious, and oh so tempting.

Clearly she'd now fulfilled that promise.

A hot wave of lust made him shift uncomfortably in his chair. What he wouldn't give to be the one to bring about the full transformation from virgin to woman. To have the cool and lovely Olivia Monteith squirming and panting in his arms. Could he make her scream with pleasure? He thought he could; at any rate he'd like to try.

Regretfully he set down his cup. Fantasies were all very nice, but in this case they were a waste of time and energy. Olivia was not for him, and the less he thought about her the better.

But how the devil could he have forgotten that long-ago interlude by the stream? The memory seemed idyllic now, the scents of summer and the splashing water; the child with her golden hair and dark-lashed blue eyes, and his own youthful idiocy. Later, they met as friends. How could he ever have imagined that she would demand he honor his reckless promise? Any union between them, sanctioned by the church or otherwise, was completely and utterly out of the question.

Nic had vowed long ago never to marry and place himself in the power of someone else. He'd been burned too badly by circumstance and was determined to live his life on his own terms, asking nothing and being asked for nothing in return.

Delicious as Olivia Monteith was, he would have to forgo her. There were plenty of other women available to him, the sort of women who knew exactly what he wanted—a monetary transaction for physical release and a very little conversation. Nic found himself looking forward to the approaching demimonde ball, an event he attended every year, and made a determined effort to put the tempting Olivia Monteith from his mind.

Chapter 2

O livia poured coffee, added cream, and sipped the delicious brew, her elbows impolitely propped on the table. It didn't matter. The breakfast room was empty, her father having long ago retired to his study to answer letters, and her mother was busy elsewhere about the house. Sunshine slanted in through the narrow windows.

It promised to be a fine day for her enterprise.

Olivia smiled to herself as she imagined what was to come. She'd composed the note and sent a servant to deliver it to Castle Lacey the evening before. A reply had come back with the same servant, a scrawl in Nic Lacey's hand.

What do you mean meet you by the stepping stones at two o'clock tomorrow afternoon? I do not make assignations with respectable young ladies. You say the matter is urgent. I don't believe you.

Olivia didn't answer him; silence was the best option. He might say he wasn't coming but she was certain he would. And if he didn't? Her certainty wavered, but she refused to let doubt color her optimistic mood. The Nic Lacey she believed him to be would meet her at the appointed place at the appointed time. Unless he had changed a great deal in the past three years, he wouldn't be able to resist the word "urgent."

Olivia set down her coffee cup, just as her mother entered the room, and the smile of anticipation she'd been unable to repress turned into a smile of welcome.

"My dear, *there* you are."

"I'm sorry, Mama, did you need me for something?" Olivia pushed back her chair and rose to her feet. She was taller and more slender than her mother, and her smooth face did not have the markings of grief that were deeply etched upon her mother's.

"No, nothing in particular. I just wondered where you were. I like to see you and know you are safe, Olivia. It gives me comfort."

It was the same old story. Ever since her sister had died her parents seemed to be in a constant state of anxiety and fear that something equally tragic would happen to Olivia. Her mother in particular clung to her, worried about her—it had been a battle to remain at Miss Debenham's for the whole year—and now she wanted Olivia to marry Mr. Garsed and live in the same village forever and ever. Although Olivia understood her parents' pain and loved them, she found such constant watchfulness and attention suffocating.

Life, she thought, couldn't be lived properly if one was constantly afraid of making a wrong move or believing something bad was about to happen. Olivia didn't want to be always frightened and she didn't want her parents to be always frightened for her. It didn't seem fair that her sister's death should result in her own demise. They did their best, but their insistence on taking the safe route was choking the life out of her, and Sarah wouldn't have wanted that. It was Sarah who had taught Olivia that life was for living and that one should never take second best. Olivia's family wanted her to marry Mr. Garsed, but in Olivia's eyes Mr. Garsed was very much second best.

Her mother was watching her, the familiar crease between her brows, her bottom lip caught between her teeth. "Olivia, have you thought about Mr. Garsed—"

But Olivia didn't let her finish.

"Shall we look at the cloth I had sent up from London?" she asked brightly. "I thought you might like a new dress, Mama. And the color would suit you."

"If you are certain, my dear," her mother said with a forced smile, "though I rarely go anywhere where there is a need to wear pretty things. It still does not seem quite right."

To Olivia's relief her mother had begun to wear bright colors again at last, after being in mourning and half-mourning for far too long. Sarah would have been horrified that she was the cause of such

drabness. Sarah had reminded Olivia of a butterfly, a joyful creature who flitted in and out of
their lives all too briefly. She'd loved to paint, the
brighter the colors the better, and she'd believed
that the wearing of black as a sign of bereavement
was an abomination.

Now Olivia scolded her mother gently. "Why
shouldn't you wear pretty things? I'm sure Sarah
would be the first to tell you you should. We will
look at patterns and you can decide on the style
you prefer."

Estelle, Olivia's and her mother's maid, was
standing at the top of the stairs as they ascended
to the sewing room.

"We are going to look at patterns this morning," Olivia said, with a conspiratorial glance. Estelle had always been sympathetic to her attempts
to ease her mother's grief.

"I'm glad to hear it, miss," Estelle replied. "It is
well past time the mistress had a new dress."

As her mother continued to make her way up
the stairs, Estelle touched Olivia's arm to hold her
back. Olivia gave her a questioning look.

"Is something the matter, Estelle?"

The maid's pretty, plump face was unusually
serious, her hazel eyes lacking their sparkle. "I
am a friend of Abbot, Lord Lacey's manservant,
miss."

"Oh?" Olivia raised her brows, playing at ig-
norance. If Estelle had something to say, then she
would say it.

"You called on His Lordship, miss." Estelle glanced about, making certain they were still alone, and her strangely secretive behavior made Olivia even more wary.

"There is nothing wrong in visiting a neighbor, Estelle, but nevertheless I would prefer it if you didn't mention this to my mother and father. They are old-fashioned and—"

"On the contrary, miss," Estelle hastened to re-assure her. "Abbot and me, we think it's a very good idea that Lord Lacey has a—a proper lady for a friend. Not one of those nasty, rackety crea-tures he seems to spend all his time with these days." As if only just realizing who she was speak-ing to, and the inappropriateness of her comment, she stopped and gave a little cough. "I just wanted you to know that if you need help, well, you only have to ask me."

This was a surprising turn of events. Did Estelle know about the proposal? Had Abbot been eavesdropping? Olivia studied the maid a moment more, pondering her sudden helpfulness and what it meant. Estelle was older than Olivia, in her mid-twenties, though her lively person-ality had always made her seem like someone younger. Instinctively Olivia trusted her, but that didn't mean she was going to tell Estelle about her planned meeting with Nic at two o'clock.

"I will bear it in mind," she said at last.

Estelle dropped a little curtsy and went on her way.

* * *

Estelle put a hand to her bosom as if she might be able to slow her heart, it was beating so fast. Miss Olivia had a way of looking at one that was quite nerve-wracking, as if those blue eyes might pierce your very soul. Not that she could possibly know the reason that Estelle was so eager to help her fulfill her wish and marry Nic Lacey.

Abbot had been listening at the parlor door. He knew everything that had been said. Amazing and scandalous as it was, Miss Monteith had asked Wicked Nic to marry her. When everyone was expecting her to accept Mr. Garsed, she had her sights set on Wicked Nic. And from what Estelle knew of Miss Monteith, she was not a young lady who was easily deflected from her goal. "Headstrong" and "determined" were just two of the words you could apply to Olivia.

"He'll refuse," Abbot had said, after he'd told Estelle what he'd overheard. "I know him. He thinks she's too good for him, and besides, he won't risk his heart."

"Then she'll just have to try harder."

"Or we can help." Abbot had wrapped his arms tighter about Estelle as they snuggled up together in the narrow bed in Abbot's room. "If they married then we could marry, too, and be together always, in the same house and the same bed. No more separations, no more you at the Monteiths and me at the castle. Imagine it, Estelle."

She did; she longed for it. Especially now that there was another consideration, something she had yet to tell Abbot, despite the increasing urgency of her situation.

After an affair lasting nearly five years, Estelle was with child.

It was a gift in one way, and a disaster in another. All this time they had snatched their intimate moments when they could. Nic Lacey was often away from home, and then they mightn't see each other for months at a time. Once Abbot had been away for almost a year, and Estelle had thought her heart would break.

She supposed she could have forced the issue. Abbot would marry her if she wanted him to, but that would not keep her from being alone whenever he traveled with Nic. Because Nic was a single man, with no wife, there would be no place for her with Abbot on his travels. And once she began to show her pregnancy she wouldn't be able to keep her position with the Monteiths; a pregnant maid was not at all the thing, and she would be asked to leave.

But if Miss Olivia married Nic, Estelle and Abbot could be together forever. It was the perfect solution, and Estelle wasn't about to let it slip through her grasp. And Abbot was with her, up to a point. Sometimes he was far too cautious and proper for Estelle's liking, such as when he refused to contemplate any of Estelle's clever plans to get His Lordship and Miss together.

That was when she decided she'd have to play

her own game, her own way, and if a little dishonesty and trickery were necessary, then so be it. Abbot didn't have to know. What did it matter about scruples when she was fighting for her happiness?

Chapter 3

Nic wasn't pleased. He was irritated and annoyed, mostly with himself. He'd sworn he wouldn't respond to the note sent to him by Olivia Monteith yesterday evening, that he would find something far more important to do, or go for a ride, or browse his father's collection of books in the library. Why should he meet her? They might be neighbors, but it wasn't as if he had an obligation to her.

But try as he might, he hadn't been able to put her from his mind. The questions kept coming, crowding his thoughts, agitating him so much he couldn't concentrate on anything else.

What did she mean by "urgent"? How could a meeting by the stream possibly be urgent? And why had she chosen him as the ultimate prize in her mad quest for a husband? Surely there were plenty of other men out there, men who would be far more eager to succumb to her charms?

Meeting with her would be a big mistake.

And yet, now, here he was, striding furiously through the woods toward the stream that marked the boundary between his land and the village, his glower dark enough to frighten the birds down from the trees.

His foul mood wasn't helped by the fact that he had run into his mother in the walled garden that morning. Not literally, of course, but they had both turned a corner at the same time and found themselves face-to-face.

His first thought, after the shock of seeing her, was that she looked old and tired. Although they lived on the same estate, she in the gatehouse and he in the castle itself, they did not see or speak to each other. His mother had not spoken to him directly since 1828. She preferred to communicate through the servants and the occasional terse note.

And suddenly there they were, inches apart.

But if he'd expected that morning to be the start of a new era of understanding, he soon realized his mistake. Her dark eyes widened, her mouth tightened, and she spun around and began to walk away with an angry rustle of her black skirts. Black, of course black. She'd been in mourning ever since his father died. He'd been told by Abbot that she still had a place set at her table for him, in case his spirit might decide to join her for dinner.

The idea made him queasy. Imagine sharing a table with his father's ghost. No, thank you. But it seemed a waste for her to be so obsessed with a dead man, when her son was still living. Was it any wonder Nic spent more time away from the castle than in it?

He strode on through the woods, feeling upset and irritable, and knowing the last thing he wanted to do was listen to Miss Monteith's fantastical imaginings of married bless. Nic slipped his fob watch from his pocket and flipped open the cover. Two o'clock, exactly. He could only hope she wouldn't turn up.

It was the last coherent thought Nic had as he stepped from the leafy trees and onto the grassy bank of the stream.

Olivia Monteith had kept their assignation, but she wasn't standing, waiting, demurely on the bank. She was balanced preciously on the stepping stones out in the middle of the deep, fast-flowing steam. The very same stones she'd been standing on all those years ago.

Nic heard himself shout. Even as his memory reminded him that this was what had happened last time, he couldn't seem to stop himself.

"For God's sake, get down from there!"

She looked up.

She was wearing a pale lemon dress, the hem lifted so that he could see her slippers as she balanced on the slippery stones, and her fine stockings molded to her trim ankles and calves. Her hair was pinned up simply, making a halo of gold for her beautiful face. Olivia Monteith was no longer a child, she was a woman, and she took his breath away.

"I'm not going to fall this time," she called to him.

Nic found he could breathe again.

"I'm going to jump."

He shouted, but it was too late. She sprang neatly from the stones and landed with a splash. A moment later she'd gone under the swift, rushing water. Cursing, he waded into the freezing stream, not even pausing to take off his boots.

She came up, spluttering and splashing wildly in her attempts to stay afloat. She started to sink again, weighed down by her clothing, just as he reached her.

"Of all the ridiculous, dangerous stunts . . ." he said, or tried to between mouthfuls of water. He wrapped an arm about her and began hauling her toward the bank. He expected her to struggle, but she didn't, and he wondered whether that was because she trusted him to rescue her or because she was half drowned.

He soon discovered it was the latter.

When they reached the bank she could barely help herself at all, and he ended up pushing and pulling her shivering body onto dry land. By the time he'd got himself out of the water, she'd crawled several feet away and was lying on her stomach in the grass, her tangled hair covering her face, and her sodden lemon dress clinging to her body. Nic turned her over, smoothing her hair away so that he could see her face properly.

Olivia's lashes were very dark against her white cheeks. They fluttered and her eyes opened, purest sapphire blue, and she gave him a feeble smile. "I knew you hadn't changed," she rasped.

A second later her eyes widened, her face took on a green cast, and she looked about wildly, trying to sit up.

Nic turned her onto her side as she retched, bringing up the water she'd swallowed. When she was done, he wrung out his handkerchief and, lifting her into his arms, proceeded to wipe her face. "You bloody fool, woman," he growled as he worked. "Are you trying to kill yourself? Or do you want me to be blamed for your death as well as—as—?"

He stuttered to a stop just in time, but she didn't seem to hear him.

Nic dug into his pocket, and his fingers closed on the silver flask that was his father's. It went everywhere with him, and he was thankful he'd thought to refill it only that morning. He tilted Olivia's head back, pouring brandy down her throat.

"No . . ." she gasped, pushing his hand away.

"Yes. More."

She gave him a mutinous look and then took another sip. The color had come back into her cheeks, and her eyes had lost their glassy stare. As he recapped the flask, she gave a sigh and snuggled against his chest. He could feel her soft bosom, and when he looked down, he realized that her pale dress was clinging to her like a second skin. He could see the full curved shape of her breasts, and more interestingly, the jut of her cold nipples.

A bolt of lust speared through him.

He might have conquered it. He hadn't forgotten that he used to be a gentleman. And then the minx lifted her long, dark lashes and gazed into his eyes with a look that a man of his experience couldn't mistake. With a groan, Nic bent his head and kissed her.

Her lips were cold and tasted of brandy, but she was enthusiastic. Very enthusiastic. He tried to slow her down, turning his attention to her cheeks, her eyelids, the curve of her jaw. She acquiesced for a brief moment, and then she took control. Olivia reached up, clamping her frozen palms on either side of his face, and held him still.

"This is what I want," she whispered, and with that she leaned forward and began to kiss his lips again.

So this was what she wanted? She was obviously a direct kind of woman. A hot and hard kind of woman. Well, he thought, he'd give it to her hot and hard.

He tilted her over his arm to get better access to her mouth, and dived in. He felt her stiffen, briefly, and then give a little whimper. Her tongue slid along his, her arms clung about his neck. If he hadn't known better, he would never have believed it was the cool and beautiful Miss Monteith he held in his arms, but some wild, passionate Gypsy wench eager to dispose of her virginity . . .

What the devil am I doing?

Shocked to the core, Nic pushed her away and

stumbled to his feet. He staggered a few steps, turning his back, knowing he was fully erect and not wanting her to see the tent in his trousers. She had almost drowned and now he was about to ravish her. Even for Wicked Nic that was pretty dastardly. Nic took several deep, calming breaths before he finally dared to turn back to look at her.

She was sitting up, still bedraggled, but she'd twisted her water-darkened hair into a knot at her nape and she was watching him with that direct, disconcerting look, as if waiting to see what he would do next.

"I apologize," he said quietly.

"I don't want you to apologize. I enjoyed it."

"I apologize anyway."

"Nic, I wanted you to kiss me. Surely you knew that? I wanted you to save me." Her face lit up. "And you did."

"What if I hadn't been here?" he retorted, the anger returning to his voice. "You could have drowned."

"But you *were* here. I've been trying to think of a way to break through the distance that has grown up between us, to bring back that easiness we used to feel in each other's company."

"So you decided to relive the past?" he growled.

"Well, it worked, didn't it?" Her blue eyes were full of laughter, as if she found the situation amusing.

He clenched his fists, resisting the urge to strangle her. If he touched her again . . . well, who knew what might happen. He was Wicked Nic, after all.

As if she'd read his mind she said bluntly, "You want me, don't you? You want me as a—a man wants a woman." That little stumble told him everything about her innocence when it came to the subject, and he might have smiled if he wasn't so tense.

"Of course I bloody want you!" he roared. "But I can't have you!"

Olivia Monteith stood up, her wet dress outlining her body in a manner that made him want to weep with desire. "Yes, Nic, you can. Marry me."

It was finally more than he could bear. Another moment and he'd throw himself upon her, and he couldn't risk that. With a muttered curse he strode away from her as fast as he could, back through the woods to his own land, and to safety.

He didn't expect her to follow him, and she didn't. He'd answered her question, and he cursed himself again for being too weak to resist her. So weak that he had to rush off and leave her, bedraggled and cold, and alone by the stream. A stream she would no doubt cross again to get home, rather than go the long way by the path and the bridge.

What if she fell in and this time there was no one there to rescue her?

Nic hesitated, slowed, then stopped. He wanted to keep walking, get home, and change out of his wet clothes, but he knew he couldn't do it. He was either a hero or a fool, but he couldn't do it. With a groan, he turned back.

Chapter 4

Olivia grimaced, her dress dripping, her slippers squishing, as she walked back to the stepping stones. She was remembering the place in the woods where she had left her bundle of dry clothing—she had no intention of arriving home in a state that would make any explanations necessary. The stones looked slippery but it would take her only a moment to cross them, while if she went the long way, by the path to the bridge, it would take at least forty minutes. She shivered despite the sunshine. She'd crossed the stones many times since she was a child, and she wasn't afraid of falling in.

Actually, the way she felt at the moment, she might simply float from stone to stone. Olivia was so full of elation and triumph, she really did feel as if she were floating as she began to cross the stepping stones. Her plan had worked—the ice between them was well and truly broken, and soon they'd be back on their old friendly footing. Nic Lacey hadn't changed, he was still the kind and generous man he had been years ago—the type of man you could rely on and trust. A hero in black sheep's clothing. She'd loved him then and she loved him now, and she knew in her heart there would never be another man for her.

And added to that, he kissed her in a way that made her body go warm and shivery and her toes curl. He'd held her as if he knew exactly what he was doing, and she liked that. Nic Lacey was a rake, a master of pleasure, and Olivia couldn't wait to benefit from his experience.

She chuckled, and then laughed out loud, remembering how she had kissed him and he had wanted her so much he hadn't been able to resist. Surely that was a very good start to their courtship?

"Watch where you're putting your feet, Olivia!"

His voice was so loud and so close, she jumped, forgetting how precarious her position was. She wobbled around to face him. He was standing on the first stone, only about three behind her, his wet dark hair dripping into his eyes, looking cross and rumpled and worried.

Her foot slipped, she tried to retrieve her balance, failed, gave a little scream, and toppled into the water.

Again.

The stream closed over her head, and she felt the tug of the current. Her slippers touched the pebbly bottom and she tried to use it as a springboard, but her legs were pulled from under her, and she found herself suddenly so disoriented she didn't know what was up and what was down.

Black swirls and eddies formed around her, her already soaked clothing weighing her down like an anchor, and she began to lose consciousness.

Olivia's last thought was the unfairness of it, that just as her life was beginning it should end.

Someone was carrying her. Her head was uncomfortably arched backward, as if her neck could no longer support it, and her throat ached appallingly. She struggled to sit up, kicking her feet and flapping her hands like a landed fish, only to be swung up and around, making her feel sick and dizzy. The next moment she was bent like a bow over his shoulder, his hand planted firmly on her bottom to keep her there, while her head now hung toward the ground, her stomach lurching with each step he took.

"Let me down!" she wailed.

"No. You'd only drown again."

"Please . . ."

But he took no notice. Olivia tried to work out where she was from the upside-down world around her. Then she knew. Nic was climbing the broad, shallow steps that led to the side terrace of Castle Lacey; he must have carried her all the way from the stream. Her stomach jolted as he half ran to the glass doors, fumbled at the catch, and carried her inside.

"Abbot!" he was shouting. "Where the hell are you, man? I need you. At once!"

After that there were hurrying footsteps and panicked voices, and Abbot saying, "Put her down here, sir," as if he attended to half-drowned ladies every day.

Nic put her down, and when Olivia's head had stopped spinning, she found herself deep in a leather armchair, wrapped in blankets, while Abbot busied himself with lighting a fire. They seemed to be alone, she thought, her gaze wandering . . . No, Nic was there, standing with his back to her and dripping all over the carpet. He was pouring a drink into a glass and he came and knelt beside her. She noticed he looked very pale, his hair plastered to his head, and his thick brows were drawn down into a frown that would frighten most people.

"Drink this."

She drank it. More brandy. It burned her throat, and she leaned back and closed her eyes, letting the restorative do its job. She could hear Abbot and Nic speaking in low voices, and then footsteps and the door closing as Abbot left. The fire was blazing away now, and she felt quite warm despite her soaking. Sleepy and warm.

"What on earth possessed you?" Nic said, coldly for a man with so much passion.

"If you hadn't yelled right behind me—"

"You were laughing. Are you insane?"

Olivia felt her face flush. "I thought you'd gone. I was crossing the stream on my way home. Why were you spying on me?"

Nic's frown grew even darker. "It suddenly occurred to me that you might do something stupid like take the short way over the stream instead of walking to the bridge. I wanted to make sure you arrived home safely."

"So you proceeded to drown me?"

His frown lifted, and something approaching a smile twitched his lips. "No, you managed that perfectly well on your own."

"Now *you're* laughing. Are *you* insane?"

"I think I must be, otherwise I wouldn't have brought you here."

"Why did you bring me here?"

His dark eyes were intent on hers. Suddenly he smiled properly, his saturnine face changing into handsomeness. "Damned if I know." But he did know. Slowly his gaze slid over her face, her throat, her bosom, taking his time, exploring every inch of her as if she wasn't wearing anything at all.

How did he do that? she asked herself, with a shiver. How did he manage to make her squirm and grow hot, just by looking? Until she was longing for . . . she knew not what.

"Perhaps I've brought you here to ravish you, Olivia. Isn't that what you said you wanted? To be ravished by Wicked Nic Lacey?"

She opened her mouth to say yes, but closed it again. Suddenly she wasn't so certain. The tension in him, as if he was barely under control, made her wary. She was not such an innocent that she didn't know some men were dangerous, untamed creatures, and rakes were particularly dangerous. Her hesitation now was pure instinct, and had nothing to do with her brain or her emotions.

"Are you having second thoughts?" He laughed quietly, moving closer and resting his long fingers on her shoulder. His thumb rubbed against her neck, making circles, and her breathing quickened. Olivia forced herself to steady it; time to take the initiative again.

"Ravish me, Nic," she said, gazing up into his eyes. "I dare you."

He was reading her, or trying to. She saw the flicker of doubt in his face, the hardening of his mouth. He bent down, so close she could feel his heat and smell the spicy scent of him and the steam as his wet clothing dried in the warmth of the fire.

"You'll be sorry if I do," he growled. "You're pushing me, Olivia. I can only be pushed so far. You don't know what I could do to you. What I *have* done . . ."

Despite his warning, she ached for him to kiss her again. "Tell me."

His gaze narrowed. "I can tell you what I'd do to you if you were one of my usual flirts. Can you pretend to be a pretty little dancer from the East End, or a refined courtesan with a dark past?"

"The dancer," she said at once, enjoying the thought. "Can I imagine myself wearing a short skirt and pink stockings? I have heard that's what they wear."

"Oh yes, definitely," he drawled. "Will you sing me a saucy song?"

Olivia considered. "I don't know any saucy

songs. Perhaps I can just kick up my legs, will that do?"

"I'm sure that will catch my attention."

"Is that all I have to do?"

"No. There's more. Later, when you've finished kicking up your legs, I'll come to your dressing room. I'll bring a bottle of champagne with me, and pour you a glass, and tell you how much I admire you."

"I'd be flattered. Will you kiss me?"

"I think so."

"Good. And then what?"

"And then, my little dancer, I'll—"

Olivia, sensing he was trying to shock her, wasn't about to let it happen. Once again she took the initiative. "Why don't you show me instead of telling me?" she said, and let the blankets fall from around her, pooling in the seat of the leather chair.

Something hot and dangerous flared in his eyes. "Don't say I didn't warn you," he murmured.

"I'd never say that," she managed, with barely a tremor.

He gave her the faintest of smiles, as if he knew exactly how she was feeling, and ran his fingertip along the neckline of her lemon dress. He stepped in closer, his hand catching her chin and lifting her face this way and that. The pad of his thumb brushed back and forth over her lips, lightly, and for a moment he seemed fascinated by the soft swell of them.

She wanted him to kiss her so badly that she was sure he could read it in her face. Her breath quickened, her skin flushed, and she could barely keep her eyes open.

"Ah, passion!" His deep voice startled her out of whatever trance he'd begun to put her under. "You want me. That's something women can pretend, but an experienced man will always know when they are genuine and when they are lying."

"I do want you to kiss me," she managed in a husky voice that didn't sound like her own. "I think, if you don't, then I will die."

"Then kiss you I will, my little dancer."

He leaned in, capturing her bottom lip between his, sucking on it gently. The sensation was exquisite, and she made a murmur of sound to tell him so. Her hand moved to stroke his cheek but he caught it, held it away, not allowing her to touch him. Firmly his mouth closed over hers, caressing, stroking, delving deeper.

Olivia felt as if she'd entered a sensual world she'd known nothing about before she asked Nic to marry her, and their kiss was taking her deeper into that world. Her skin was feeling hotter and more sensitive, there was an ache between her thighs, and with it came a need she still only half understood.

Nic finally lifted his lips from hers. "Inexperienced," he murmured, "but sweet, very sweet." His fingers slid into her fair hair, releasing it from its pins and fanning it out around her shoulders. The damp strands were already drying. He pressed his face against her hair, breathing deeply, nuzzling against her.

"Nic?" she said, trying to see his face, but he held her too close. "What are you doing?"

"Smelling your scent," he spoke against her hair.

She rested her cheek against his shoulder, breathing in, and thought that he was right. She could smell the essence of him, too, and she liked it.

"I've seen what you look like with your clothes on," he said, his voice muffled, "but I need to see you without them. Corsets and petticoats can hide a multitude of sins."

She pushed him back so that she could read his face, his eyes. They were sleepy, his eyelids sunk low over them, but there was a gleam there that made her heart begin to beat faster.

"I could make an exception. In your case." He stroked her lips with his fingertips, running them down over her jaw until his hand was resting on her chest, his fingers splayed. "I don't think clever undergarments have anything to do with your figure."

"But I wouldn't want to disappoint you," Olivia said breathlessly.

He gazed into her eyes a moment longer, and then he slid his hand down over her bodice, over her breast. He cupped her flesh, tenderly, as if testing to see how well it fit into his palm.

Olivia gasped, her eyes widening, gripping the arms of the chair as if she needed to steady herself.

"Very nice," Nic murmured, still squeezing her gently. "Full and yet firm. What color are your areolas? I like pink, but I won't quibble. I can feel your nipples, too. Little hard buds. I'd like to roll them with my tongue and take them into my mouth."

This image was so vivid in Olivia's mind that she almost felt as if he had done just that, causing her breasts to feel full and almost painful with desire. Seeing her predicament, he smiled again, and now there was a hint of color in his tanned cheeks. "You'd like that, too, wouldn't you, Olivia? I can see it in your face. You really are a passionate woman."

"People . . . people call me icy and controlled."

"Do they? Well, they don't know you at all, do they, Olivia?"

No, they didn't. Only her friends knew the real Olivia. Nic was her friend, or he used to be. "Nic," she breathed, and lifting her hand, rested it against his lean cheek. She had meant to ask him the question, but now, gazing into his eyes, she found that words were beyond her. What she really wanted was to be with him. To be his.

He knew. How could he not? For a breathless moment she thought he was going to oblige, but then his eyelids closed, briefly, and when he opened them again the sleepy look was gone. His voice was like a frosty morning. "I want you to undress now. Every stitch. I want to see what I'm buying. I never sign off on a deal until I've seen the merchandise. If I don't like what I see, then I'll leave you a tip and pass you on to my friends."

Shocked by the abrupt change in him, Olivia felt her passion give way to anger. "Are you really capable of such callous behavior?" she demanded. "You would really force a woman to disrobe before you so that you could look her over like a—a beast? Before you hand her over to the next man?"

He shrugged indifferently. "Of course. Why not? I've had no complaints. If I choose a woman, she and I are together for an agreed period of time, and during that time we give each other pleasure, and when it is over she is well paid. Both parties get exactly what they want."

Olivia's ideas of men and women and love were far more romantic than his, and she found his attitude disappointing and difficult to comprehend. "And you've never felt inclined to keep a woman with you for longer than the agreed time?" she asked, struggling to understand. "You've never fallen in love?"

His smile widened. "Olivia, " he mocked, "this isn't about love. It's about pleasure, and pleasure grows stale. Moving on to greener fields is the only way to keep it fresh." He glanced away. "I think I've said enough for now. I don't want to completely destroy that attractive naïveté of yours."

Olivia reached out and caught his hand before he could withdraw, forcing him to remain facing her. "Do you know what I believe, Nic?"

He sighed. "I'm sure you're going to tell me."

"I believe pleasure is more than a brief liaison with a stranger. Or it can be, if you make the right choice. Life doesn't have to be about fighting off boredom and a constant search for greener fields. If you make the right choice of partner, every day of your life can become an adventure in itself."

Nic's hand turned in hers, and he held it lightly, looking down at her long fingers and pink nails. "That is where we differ, Olivia. That is where our roads divide. *I* am not looking for the right choice, just a woman to take to bed with me."

"Why don't you let me try and persuade you?" she urged. "You used to like to listen to me talk."

"That was a long time ago. We've changed."

"But we haven't! Don't you see? We're still the same two people."

"Olivia . . ." His lips brushed hers, barely, and then abruptly he straightened and moved away.

It wasn't nearly enough. Olivia gave an involuntary cry of protest before she heard the voices beyond the door, and then the hurrying footsteps coming closer. Dangers Nic had no doubt already been well aware of.

"You're lucky," he said. "You've escaped from this with nothing more than a dunking. Don't risk yourself again, Olivia. Go home and marry someone who won't ruin your life and break your heart."

Olivia wanted to tell him that she had no intention of taking the safe way home, no matter how many times she fell in. And she didn't believe he would ruin her life or break her heart, not deep down, no matter how often he said it. But it was too late; the door was opening.

"Miss Monteith!" Estelle cried, looking worried, and behind her Abbot, flushed from hurrying to keep up. "Oh dear me, miss," the maid gasped, a hand to her heaving bosom, "you are very wet!"

Olivia managed a laugh. "Yes, I am very wet, Estelle."

"I brought you some dry clothing," Estelle said, glancing at Abbot, who was carrying a bundle, and some message seemed to pass between them. "I don't want you to worry," she went on. "No one knows about this but us."

"And no one will ever know," Nic added, giving them both a stern look. "Miss Monteith had an unfortunate accident in the stream, that is all. No need to turn this into tittle-tattle for the amusement of the village."

Estelle was helping her up. "Come with me, miss. Abbot tells me there is a room prepared for you, with a nice warm fire. You'll soon be yourself again."

Olivia doubted she would ever be the same again, but she allowed Estelle to lead her from the room.

* * *

"Thank you, Abbot," Nic said. "I am grateful, as always. If we can manage to keep this blasted incident hushed up, then no one will suffer for it."

"Of course, sir. I would hate to see your reputation blackened even more than it already is."

"Yes, that would be a tragedy," Nic said dryly, pouring a brandy for himself. Abbot had come at just the right moment. A second more and he'd either have taken her maidenhead on the hearth rug, or frightened her out of her wits in order to escape the net he felt closing around him. *Haven't you ever fallen in love?* The devil he had! Nor was he going to.

Abbot was choosing his words carefully. "Miss Monteith appears to be a very headstrong young lady, my lord."

"That's putting it mildly."

"A young lady who knows what she wants."

"Well, she may think she knows what she wants, but we know better, eh, Abbot? Young ladies like Miss Monteith are not for the likes of me. Besides, what would I do with her? She'd drive me to distraction within a week, wanting me to reform all my wicked ways. I can't have that."

Abbot's smile lacked humor.

"No, Miss Monteith is not for me. As you are aware, I like my ladies to be anything but ladies. They should know their business and go about it cheerfully, and then leave. No tears, no regrets, no expectations. That is the way I prefer it."

"As you say, my lord."

"Yes, *exactly* as I say, Abbot. Now see to a bath. And, damn it, bring up the best brandy. I think I deserve to celebrate my elevation to sainthood."

"Sainthood, my lord?"

"Only a saint could withstand Miss Monteith's charms, Abbot."

And with those final words, he sank into the chair recently vacated by Olivia and stared moodily into the fire.

Chapter 5

Olivia was certain she'd escaped any reper-cussions—she arrived home in dry clothes, and no one seemed the least bit suspicious when she explained she'd been out walking and enjoy-ing the sunshine, and had forgotten the time. However, during the night she developed a head-ache and a rising fever, and by morning she was very ill indeed. Her mother called the doctor, and he declared Olivia had contracted a chill, possibly influenza.

"But she will be well again?" Mrs. Monteith asked, beside herself with her fears.

The doctor was used to dealing with worried relatives. "Your daughter is a strong and healthy young woman. Give her plenty to drink, keep her quiet, and she will soon be her old self."

By the following day the fever had broken, leaving Olivia weak and listless, so that it wasn't until the fifth day of her illness that she was al-lowed out of bed. Estelle helped her downstairs to the parlor, where she was confined to the chaise longue.

It was torture.

Olivia longed to go out into the garden, to stretch her legs and take deep breaths of fresh air, but instead she was a prisoner of overheated rooms and medicinal tonics and questions about her every symptom. Since Sarah died she'd frequently felt as if she was being held captive by the love and anxiety of her parents. Sometimes in the past she had longed to scream in frustration, only to feel guilty and ungrateful moments later. On the occasions when she did speak sharply, her mother didn't reprimand her or appear hurt—she simply gave Olivia what Olivia secretly thought of as "the look." It always had the effect of making Olivia feel lower than low for what she had said or done, or what she hadn't said or done.

"There," Mrs. Monteith said, tucking the rug about her daughter, and rearranging the pillows, "that's much better. Now you can look out of the window and be safe inside."

"Thank you, Mama."

"Mr. Garsed has called every day," Mrs. Monteith reminded her for the umpteenth time. "Such steadfastness shows a man of dependable character, Olivia."

"Or a man with very little else to do," said Olivia.

Her mother gave her "the look," and instantly Olivia felt selfish and ungrateful.

"Lord Lacey sent a lovely bunch of flowers," Estelle piped up, as she refreshed Olivia's lemonade.

"Did he?" Olivia said, surprised and pleased, turning to the maid.

"And he sent a note," Estelle added, with a sideways glance at Mrs. Monteith.

"Can I see it? Mama?"

Her mother looked chagrined, but rallied. "It was very kind of Lord Lacey to think of you, dear. I must say I didn't expect such consideration; he's not exactly the sort of man who pays attention to the social niceties. Why, he's hardly ever at home! One wonders how he knew you were ill."

"Mama, where is the note? Surely it would be impolite of me not to read it?"

"You're right, of course, my dear." Her mother gave up puzzling over Lord Lacey's motives and left the room. Estelle shot Olivia a conspiratorial smile.

"Wicked Nic sent you flowers, miss! I think that's a first for him. Well, where proper young ladies are concerned, anyhow. Do you know what Abbot says? He says that Lord Lacey takes great care to keep his real thoughts to himself, and that no one really knows him."

"He was very forthcoming with me the other day," Olivia said wryly. "I gather that he's easily bored and needs to be constantly finding new, eh, companions."

Estelle tucked a loose strand of hair under her mobcap. "Or rather than bored, it could be because he doesn't like them to get too close to him. Lord Lacey is a very solitary man, miss."

Olivia hadn't thought of that, but now she could

see it might be so. What better way for Nic to prevent any woman from getting close to him than by changing them like rides on a merry-go-round. And why didn't he want anyone to know him? To love him?

Just then her mother returned with the note, her eyes triumphant. "Olivia, Mr. Garsed is here to see you," she said, giving her daughter a hasty inspection, smoothing down the white lace collar on her dress and fussing with her hair.

"I must get up, Mama," Olivia declared, attempting to rise on wobbly legs. "I can't receive Mr. Garsed like this."

"Nonsense, you have been ill. Besides"—and a knowing smile hovered at the corners of her mother's mouth—"gentlemen seem to find convalescing women very interesting. I've never understood why."

"I don't know where you get these ideas from, Mama," Olivia grumbled, as her pillows were rearranged yet again and the rug straightened about her legs. But at least she had the note now—she'd taken it from her mother's hand while she was distracted, and she slipped it into her sleeve as a treat for later. Not a moment too soon, as the door opened and Mr. Garsed entered.

Nic Lacey rode his horse through the village, past the little church with its blunt tower, and the neighboring ramshackle rectory, and the two alms cottages, inhabited by the deserving poor. The village of Bassingthorpe had been set-

tled around the castle, when his Norman ancestors arrived to claim the land for which they'd
fought and died. In those days they'd lived
crowded together with their men-at-arms in a
wooden tower upon a motte, but eventually that
was replaced with stone, and over the centuries
the castle had grown with the fortunes of the
Lacey family.

The village and tenants who once belonged
to them had grown, too, other families rising to
prominence, like the Monteiths, who had been
yeomen in the eighteenth century but had wisely
invested their money in property and factories,
and were now wealthy. Until recently such new
wealth was despised by the old aristocracy—it
still was in many quarters—but these days self-
made men were looked upon as the backbone of
Britain and the way of the future.

Olivia was right in that, at least. As for all the
other things she'd said to him . . . she couldn't be
more wrong. This situation was unique for him.
He hadn't been stalked by a woman like Olivia
before. Oh, he was aware of the fascination vir-
ginal young ladies had for a man like him, but
the warnings of their parents and their instincts
for self-preservation usually tempered any wild
urges they might have to throw themselves at his
feet.

It was the ladies of the demimonde, the ad-
venturesses, with one eye on his money and the
other on his title, who tended to pursue him,
and he'd had many memorable encounters with

such women. But he could honestly say that the encounters that currently occupied his thoughts were rather different. Beautiful Olivia Monteith had lodged herself in his mind as no one else ever had, and he wasn't sure how to eject her.

Nic looked up and found that his horse had halted outside the Monteith house, its warm pink bricks and mullioned windows gracefully aging within the treed park. He frowned. He hadn't intended to call on Olivia Monteith—the flowers and note were enough for what was after all only the concern of a neighbor. And yet, now, here he was. He could simply ride on, and that was what he should do, but even as he thought it, he was inexplicably turning into the gate.

That was when Nic realized he wasn't the only one visiting Olivia today. Theodore Garsed was just dismounting from his flashy chestnut, his riding boots gleaming with so much polishing they made Nic's eyes water. He disliked the man, and for the second time in as many minutes he considered turning away and riding home, but something stubborn rose up inside him, something he preferred not to inspect too closely.

"No, damn it," he muttered, "I'll not be run off by a peacock like Theodore."

"Lord Lacey." Garsed had seen him, his eyebrows rising with prim disapproval. "Have you business with Mr. Monteith?"

"No, Theodore, I've come to visit the invalid."

His eyebrows rose higher. "I didn't know you were acquainted with Miss Monteith," he said, as if such a possibility was beyond his comprehension.

Annoyed, Nic didn't bother answering.

"Well, I suppose there's no harm in it," Theodore went on with a doubtful air, as if it was his business to filter any visitors who called on Olivia. "You won't stay above half an hour, will you, Lacey?"

I'll stay as long as I damned well please! Nic swallowed the retort down. "What are you doing here, Theodore?" he said instead.

Theodore's expression grew smug and he leaned toward Nic, his voice taking on a confiding note. "Can you keep a secret, Lacey? Miss Monteith and I are soon to become engaged. It's not official yet, so you need to keep it to yourself, but it's more or less a fait accompli as far as her mother is concerned."

Nic felt as if someone had punched him in the stomach. Olivia and Theodore Garsed? It was so ludicrous, he was inclined to dismiss it as mere wishful thinking on Theodore's part. Surely if it were true then Olivia would have mentioned it to him when she proposed?

"She's a little in awe of me, I believe," Theodore added with a man-of-the-world chuckle. "Only to be expected. Do you know, last time I was in Bond Street I had at least a dozen gentlemen stop me and ask where I got my waistcoat and the name of my tailor?"

Nic bit his tongue on what he'd really like to say, and cast an eye over Theodore's attire.

His fair hair was carefully brushed and styled, disguising a hint of a bald spot on his crown, and he was wearing a jacket nipped tightly to his waist and excessively padded at the shoulders. Probably because he wanted to disguise his growing paunch, Nic thought unkindly. Theodore liked to give the impression that he was sporty, but in reality he was a sedentary gentleman who enjoyed his food far too much. In a few years' time he'd have run to fat.

He tried to picture Olivia on Theodore's arm, and couldn't. Revulsion rose up inside him at the idea that this man might possess a woman like Olivia. That he might touch her soft skin and lie upon her body, plunging inside her. The images disturbed him, and Nic decided right then that he was going to put a spoke in Theodore's wheel.

A woman servant answered the door, her eyes swiveling from one gentleman to the other. "Miss Monteith is in the parlor, m-my lord . . . sir."

Theodore seemed to know his way about intimately, waving away the offer to show them in, and striding ahead. He was the first one through the parlor door, warbling a greeting, while Nic paused in his wake.

"Mr. Garsed!" Mrs. Monteith was breathless with excitement—it was quite clear she favored his suit. "Do come in and see how well dear Olivia is doing. She has the roses back in her cheeks."

"Miss Monteith will never be anything less than exquisite in my eyes," Theodore replied, hurrying to take Olivia's hand and raise it to his lips.

"Mr. Garsed." She smiled up at him with her serene and beautiful smile, and Nic wondered if Garsed saw the hint of panic in her eyes, or was it only he who noticed it? He knew then that it was true and not some lurid fantasy of Theodore's—he really did intend to marry her.

"There's someone else to see you," Theodore interrupted, the note of disapproval heavy in his voice.

Olivia's gaze slid by her suitor and fastened on the second visitor standing in the shadows. And Nic could have sworn that her eyes flashed blue fire as he entered the room.

The greeting he received was very different from Theodore's. Mrs. Monteith gasped and then rattled off a "How do you do, Your Lordship?" while clearly wishing him to the ends of the earth. Estelle, the maid, gave a hasty curtsy. But Nic was more interested in Olivia.

She kept her smile in place, although the color in her cheeks deepened, and when he took her fingers in his he felt them tremble. "Lord Lacey," she said, "how . . . unexpected."

"We are neighbors, Miss Monteith. Why is my visit unexpected?"

If she noticed his paraphrasing of her own words when she'd called on him, she gave no sign. Besides, now that he was close to her he saw that she had indeed been ill. Her face was wan and pale, and there were shadows beneath her eyes. There was a fragility about her, too, that hadn't been there before, and he was tempted to sit down beside her on the chaise longue and try to instill some of his own vigor into her.

"I hope you have been taking your medicine, Miss Monteith," Theodore said archly, waggling a finger in front of her nose.

Olivia glanced away. "Religiously, sir. I really am much better. I wish I could walk outside in the sunshine. It is very stuffy inside, and I'm sure I wouldn't take any hurt."

She sounded wistful, but a chorus of voices rose in protest.

"Why not?" Nic said, loud enough to break through the racket. "The sunshine will do you the world of good, now that you're on the mend."

There was a silence. Mrs. Monteith was frowning, but it was Theodore who reprimanded him. "You should leave the matter of Miss Monteith's health to those who know her best, Lacey."

Another uncomfortable pause. Olivia broke it by suggesting, with her calm smile, that both gentlemen sit down, as staring up at them was making her neck ache.

Theodore sat, perfectly at home, and began a long and detailed description of the quail his cook had placed before him for last night's dinner. Irritated and bored, Nic tried to catch Olivia's eye, but she was giving every sign of listening to her beau with fascinated interest.

"Mr. Garsed is quite a gourmet," Mrs. Monteith explained fondly. "Do you have a French chef, Lord Lacey?"

"My cook has been in the family for years, Mrs.

Monteith. I can't say she's ever tried her hand at quail, but her jam roly-poly is to die for."

Olivia laughed, and Nic turned to her with a smile.

Theodore shuddered. "Good God, man, you need to dismiss her immediately and find yourself someone who is au fait with the latest dishes."

Nic's smile faded. "Is that what you would do, Theodore? Dismiss her without reason? Out with the old and in with the new?"

"Most definitely. If you like, I can give you the name of a superlative chef. Expensive, but well worth it."

"That is very kind of you, Mr. Garsed," Mrs. Monteith gushed. "I'm sure no one is more to be relied on than you when it comes to fashionable food."

"I pride myself on it, Mrs. Monteith."

"I wonder if my cook would thank you, Theodore," Nic drawled, lounging back in his chair, one hand jammed in his pocket, his dark hair falling over his brow, his eyes gleaming with malice. "She and her family have been with my family for generations, and our loyalty to each other is a matter of pride. I don't think she'd understand if I sacked her because she couldn't cook the latest recipe from Paris."

Theodore, flushed and humiliated, rose to his feet. "You're willfully misunderstanding me, Lacey. But I refuse to be insulted by a man who eats jam roly-poly." And he shuddered.

"Oh? What a shame."

"Lord Lacey," Olivia said sharply.

He met her reproving gaze and then shrugged and said mildly, "Miss Monteith wants me to apologize, Theodore, so I will. No need to throw a tantrum."

"I have never thrown a tantrum in my life, Lacey. Far too undignified."

"You disappoint me. I hoped you were going to call me out. I am a crack shot, you know."

Mrs. Monteith gasped and clasped a hand to her breast. "A duel, oh Lord no . . ."

"I have no intention of upsetting Miss Monteith by calling you out." Theodore bristled, even redder than before. "I value her peace of mind."

"Lord Lacey isn't fighting a duel with anyone," Olivia interrupted in a firm voice, casting Nic a warning glance. "Are you, my lord?"

Nic hesitated, sorely tempted, and then he smiled at her, an unapologetic smile, and shook his head. "No, Miss Monteith."

"Well, thank goodness for that," Mrs. Monteith exclaimed.

"I forgot to tell you that I've heard from my brother, Alphonse, Miss Monteith. He's visiting me. You have met him before . . . ?"

Olivia looked as if it hadn't been a pleasant experience, but she rallied a smile. "I have, Mr. Garsed. I look forward to renewing the acquaintance. Will he be staying long?"

"I don't know. With my brother, Alphonse, one never knows."

Just then the mantel clock chimed the half

hour. There was an expectant silence. Nic knew what that meant: Polite society decreed that half an hour was all the time one was allowed for a visit in this situation. Theodore would also be well aware of such a decree—in fact he had mentioned it on their way in—and, unlike Nic, he would never flaunt such a basic rule of etiquette.

As Nic expected, Theodore cleared his throat loudly, and when Nic didn't move, he spoke with a blustering attempt at authority. "Is that the time? We really should be leaving." And he gave Nic a pointed look.

Nic brushed at his cuff and remained exactly where he was.

"Miss Monteith needs her rest," Theodore said petulantly, deflated.

"Of course she does," Nic agreed, remaining where he was.

Mrs. Monteith looked as if she wished she could order them both out, but she was too polite, and after hovering in the doorway a moment, she gave up on Nic. Theodore murmured something close to her ear, and with a hunted glance at Olivia, she accompanied him through the doorway. Nic could hear Theodore's complaints fading into the distance.

The room fell silent, and at last Nic was exactly where he wanted to be. Alone with her.

Chapter 6

The parlor was very quiet, apart from the ticking of the clock, and Olivia was beginning to think she wasn't strong enough yet to be alone in a room with a man like Nic. His magnetism, his presence, shook her to the core. But she wasn't a coward, and she forced herself to look up.

He was watching her with a smile hovering around his mouth, his dark eyes intent. His long body was folded into the chair, graceful without the conscious pretentiousness of Theodore. Nic Lacey was charismatic without even trying.

"You were disgraceful," she said reprovingly.

"I meant to be. I wanted to save you from a fate worse than death—marriage to Theodore Garsed."

"You . . . what?"

"He informed me while we were waiting outside the door that he intended to marry you. Why the hell didn't you tell me that the other day?"

She closed her eyes and rubbed her fingers across her brow, as though her head was aching.

"Because it was none of your business. And for your information I have no intention of marrying Mr. Garsed, no matter what my mother hopes and believes."

Nic stood up and crossed to the chaise longue and sat down beside her. She felt the size and warmth of his body like a shock; her flesh was actually tingling with the promise of contact.

"Olivia?" he said, and when she didn't answer he slipped a finger under her chin, tilting her face toward his, forcing her toward him.

She dropped her dark lashes lower, hiding her thoughts from him.

Nic spoke softly. "He's not the man for you; don't let him convince you he is."

She bit her lip. What was he trying to do? Save her from making a matrimonial mistake? How ironic that he could see that Theodore was completely wrong for her and yet could not see that he was completely right.

He tucked a strand of hair behind her ear, his fingers warm and tender. "I can fight a duel with him. Drive him off for good. Would you like that?"

Olivia's head was filled with the shocking image of Nic standing over Theodore's lifeless body, the gun smoking in his hand. "No, I don't like that! You'd hurt him."

"He might hurt me."

"I doubt it. At least, not according to your reputation." She took a breath, gathering her courage, and looked directly into his dark eyes. "Nic, are you really offering me advice on who I should take as my husband?"

He was very close to her; she could feel his warm breath on her lips. If she'd thought her recent illness might protect her from wanting to kiss him, she was mistaken. In fact her status as a convalescent seemed to have made her even more receptive to his seductive charms, she thought, as a warm rush of desire overcame her and she had to concentrate to hear his reply above the pounding in her ears.

"I've seen far more of the world than you, Olivia, and this man would make you extremely miserable, believe me."

She lifted her hand and placed it lightly on his shoulder. "So . . . you don't want me to marry Theodore? Is that what you're saying?"

His face grew serious. "I don't want you to marry Theodore."

She smoothed his lapel with her fingers as she thought about what she was going to say next. The moment seemed so intimate, she was loath to break it. "Nic, there is another way to stop the wedding."

He knew what she was going to say. She could see his dark eyes fill with the knowledge. His smile was regretful, as if he was turning down a second helping of his beloved jam roly-poly. "Olivia, Olivia," he murmured. "If you think you're unhappy now you have no idea how unhappy I would make you."

"But if you don't want Theodore to have me—"

He groaned softly. "I don't want anyone to have you. Only me."

"Then marry me, and then you can have me."

"You don't know what you're saying—"

"I do know!"

He kissed her, blindly, tasting her lips, and then he kissed her again, deeper this time, delving inside her mouth, as if he couldn't help himself. "You're killing me," he said, coming up for breath. "God, I want you. But if I took you . . . the consequences for you, for both of us . . ."

"Surely that's my decision to make." She was growing a little desperate in the face of his determination to reject her. "You're a rake! What self-respecting rake would refuse such an offer?"

"But you want more than my body inside yours," he said bluntly. "Don't you? You want my honor. You want a marriage of hearts and minds. You want what I cannot give."

"Can't or won't?"

He stood up, leaving her cold and alone on the chaise longue. "Good-bye, Olivia."

Olivia gazed up at his hard, implacable expression. She could weep and beg, she could shout and sulk, but none of that would work with a man like Nic. So instead she smiled her serene smile, a hint of mischief in her eyes. "I'm glad you came to call, Nic."

He hesitated, taken by surprise, and then he

laughed and bowed. "My pleasure, Olivia," he said, a world of suggestion in his voice.

"Olivia!"

Mrs. Monteith had returned to the parlor unheard, and now she looked as if she didn't know whether to shriek or faint. Nic gave Olivia a brief, mischievous look, and then he was gone.

"Olivia, how could you allow that man to speak to you in that way? Don't you know what he is? Your reputation—"

"You didn't pay much attention to my reputation when Mr. Garsed kissed me after dinner when you invited him for Christmas."

"That was different."

"Why was it different?"

"Don't be obtuse, Olivia. You know why. Mr. Garsed is a gentleman whose intentions toward you are proper—he wants to marry you. Lord Lacey is a—a rake, and his intentions toward you can only be a source of disgust and concern to me and your father. Any respectable person would feel the same. He intends to lead you astray, Olivia. He must never set foot inside this house again."

The two women glared at each other, both determined not to agree, and it was only when Mr. Monteith cleared his throat behind them that they became aware of his presence.

"What on earth is going on?" he demanded irritably. "This shouting can be heard all over the house. My dear? Olivia?"

Olivia's father rarely interfered in his wife's

arrangements. He spent his time in his study or else in London, dealing with business. In fact, Olivia often thought that he'd become distant and withdrawn from family life since her sister died, as if now that she was gone, he no longer had an interest.

"Lord Lacey has just paid a call on Olivia," her mother explained, her mouth a grim line. "They were alone in the parlor for several moments, and when I returned from farewelling Mr. Garsed, he was leaning toward her in a very intimate manner."

"Good God. Lacey? But he is the man who—"

"Exactly!" said his wife, bursting with triumph.

"Olivia," Mr. Monteith said, in his heavy, measured way, "you should never be alone in the company of a man like Lacey."

"He's our neighbor, Father, surely it would be unkind to cut our neighbor?"

"I don't mind if you nod to him in passing, but from what your mother has said it was more than that. You were alone with him in the parlor for several moments."

Olivia had a strange urge to burst out laughing. Several moments was only long enough for Nic to kiss her, and certainly not enough time for him to do all the things she wished he would. In the end all she could manage was, "Lord Lacey would never hurt me."

But her father wasn't listening. "You may well think him charming, but there's another side to him. There have been incidents in the past, behavior that the Lacey family have tried very hard to have hushed up. Some of the things I've heard . . ."

"What have you heard, Father?" she asked curiously.

"No, Olivia, I won't soil your ears with such tales. My job is to protect you, and that I will do to the best of my ability. Let me just say that he's not a man to be trusted with an innocent young girl."

Now was the moment for Olivia to promise her unwavering obedience; but she didn't. She couldn't. "I will be twenty-one in a few months' time, Father. I am not an innocent young girl. I am a grown woman and I know my own mind."

They were staring at her as if she had suddenly grown two heads, and both of them with horns.

"Olivia!" hissed her mother, wide-eyed with shock.

Her father looked even graver than usual. "You may think yourself all-knowing when it comes to the world outside Bassingthorpe, Olivia, but I assure you, you are far from it. Lacey is not the man for you. He would make you dreadfully un-happy. He would take you from us. Your mother wouldn't be able to bear losing another child."

"Sarah died, Father. She was ill and she died. I have no intention of such a thing happening to me, but I can't know it won't. I can only promise to do my best to live a long life, and I certainly have no plans to get lost."

"Olivia!" her mother gasped, white-faced. "This isn't a subject for levity."

"Mama, I promise you I am being very serious. Besides, Sarah herself always told me that I should insist on the best and only the best, and scorn to take second best. I am only trying to follow her—"

"Stop it." Her father had had enough. "I don't want a Lacey . . . I don't want him in this house again," he said, hardly raising his voice, and yet his tone stopped Olivia midsentence. "Is that clear?"

"Father . . ."

"Is that clear, Olivia?"

It was useless to argue. They would not listen and they would not see. They had made up their minds that Nic was the villain and the only way to save her was to hand her over to the hero, in this case Theodore Garsed.

"Yes," Olivia said dully, "it is very clear, Father."

Her father was pleased with her, now that she'd given up the fight to be independent. He drew her into a warm embrace and kissed the top of her head. "You have been ill, my dear. That has made you a little testy, perhaps. When you are better you will realize I am right. We know what is best for you, and you must follow our advice, not Sarah's. Theodore Garsed is a good man. Your mother is very keen on him."

Then *she* should marry him, Olivia thought mutinously. She was glad when they decided she'd had enough excitement for one day, and left her to rest on the chaise longue.

Alone and beaten into submission.

Or so they thought.

But Olivia had no intention of giving up. She'd sworn to the other members of the Husband Hunters Club that Nic Lacey was her chosen husband, and nothing had changed. In fact, after today, when he'd told her he wanted to save her from Theodore Garsed, she was more certain than ever that Nic was the man, the *only* man, for her.

And she was more determined than ever to have him.

The church bell was ringing as Theodore took the path by the village pond and into the woods that bordered Nic Lacey's land. Ahead of him, Nic was riding slowly, evidently deep in thought. Theodore was not sure yet what he was going to say to the other man, but he knew he must say something.

He was still reeling from the realization that His Lordship was a rival for Olivia's affections. The way Lacey had ogled her! How had this happened, and right under Theodore's nose? Well, he had to put a stop to it. Lacey's reputation was of the worst, and if Theodore was officially engaged to her, he'd have ordered Lacey from the house. As it was he'd been insulted and routed, and forced to leave Olivia alone with that rake.

Theodore ducked under an overhanging

branch just in time. After he'd rearranged his hat, he peered ahead through the shadowy woods and saw that Lacey was still there. Mrs. Monteith had been in a terrible state, but he'd sworn to her she could rely on him to do everything in his power to save her daughter.

"I know how you feel about a duel, my dear madam, but believe me, if necessary I will face Lacey at dawn and finish him once and for all."

Brave words, and he was certain he'd impressed Mrs. Monteith with his fervor, but in reality he knew he was at a disadvantage. There were rumors that Nic Lacey had shot a man in scandalous circumstances in Paris, and there had been other encounters in the time since. Theodore wasn't much of a shot, and he wasn't very courageous, either. He couldn't really see himself turning up at dawn and taking turns to try and put a bullet in his opponent. Such barbaric behavior was repellent to a gentle soul like Theodore—he was a poet at heart, not a soldier. Now, if it was his brother, Alphonse, standing against Lacey, things would be very different!

Ahead of him there was a cry. He looked up and saw Nic Lacey's horse rearing up on its hind legs. Something, a bird perhaps, had startled it. Lacey, taken by surprise, clung on briefly, but the next moment he was thrown and landed heavily on the ground.

Theodore didn't move, staring at the scene before him, certain that in another moment Lacey would get up. But as the seconds ticked by, Lacey remained unmoving, while his horse wandered a few paces away and began to crop the grass.

I should go and see if he's badly hurt, Theodore thought. *I should go for help.*

But like Nic Lacey, Theodore didn't move.

His mind was racing.

If Nic Lacey was seriously injured, if he was—God forbid!—dead, it would be a tragedy, of course it would be, and yet there was another side to the coin. With Lacey out of the way, Theodore's difficulties would be over. Olivia would be safe and everything would go back to being comfortable, and Theodore need do nothing courageous at all.

No duels, no messy arguments, no fisticuffs.

But could he really be such a coward? No, he told himself firmly, not a coward. He was simply using his reasoning and his intelligence to extract himself and Olivia from a potentially tricky situation. If Lacey had an accident on his way home, it had nothing to do with Theodore. If he hadn't just happened to be here, completely by coincidence, he would never have known.

Decision made, he turned his mount around and rode back the way he'd come, leaving Nic Lacey alone to his fate.

Chapter 7

Olivia was glad to be alone. After yesterday's excitement she had been exhausted and eager to go to bed, but this morning she was almost herself again. Her mother had agreed she could sit in the garden, as long as she wore her warmest shawl and tucked a rug about her feet. It was better than nothing.

She reached into her sleeve and took out the note Nic had sent with his flowers. Olivia had read it several times already, but it didn't hurt to read it again. Not that it was in any way improper—he wished her a speedy recovery—she simply liked to see his heavy scrawl and the way he signed his name: "Lacey."

She closed her eyes and sighed, remembering his kisses. How could she ever make do with good-enough when she'd tasted paradise? If he thought he was going to be noble and she was going to give up, then he was making a grave mistake. There was an overflowing well of passion inside her, and she refused to dam it shut or let it dry up. She wanted to live her life to the full, and he was the man to help her do it.

"Miss Monteith?"

Olivia opened her eyes, blinking against the sunlight. Estelle was standing in front of her, hands twisting in her apron, looking worried.

"What is it, Estelle? My mother—"

"Mrs. Monteith is chatting with one of her friends in the parlor. It's Lord Lacey I've come about, miss."

"Lord Lacey?"

"He was thrown from his horse. He's not badly injured," she hastened to add, seeing Olivia's eyes widen, "but his lame leg was twisted. He's having trouble walking. Abbot thought you might like to know."

"I did. I do. Thank you, Estelle."

She wanted to go to him and see for herself that he was all right, but Olivia knew that even if she could, she wasn't up to visiting yet. This was her first day outside in a week.

"Can you tell Abbot to inform Lord Lacey that I wish him well," she said, calming herself. "Very well."

Estelle smiled. "I'll tell him, miss."

"How—how did it happen?"

"Lord Lacey was on his way home from calling on you, miss. Some creature frightened his horse, and he was thrown. He lay there for an hour or more before he was discovered and help was sought."

It sounded appalling, and Olivia was only glad

that Nic hadn't been killed. As it was, Estelle said he was having trouble walking, and Olivia wondered if his injuries were permanent. She had a momentary image of herself gravely nursing him through his pain. She could straighten his pillows and lift his head so that he could drink, and spoon thin beef broth into his mouth when he was hungry. Olivia pictured him gazing at her in earnest adoration and declaring how wrong he had been to reject her.

It was nonsense and she knew it, but sometimes it was pleasant to tell oneself fairy stories. In reality Nic Lacey was far more likely to curse his leg, and her, than obediently take his medicine and suck broth from a spoon. He'd probably send for some of his lady friends to cheer him up.

Her smile faded.

Nic Lacey might be a rake with a string of women in his past, but Olivia was determined that once she caught him there would be only one woman in his life.

And that was Olivia.

In Castle Lacey gardens, Nic sat gloomily in the chair Abbot had set for him, his leg resting on a mountain of cushions and the damnable walking cane close by. The scent of flowers was pleasant, the sun was warm, and the drone of bees made him sleepy. But he chafed against his forced inactivity. He was being made to feel like a cripple and he loathed it, but he'd been warned of the consequences if he didn't do as he was told.

"Rest or you may never walk again," the doctor had told him with chilling bluntness.

"I'm sure you can get me on my feet again," Nic retorted, gritting his teeth as the physician poked and prodded at him. "You've done it before."

"I can only do so much, my lord. Your leg never set properly after you broke it the first time. I warned you then that if you didn't go to London for the best possible treatment you'd always have trouble with it, but you chose to ignore my advice."

"Yes, yes, so you've reminded me innumerable times before."

"And you never take the slightest bit of notice. Well, this time, my lord, you will listen to me or I will wash my hands of you."

Nic ground his teeth. Even he knew the doctor was right, but he hated to admit it. "I will take your advice and rest," he bit out. "Now leave me alone, devil take you!"

"Very wise, my lord." Unperturbed, the doctor gave him one more stern look, clicked his bag shut, and left.

After several dreary days confined to the house, Nic was finally allowed to begin to exercise. Just a few minutes at first, until now he could walk about the garden, with the help of his cane, and without having Abbot hovering over him like a demented nursemaid. It still hurt, of course. Sometimes the pain left him faint and his breathing ragged, but he refused to let it beat him. And he refused to contemplate turning down his invitation to this year's demimonde ball, as Abbot was hinting he should.

They'd had another to-do earlier, before Abbot put him out there in the garden and left him to his own devices. Abbot seemed to be prone to the sulks these days, but Nic wasn't going to let it spoil his day. He'd go to the ball and find some smiling beauty to take to Paris with him, and they would have a splendid romp.

Until it was time to come home again.

Nic's mood turned even gloomier, and he sat contemplating his leg, and remembering the day he had broken his thigh bone. The pain had been excruciating. He remembered the doctor telling him to get specialist help in London, but at the time it'd been impossible to leave the castle. Even though he was damaged and in agony, there was no one else to take charge with his father dead and his mother half mad with grief. He shivered, as if a cloud had slid over the sun.

Those days were some of the worst ones of his life, and being here at the castle was a constant reminder. Another reason to get away as soon as possible.

The sound of voices drew his attention and he looked up. Abbot and two women were standing at the end of the long walk. As he watched, Abbot and one woman walked away, and after a moment's hesitation, the second woman began to come toward him.

Nic shaded his eyes.

She wore a white dress that seemed to float about her slippered feet, and her parasol cast shadows but could not dim the glow of her golden hair. Or her beauty. She was a woman in a million, a rare jewel. She took his breath away, scattered his wits, and left him in a state of permanent arousal, and that was the problem.

Olivia Monteith was the very last person he wanted to see right now, when he was at his lowest ebb. He felt as if he'd already said goodbye and relegated her to the past, and that was where he expected her to stay. That was what he'd done last time he felt threatened by her, when they used to meet by the stepping stones— the day he'd looked at the child and seen the budding woman.

Now here she was, and the fact that the sight of her made his chest tighten and his pulse give a little jump angered him.

"Lord Lacey." She'd stopped before him, and he noted the cautious expression in her eyes as she looked down at him, as if she suddenly sensed danger.

Good! Let her beware. Let her turn around and run home as fast as her legs could carry her. But Olivia being Olivia, she didn't run away. She stood firm and said what she'd come to say.

"I'm so sorry to see you hurt," she said. "Is there any—any lasting damage to your—your—"

"My leg?" he demanded, furious and not bothering to hide it. "Am I even more of a cripple than

I was before? Don't try and wrap it up nicely, Olivia, ask away. There's nothing I love more than to discuss my physical infirmities."

She glanced to one side—a gesture he'd noticed before when she was embarrassed or anxious. "Don't be cross, Nic. I was worried. I couldn't come before, but I'm here now."

"I'm surprised the faithful Theodore isn't here with you, just to make certain I don't contaminate you."

Her eyes widened, but before she could accuse him of being jealous, he gave her thoughts another direction.

"Or ravish you."

"Estelle is with me." She looked over her shoulder at the empty walk, gave a shrug. "Somewhere. I think she went off with Abbot."

"Somewhere?" With a groan he covered his face with his hands. "You need her here, by your side, Olivia. You're not a fool. Do you want your reputation to be ruined?"

"Nic . . . you're in pain," she said, "but I know you'd never hurt me. I trust you."

There was no way to reply to a statement as ludicrous as that.

"How did you break your leg?" she went on, when it seemed he wasn't going to try.

He nodded beyond her, toward the end of the long walk where the ruins of the old bailey wall still stood. "I was climbing and I fell."

"You were climbing?" She stared wide-eyed.

"My father was an enthusiast and he taught

me from a young age. He climbed in Wales and Derbyshire. I was never as good as he, but I could scale that wall well enough. The last time . . . well, I was upset and probably a little drunk. I took a misstep and fell. They wanted to send me to London but I refused. My father had just died and my mother needed me."

"You pretend to be wicked, Nic, but at heart you are a good man."

"Olivia, I'm not your knight in shining armor," he growled, sinking lower in his chair.

"Certainly not," she replied with a shudder. "And I'm not one of those pitiable damsels in distress."

Something in her words and her manner caught his attention, lifting him from his gloomy self-pity. "So how do you see yourself?"

"A free, independent spirit."

He showed his teeth. "I hate to burst your bubble, but there's nothing independent about a woman of your class and situation. Eventually you will see that and settle down and do as you're told."

"Never!"

She sounded fierce and determined, and he wondered if she could manage to escape the bindings and chains her family and society had already fashioned to snare her. Not maliciously, perhaps, but nevertheless their rules and unspoken laws were meant to stop her from being exactly what she wanted to be: free.

Now that he understood her situation a little

better, Nic wondered if that was why she had fixed her sights on him, as an antidote to Theodore. Well, if that was so, then he would have to do his best to disabuse her of her foolish belief.

"I turned my back on you before," he said bluntly. "Would a man with a good heart do that?"

Olivia was making herself a comfortable seat on the grass beside his chair, her skirts drifting about her, her parasol rolling to one side on its fringed rim. She looked up, surprised. "What do you mean?"

"I mean those trysts you remember so fondly. Did you never wonder why I stopped coming?"

A cloud came into her eyes. "I wondered why. I visited the castle once, perhaps twice, but you were away. You were away a great deal. I suppose it occurred to me that my parents had discovered our meetings and warned you off. I resolved to wait until I was older and could do as I pleased. I told myself that if I still felt the same about you when I reached my majority, and you were still free, then I would make my feelings known to you."

He gazed into her passionate upturned face for a long moment. There was such a look in her eyes. And he understood. He understood only too well. But understanding did not mean it was in his power, or his wish, to help her.

"Well now you know," he said cruelly. "You bored me and I dropped you." He moved to stand up and then gasped as the now-familiar agony en-

veloped his leg. For a moment black spots danced
before his eyes, and it was all he could do to stop
from crying out.

"Poor Nic." Her soft voice came through the
pain. As his head cleared, he found she was kneeling beside his chair, her arms about him, holding
him, with his face pillowed against her breast.

"If this is a dream then it's a good one," he murmured, and sighed, beginning to enjoy himself
despite his discomfort.

Olivia either didn't hear him or believed his
words were induced by his suffering. "Is there
nothing they can do for your leg?" she said.
"Surely, in this modern age of medicine and science, there is something."

"It has been suggested I have it rebroken," he
replied, his voice muffled by her sweet, lush flesh.
"However, I don't fancy it."

She shuddered and held him closer. "I wouldn't
fancy it, either, but if it was the only way to make
things better . . ."

He could feel the beating of her heart. He wondered what she'd do if he unfastened her dress
and unlaced her stays and began to fondle her
in the way he wanted to. If he laid her down on
the soft grass and lifted her skirts and used his
tongue and fingers on her until she came. And
then, when she was hot and wet and ready, he'd
begin the long, slow dance of pleasure.

"Olivia," he groaned.

"Poor Nic, is it so bad?" She was stroking his
hair now. In another moment she'd be kissing his

brow and he'd have her on his lap, with her legs in the air.

"Olivia, I may appear to be a helpless invalid but I am a virile man. If you don't move away from me I will prove it to you."

He sounded dangerous, and, startled, she leaned back. He could see she was flushed, tendrils of her hair loose about her face, and her blue eyes were brighter than ever.

Nic did the only thing he could do. He showed her just how much danger she was in.

"Give me your hand."

It said much for her innocence that she immediately held out her hand. He took her fingers in his, and before she could struggle or protest, brought them down to the hard rod between his thighs and pressed them there.

"This is what you do to me," he rasped.

Olivia stared into his eyes, her own perfectly round.

"Now run away, little girl, before you really are lost forever," he added, for good measure.

She moved as if to do exactly that, but once more he'd underestimated her. Instead of snatching her hand away and running, she leaned against his shoulder and looked to where her hand lay beneath his. Her gaze slid to his again, before her long, dark lashes fluttered down, and slowly, tentatively, she began to explore the bulge in his trousers.

Her fingers stroked his shaft, closed around it, and he heard her breath quicken, as if she found him exciting and fascinating. His own chest was rising and falling heavily, his limbs like lead, all sensation focused on that cursed organ between his legs as she continued to fondle and pet it.

Had he really expected her to scream and flee in terror? Or faint in outrage? He was a fool; this was Olivia he was dealing with, the woman who'd jumped into the stream so that he could save her.

"Nic." Her breath tickled his chin and her hair tickled his face. "I feel . . . I feel . . ."

Nic knew that if he turned his head he could find her mouth, and if he wanted, he could unbutton his trousers and show her how to pleasure him like the most practiced whore. And suddenly he was sickened by himself.

"Enough," he groaned, and pushed her away.

She fell back onto the grass, giving a little cry of hurt and surprise, and he had a glimpse of her stockings and petticoats before she pushed her skirts down again, and clambered to her feet.

"Go," he said, turning his face away and refusing to look at her. "No more visits, no more games. This nonsense is over."

"I don't understand what I did wrong," she cried. "Tell me what I did wrong. At least look at me!"

Nic forced himself to turn. She was flushed and upset, her eyes still bright with desire, or was it anger? He knew he'd been insane to let her imagine, even for a moment, that there might be something between them. He was insane to think he could frighten her away.

"Listen well, Miss Monteith." He sounded implacable. "I will be leaving here in two weeks for the demimonde ball, where I'll find some pretty dancer, and after that I'll take her with me to Paris for plenty of sordid dissipation. That is my world, and it's not for you."

"Nic, how do you—"

But he wasn't going to listen to her. "This is the last time you visit me. If you come again I will have Abbot throw you out."

She glanced away, and seeing her parasol lying on the ground, bent to pick it up. Her hands twisted the stem.

"Good-bye, Lord Lacey," she said at last, and if there was a faint tremble in her voice it was hardly noticeable. He watched as she turned and walked away, her back straight, and reached down to massage his aching leg.

You really are a bastard, Nic Lacey, he told himself. *Couldn't you have been nice to her?* But it wasn't possible to be nice to Olivia Monteith. She would consume him, he knew it, he'd known it the last time. She would destroy them both. In the long run it would cause far less pain and damage if he was mean to her. She didn't realize it now but one day she would. She would see that she had had an extremely lucky escape from Wicked Nic Lacey.

Chapter 8

"I won't cry, I will not cry," Olivia murmured to herself as she walked through the garden, blind to the beauties of perennial borders with their swaying foxgloves, and pleached arches of pear trees, and climbing roses of extravagant blooms. He'd made her feel as if this was her fault, and she knew he'd planned it that way. But he couldn't destroy the feelings she'd had when she'd touched him and seen the desire in his face and his eyes. Desire for *her*, whatever he tried to tell her.

She'd been so certain she could win him over, and she wondered now if it had been that very certainty that was her downfall. Had she gone about it all wrong? She had tried to persuade Nic to her point of view by being herself—respectable, innocent, wide-eyed. But he'd seen her as someone to be protected from his reputation, an untouchable creature, totally off limits. English society was very strict in its boundaries; it worshipped the purity of respectable womanhood. Nic might be a rake,

but she did not think he would ever set out
consciously to ruin an innocent young lady, no
matter what he claimed to the contrary.

So, instead of seducing her, he'd been nobly
protecting her.

Olivia needed to adjust her strategy. Husband
hunting involved taking risks, and so far she had
taken very few, and none of them particularly
dangerous, no matter what Nic said. She'd always
known he wouldn't harm her, so where was the
risk? If she wanted him then she must be prepared
to throw caution to the winds.

Excitement gripped her. Yes, what she needed
to do was shrug off the trappings of Miss Olivia
Monteith and plunge into Nic's world. She must
mingle with the shadowy, disreputable women
of the demimonde. She must show him that she
wasn't a statue on a pedestal, but a living, breathing woman, and that she was not untouchable
where he was concerned. In fact she was very
touchable indeed.

He wanted her. Now all she had to do was
show him that it was all right to want her, to take
her, and to love her. She was perfectly willing to
go to Paris with him and be dissipated, in fact
she would insist upon it. They could be happy
together.

If only Nic would allow himself to be happy.

Her steps slowed and she stopped, staring
blindly at a statue of Pan set in the midst of a
lily pond. She still burned with the sensations
he'd created, excitement and need and daring.

Whenever she was with him she felt that, but more, she felt alive, so that the rest of her life became dull and flavorless by comparison. Not being with him was something she could not contemplate; not being with him made her feel desperate.

"I will have him," she breathed. "I love him!"

"I beg your pardon?"

The imperious voice came from right behind her. Olivia turned and found a woman in a black silk mourning dress, wearing a black bonnet with a black dyed ostrich feather on her head. Her face had once been beautiful, but time and grief had aged it, pulling her mouth down at the corners, and turning her youthful skin to the consistency of crepe. But her eyes, Olivia saw with a jolt of shock, were Nic's eyes—dark and intense and passionate.

"Lady Lacey," she said, recovering herself. "I'm sorry if I intruded upon your solitude. I didn't realize—"

"Who are you? I did not know I had a visitor, and you certainly are not one of the gardeners." Was there a twinkle of a smile in her dark eyes? It gave Olivia courage.

"I have been to call on your son, my lady."

In an instant Lady Lacey's expression had hardened, the smile quite gone. Her voice into even haughtier heights. "I do not believe it proper for a young lady to visit my son without a chaperone."

"I have my maid . . ." Olivia glanced about, as if expecting Estelle to pop up from behind the shrubs. "And we are neighbors, my lady. I am Olivia Monteith."

"Monteith? I have heard the name. Weren't your family once our tenants? You had an elder sister—"

"My father is a businessman, my lady. A banker." Olivia tried not to be annoyed by her attitude. "We haven't been tenants of the Laceys for over fifty years."

Lady Lacey dismissed that with a wave of her hand—the Monteiths might have risen in the world but they were evidently still beneath her notice. "You should go home, Miss Monteith. My son is not to be trusted with young women. You are not safe here."

"I beg your pardon, my lady, but I disagree," Olivia said, her voice calm, while inside anger was beginning to simmer on Nic's behalf. "I trust your son and I feel perfectly safe with him. He would never hurt me."

Lady Lacey seemed startled by Olivia's answer, or perhaps she just wasn't used to being contradicted. "Would he not? How do you know what Dominic would do, Miss Monteith? You know nothing about him."

"Yes, I do. He isn't the man he pretends to be, my lady. But surely you must know that— he is your son. You must know him better than anyone."

Lady Lacey's face twisted, as if some great emotion had caught her unawares. "My son. Yes, he is my son, I cannot deny that. But he has destroyed himself, and me, and I can never forgive him for it."

The outburst was bitter and shocking, and Olivia searched for an answer. She knew there was something, an awful scandal—her father had hinted as much, as had Nic himself. *I have done things* . . . But surely his mother, of all people, would be on his side whatever awful crime he might have committed? And Olivia did not for a moment believe it was so awful.

"Lady Lacey, I do not pretend to know what it is that he has done," she began tentatively. "But I am sure that—"

"You are sure that what, Miss Monteith? That he is very sorry? Please, keep your opinions to yourself. You are ignorant of our circumstances, more ignorant than you know. Now, will you please leave me."

"Lady Lacey—"

"I am not in the habit of asking for something twice, Miss Monteith." Her voice was icy. "Leave me. Now."

For the second time that day, Olivia walked away, her back straight, her fingers clenched on the parasol. Tears stung her eyes but she would not let them fall. Perhaps Lady Lacey was right, perhaps she was ignorant and foolish and knew nothing of Nic. *I was bored.* His words came back to her. At the time she'd believed he was simply

trying to drive her away, but now she wondered
if they were true. She had loved Nic all her life,
but what if she had been in love with a man who
didn't exist?

Olivia stood alone in the gardens, remembering the past, every treasured memory, from the
age of ten until just a few moments ago. There
were reasons to doubt, yes, but there were also
reasons to believe in her vision of Nic. *Olivia*,
he'd groaned as she held him against her breast,
and she'd heard all the longing in his voice, all
the need he could not express for fear of hurting
her or being hurt.

Whatever the real reason for his abandoning
her three years ago, she would discover it, and she
was certain it was not due to boredom. Nic, the
Nic she knew, wouldn't do that.

"I am not going to be beaten," she told herself for the second time. So Nic thought of her as
too fragile and innocent to be in his company?
He would not soil her with his presence? Olivia
smiled to herself, her plans crystallizing in her
mind. What better way to convince him otherwise
than to go to the demimonde ball? And Estelle
would help her.

Gripping his cane in one hand, Nic heaved himself up from his chair. Slowly, painfully, he began
to make his way down the long walk, every step
exquisite agony. He refused to rest any longer like
a cripple. He must get away from Castle Lacey
and leave behind the memories of his past.

The demimonde ball was less than two weeks off, and he was damned if he was going to miss it. He needed the hot forgetfulness of being with a stranger, when nothing mattered but losing himself in the pleasure of the moment. No past, just the here and now.

Then why did an image of Olivia's face pop into his head, as he ordered her to leave? Betrayed, abandoned. And why could he think of nothing but the sweet anguish of her hand stroking his cock?

Irritably, he turned down another avenue, which ran beside the old bailey wall. He remembered his father scaling that wall, turning his head to grin down at him, urging him on. *Come on, son, you can do it. You should see the view from the top. This will all be yours when I'm gone, the Lacey estate.*

His mother always said that one day his mountaineering father would fall and kill himself, but in the end it wasn't he who fell, it was Nic. And it was Nic who killed his father.

He stopped and placed his hand against the wall, feeling the warmth of the sun on the aged stones. Hard to believe he'd been happy once, hard to believe it could have been destroyed so completely in a moment of bad decision.

He heard the sound of a step and he turned, just in time to see his mother's black skirts swirl as she spun around and made her way swiftly back the way she'd come. No words, no glances, nothing. He didn't exist for her; he hadn't existed since 1828.

Nic didn't feel this was his home, not any longer. He could never be happy here with the past suffocating him, and now there was Olivia to confuse matters. It was time, he thought bitterly. Time he left Castle Lacey, and with any luck he wouldn't be back for a very long while.

Abbot stroked Estelle's bare back as she snuggled closer to him in the narrow bed. They'd taken advantage of Olivia's visit to slip away to his room and spend some time together.

"He plans to send her away once and for good," Abbot explained, as they lay quiet, pondering their situation.

"Can't you persuade him to see her again?" Estelle murmured at last, her breath soft against his neck.

"He won't. He thinks he's being noble, or as noble as it's in his nature to be."

"I thought he was a rake. Don't rakes seduce girls?"

"Lord Lacey may be a rake but he has his self-imposed limits."

"Scruples! What sort of rake is he if he has scruples?" Her voice trembled. "There must be a way. There has to be a way."

Abbot tried to move aside to see her face, but she clung closer. "Estelle? What is it? Are you crying?"

"They have to marry, they have to . . ."

Her tears were hot and damp against his skin, trickling down into the bedclothes.

"My love, tell me what is wrong?"

It took a while but eventually she did tell him. And Abbot, stunned, didn't know whether to laugh or cry.

"I'm going to be a father?"

Estelle nodded, wiping her cheeks, watching him anxiously.

"Then we need to marry."

Her eyes met his, filling with tears once more, and that was when he saw the problem. Married or not, they would remain separated, unless . . .

"We need Nic to marry Olivia," Estelle spoke his thoughts aloud. "And as soon as possible. That is the only way we can be together, Abbot."

"Estelle, you know I can only do so much to bring this about. I will not force Miss Monteith into matrimony with Lord Lacey, not if they end in misery."

"So we end in misery instead," she said dully.

Abbot didn't know what to say to her. His position, his loyalty to his master, were integral to him as a person. How could he put his own needs first? And yet he wanted to. Right now, he wanted to carry Estelle away from here and keep her safe. But that was a fantasy and this was real life. Estelle needed him to be strong, but she also needed him to be honest.

"No, my love, that will not happen," he said firmly. "Everything will be all right. Even if I have to leave you for a time, be assured you will be safe and well looked after. I will not abandon you. I would never do that."

Estelle's eyes grew sad, but she quickly buried her face in his shoulder. He held her, telling himself she would just have to accept that perfect happiness might not be for them. He knew of many other couples in their situation, and they managed with what they had. He was old enough not to expect miracles, but Estelle was young and idealistic. He hoped she would be content, but he had a niggling feeling that she wouldn't, and she was already making her own plans.

Chapter 9

Nic, elegant in his black and white evening wear, stood with a glass of champagne in his hand and observed the ebb and flow of the crowded ballroom. Guests were arriving and greeting one another, their voices rising above the soft music of the orchestra on the dais at the far end of the enormous room. Above, a chandelier the size of a small moon shone down on glossy hair and glittering jewelry and the finest clothing money could buy.

A casual visitor might have imagined these were lords and ladies, the aristocracy come out to play, but if he looked harder, he'd notice that the evening gowns were far more risqué than any true society hostess would dare wear, and the manner in which the men and women were gazing at each other, the experience and come-hither in their eyes, was a world away from innocent flirtation.

The truth was, these women were not respectable matrons and debutantes; they were whores and dancers and actresses, and they were seeking a meal ticket in exchange for their professional expertise. A few of the men had brought along their mistresses, but the rest of the women were on the lookout for a lover for the night, or even a billet for a month or more, if the conditions were right.

That suited Nic perfectly.

Apart from satisfying his physical needs, Nic wanted a companion who was intelligent enough to hold her own in conversation with him—when he felt like conversing—and who was familiar enough with his privileged world, even if she did not originate from it, not to embarrass him with too many faux pas. More importantly, he wanted someone who wasn't foolish enough to believe their liaison was anything more than a business transaction.

There was a surprisingly large number of women out there who were happy to agree to his terms. They had a living to make, and they did not want anything permanent, and that was the way Nic liked it.

He sipped his champagne and enjoyed the view. For the past six years he'd been to every demimonde ball, and this was the part he looked forward to the most—watching the arrivals, catching the sly glances and the suggestive pouts. Then came the difficult task of making his choice, circling his prey, and consummating the bargain.

He'd never been refused. He was wealthy and reasonably good-looking. It was true that his temper was sometimes uncertain and he was lame, but he was known as a generous protector. When he was done with them, his mistresses were always left well rewarded.

Nic's gaze lingered on a brunette with a wide mouth, her bosom bursting from her emerald green bodice, and moved on to a redhead with wild springing curls and a trilling laugh. There was a yellow-haired creature in red, and a Gypsy-like dancer with flashing eyes and a temper he'd like to tame. He'd been standing there for an hour, and he didn't have any complaints, he was spoiled for choice, this was his favorite part of the demi-monde ball, and yet . . .

And yet he didn't feel the same as he usually did.

There was something wrong, and for some reason he couldn't explain, the usual excitement and anticipation just weren't there. Instead he felt irritable and restless and . . . yes, *bored*. What the devil was wrong with him? All these stunning women perambulating around the room and he couldn't see a single one he was inclined to make the effort to pursue!

Disgusted with himself, Nic reached for another glass of champagne from a passing servant. He had a trip to Paris planned, and he was damned if he was going alone. Perhaps if he invited both the brunette and the redhead into a private room, and gave himself up to the hot sensual pleasures of the flesh, he'd feel more like his old self? Nic smiled as he imagined a ménage à trois, each woman vying with the other for his attention.

But the next moment he was cursing under his breath as he realized that he'd been picturing the two women with the same face. A face he knew all too well and was trying hard to forget.

Olivia Monteith's face.

As soon as Olivia stepped through the door, she entered another world. A darker, far more sensual world than any she was familiar with. Beautiful women in revealing gowns circled the room, as elegant as gazelles, and gentlemen prowled among them, like sleek jungle lions, hunting.

A shiver ran over her flesh.

In all the preparation and fuss of getting there, she had not allowed herself to consider that what she was doing was dangerous, but she knew that if she had . . . well, she would have ignored the warning. After all, she was hunting, too—husband hunting. She was on the scent of Wicked Nic Lacey, and when she found him she'd lure him into her trap and close the door.

Estelle had been very helpful, seeing to her travel plans and her stay, incognito, in an inn at a nearby town—information, she said, she'd learned from Abbot. Olivia soon discovered she wasn't the only single lady staying there, and what was normally a situation for censure and comment provoked no questions at all, not even a curious sideways glance. Understanding followed. The demimonde ball, held in a grand manor house outside London, was a lucrative yearly event, and the innkeeper had no intention of making things awkward for his customers.

Estelle also chose her clothing for the ball, smuggling it into her room at Bassingthorpe. She'd liberated it from the attic, and after a thorough cleaning, and various additions and alterations, it was ready. Olivia laughed when she tried on the dress for the first time, unbelieving that anyone would be seen in public in anything so revealing, but Estelle insisted there would be far more eye-catching outfits than this. Now, of course, she understood that the dress was perfect. Estelle had known exactly what Olivia needed to wear in a place where the woman who created the most attention attracted the wealthiest protector.

Black silk and velvet.

The dress was tight at the waist and indecently low over her breasts, accentuating her curves, while its starkness framed her fair beauty. The other women had gone for bright colors, to draw the eye, or pale shades, as if to mock their long-lost innocence. In her black dress, Olivia stood out like a raven among the pigeons. She was already being ogled, and although she had yet to see the man she had come to capture, she told herself that it wouldn't be long before he spotted her.

"Pretend you're at a debutante ball, miss," Estelle had advised her. "Abbot told me that the principle is the same, really, because the prettiest, most outstanding ladies go to the highest bidders."

This seemed a cynical attitude, but Olivia found it did help to think of the exercise in such terms.

After the first moment of awkwardness, she set her chin high, and thrust back her shoulders, and strolled into the glittering ballroom as if she had been born to be a demimondaine.

She soon discovered that many of the women knew one another, and there were some curious and resentful glances cast in Olivia's direction. Ignoring them, and the stares of the gentlemen standing around the perimeter of the room, she began to circle with the others.

It didn't take Olivia very long to pick up their manner of walking—swinging her hips and tossing her head. A wicked smile curled her lips as she perambulated, wishing her four friends from the Husband Hunters Club could see her now. They were the only ones she would ever be able to tell about this adventure, and she was looking forward to describing to them, in lurid detail, the grand ballroom and its colorful occupants.

A gentleman taking snuff stopped with his fingers halfway to his nostrils to ogle her chest. Olivia glanced down, realizing her décolletage was slipping. It was already so low that it barely clung to the upper swell of her breasts and was dangerously close to exposing the pink circles of her areolas. Olivia gave the neckline a surreptitious tug. It was all very well to play at being a demimondaine, but she had no intention of showing her naked body to anyone but Wicked Nic Lacey.

The snuff-taking gentleman was trying to catch her eye, but she ignored him, setting out to circle the room again. If she didn't find Nic soon she'd have to rethink her plans. Perhaps he'd changed his mind, perhaps he wasn't here after all and this had all been for nothing . . .

And then she saw him.

His long body was folded against the wall, and he looked devastatingly handsome in his evening wear. A swath of dark hair had fallen over his brow, giving him an even more rakish appearance than usual. How could any woman not give him a second, or even a third, glance? As she watched, he sipped from his glass, his eyes narrowed as he surveyed the passing parade of women, coolly assessing them. He was like a groom at a horse fair on the lookout for a new mare.

The metaphor made her flush. Such thoughts were not for respectable young ladies. But Olivia had discovered she was different from the others of her class and position, and if Nic didn't know it by now, then he soon would.

He sipped his champagne again. She was directly in his line of sight now, but he seemed to be concentrating on the redhead next to her, the one with the appallingly horsy laugh. Just as she thought he'd never see her, and she'd have to go around again, his gaze shifted and he looked straight at her.

Nic's expression went blank with shocked surprise. He straightened up, and she saw anger flash into his dark eyes, as they slid over her black dress and lingered on all that bare, exposed flesh. Anger turned to outrage as his gaze returned to hers, holding her frozen for a brief moment that seemed an eternity, before her steps took her past him.

She realized she was trembling.

Olivia knew she was a little afraid of his anger, but at the same time, the memory of his eyes scalding her bare skin was exciting and shocking, almost as if he had physically touched her. She knew it was up to her now. To soothe Nic's temper and show him that she was not the untouchable young lady he believed her to be, and that there was absolutely no need for him to be noble.

"What in Hades are you doing here, Olivia?"

She jumped before she could stop herself as his angry voice rasped in her ear. He slipped his arm through hers and pulled her against his side, holding her there. She stumbled a little, steadied herself, before turning her head to look up into his face. She could see the emotion boiling in his dark eyes, turning his smile into a sneer. He was spoiling for a fight, but she wasn't about to give him one.

"I don't think my presence here is any of your business, Lord—"

"Nic or Lacey." His voice was a furious hiss. "Tonight we are men and women first, lords and ladies second."

"I wouldn't have thought there were any ladies here."

"You'd be surprised who's here, Olivia." His breath felt warm and intimate against her cheek.

"And you haven't answered my question. What are you doing here?"

"I did answer your question. It's none of your business."

"You knew I'd be here, didn't you? Answer me."

His fury was making him incautious, and others had noticed. They were openly watching and enjoying the scene, as if they were spectators at a cockfight. Olivia pulled away from him, forcing herself to smile gaily, as if he wasn't glowering at her as if he'd like to throttle her.

"No, I won't answer you. I'm here for my own personal and private reasons." She widened her eyes at him. "And those reasons have nothing whatsoever to do with you, Nic. Why on earth did you think they did?"

Before he could let fly with a blistering reply, they were interrupted by the snuff-taking gentleman, who suddenly appeared on Olivia's other side, leering.

"What do you want, Neville?" Nic growled.

"Lacey, you're monopolizing the most fetching woman in the room," Neville protested, his pale eyes sliding down over her breasts and lingering where the velvet teetered on the verge of slipping. "Come with Neville, my beauty. He's far better tempered than this moody brute."

Olivia never liked men who spoke of themselves in the third person—she always believed they secretly thought themselves more important than anybody else, like royalty.

"Oh, I don't mind a man with passion," Olivia said airily.

"Neville has passion," he rumbled. "He's a fire-brand of passion."

She opened her mouth to give him a set-down, but Nic was too quick for her.

"Keep the devil out of this, Neville," he said nastily. Sliding his arm around Olivia's waist, he turned her and led her out of the crush.

"That was rude," Olivia said reprovingly, although she was secretly delighted by his possessive attitude. She was enjoying herself very much, but it wouldn't do to let Nic see that.

"You don't know what rude is," he snarled, tugging her toward a secluded alcove, where there was just space enough for a sofa and a potted fern on a plinth.

Nic untied a gold silk cord that was holding up a looped, red velvet curtain and let it fall, effectively creating a separate room. Inside, it was surprisingly private, while the noise from the ballroom beyond became a background hum.

"What possible reasons could you have for coming to a place like this?" he said in a voice that probably brought dread to the hearts of most people.

But not to Olivia. "The same reasons as you, I expect," she said mildly, seating herself on the sofa and arranging her skirts.

He raised his eyebrows in mocking disbelief. "You're looking for a lover for the night? I very much doubt—"

"Nic, I have a secret." She lowered her voice, her heart beginning to beat faster. "I am not quite the angel you think me. I find myself drawn to excitement and to danger. I want to experience all that life has to offer. When you spoke of the demimonde ball, I knew I had to see it for myself. That is why I am here."

He stared into her eyes as if trying to read the lies, and then his gaze dropped down to her neckline, and she recognized the sear of heat in their darkness. Olivia looked down, too, and saw that her bodice had slipped again, only this time her pink areolas were partially visible, and the hint of one nipple. In another moment she would be half naked before him.

That was when Olivia knew for certain that she was no respectable young lady.

Because she was looking forward to it.

Nic tasted the sweet tang of lust. It tightened his muscles and tendons, and jolted his body into readiness. If she was anyone else but Miss Olivia Monteith, he'd be kissing her by now, his hands busy freeing her from her bodice so that he could caress her until she begged for more.

But she wasn't anyone else. She was Miss Olivia Monteith, and it was up to him to keep her safe from scoundrels and seducers like himself.

He closed his eyes with a groan, and when he opened them again found she had tugged up her dress to a more respectable level. Although—he swallowed—not by much. The swell of her breasts threatened to overflow again at any moment, and Nic was finding it difficult to breathe normally.

He tried to concentrate on her expression, and the words she had just spoken. *I have a secret.* Nic was certain she was playing games with him, but her smooth face and unflinching gaze made it difficult for him to tell her true feelings from her lies. Olivia Monteith addicted to danger and excitement? Olivia Monteith eager to experience life on the edge? Impossible! Girls like Olivia were made to be placed on a marble pedestal, far above the dirt and grime of ordinary life, where they could be an inspiration to lesser mortals.

"Should we be hiding in here, Nic?"

He frowned at her, forcing his wits to focus. "Hiding?"

"Well, I don't think this can be the way things are done at functions like this. How will I ever meet any nice exciting men if I'm shut up in here with you glowering over me like a dog with a bone?"

Something inside him jolted, and an angry protest rose to his lips. *Nice exciting men be damned!* He bit it back. That was probably exactly what she wanted, to push him to the point of insisting he take her home. Then his evening would be ruined, as well as his visit to Paris, and she'd have him in her clutches once more.

"You are neither my relative nor my guardian," Olivia was saying calmly, giving her bodice another upward tug. "You can't stop me from doing as I please, and my pleasure is to enjoy myself."

"Olivia, the men who come here are only concerned with finding a pliable woman to take to their beds. Don't tell me that is what you want, because I won't believe you."

She laughed. "You must think me very simple not to know that, Nic. Of course they want to take me to bed, and—" she leaned closer again, bringing with her a heady waft of perfume—"I am more than willing to go. If I am to spend the remainder of my days with Mr. Garsed, I'll need something very special to remember, to distract me from the boredom."

He stared at her, openmouthed. She couldn't possibly mean that. No, she was still trying to bamboozle him into saving her, like some knight in shining armor, no matter how much she had once protested to the contrary.

"You speak of the bedroom as if you know all about it," he sneered. "You can't convince me you are anything but an innocent, Olivia."

"Well, I know a little," she said thoughtfully. "You let me touch you, remember, so I know what a man can feel like. Of course I don't know everything, but I am very keen to learn. Do you want to show me?" she added innocently. "So I don't make a fool of myself? I'd hate to be laughed at in such experienced company."

Yet again Nic found himself without anything to say. She wanted him to "show her" what to do? He knew in his black rake's heart he wanted nothing more than to be her tutor in all things sensual, but instead he was clinging by his fingernails to his tattered gentleman's honor. Just.

"Go home, Olivia. You will be hurt and ruined if you stay here, and I won't be able to protect you."

"I don't want you to protect me," she retorted crossly. "I didn't come here to be a burden on you. I want to enjoy myself. Now, are you going to let me go?"

He looked at her a moment more, trying to read past her defiance, and then he shrugged and held the red velvet curtain aside. Outside their secluded alcove the ball was more boisterous than ever. A couple stood by the wall, just beyond the alcove, their mouths seeking, their bodies pressed tightly together. The woman's skirts were pulled up and the man's hand was busy beneath her silks.

Nic glanced at Olivia and thought she turned a little pale at such blatant lust, but when she noticed him watching, she made a point of standing and viewing the scene with open curiosity.

"This uninhibited behavior is very refreshing," she said. "Have you ever—"

"Not in public. Not here," he spoke between his teeth.

"So you prefer closed doors and privacy, rather like any other gentleman?" She sounded disappointed, blast her.

"I went to an orgy in Rome once," he said, "but I don't remember much after the first hour."

Her blue eyes flickered to his and away again.

"What a waste, Nic, if you can't remember it. I'm sure when I go to an orgy I will want to experience every second of it over and over again."

"You're not going to any orgies," he almost shouted.

Olivia glanced at him again, and this time she smiled. He narrowed his eyes at her as she reached out and twisted a dark strand of his hair around her finger, smoothing it back from his neck and his collar. Her touch made him ache, and he wondered how he managed not to haul her into his arms and kiss the life out of her. Perhaps because he knew that he'd find it hard to stop.

"I think I might go and meet some of these interesting people now, Nic."

"Please yourself," he growled.

She hesitated, as if she expected him to argue, but Nic wasn't going to argue with her any more. If and when she wanted help to get home, she could come to him and ask nicely. In the meantime he wasn't going to waste any more time on her. He was there to enjoy himself, and, goddamn it, that was what he was going to do.

Chapter 10

Despite what she'd said to him, Olivia admitted it would have been nice if he'd accepted her offer to be the one to introduce her to the art of pleasure. She supposed it was still difficult for him to see past his vision of her as his respectable young neighbor, but she was determined that by the end of this evening he would be looking at her through newly opened eyes.

With that in mind, she set out to be as outrageous as she possibly could. Men flocked to her, so there was no need to seek them out, and she flirted and laughed and tossed her head, trying not to show how secretly horrified she was by some of their remarks. At least, those that she could understand.

The other women, at first wary and occasionally hostile, seemed to become more friendly as the night wore on. One even insisted on fetching her a drink to quench her thirst, and the sweet, syrupy liquid was rather like lemonade. Olivia had no qualms in accepting a second glass. Afterward, things became a little blurry around the edges, and it crossed her mind that the kindness might have been a trick, in order to remove a rival. But by then it was too late.

"I am tipsy, quite, quite tipsy!" she cried.

Olivia tilted back her head and watched the chandelier spinning around, and it wasn't until she nearly fell that she realized it was actually she who was spinning. Her skirts belled out, her loosened hair whipped about her face, and she laughed aloud with the sheer joy of being alive.

As night slipped into morning, the noise grew louder and the company slipped further out of control. Some of the couples disappeared into dark corners, or the rooms upstairs, or else rode off in their carriages. Several of the dancers were putting on an impromptu show amid wild shrieks of laughter and applause. Nic had found a woman— or she had found him—and now she was clinging to his side like a burr. He thought it was probably so that she didn't fall over, rather than because she fancied him—she had drunk a great deal of champagne.

Nic was surprisingly sober. He smiled politely at the high jinks around him but he wasn't enjoying himself. He'd been keeping an eye on Olivia as she flitted from one besotted gentleman to the next, cleverly holding them at arm's length, then moving on before it became awkward. Once, he lost sight of her, and he found himself searching the room in a state of pure funk until he found her again.

If she noticed his nursemaidish attitude she didn't show it. Never once did she turn to see if he was there, or try to catch his eye. He alternated between wanting to take her into a corner and show her exactly how frustrated he felt, and wanting to bundle her up, toss her over his shoulder, and take her home.

"Mmm." The dark-haired beauty at his side licked her lips. "Do you want me to kiss you? I am famous for my kissing." Her gaze slid down over his trousers and she licked her lips again, so that he couldn't mistake her meaning.

"I'm sure you are."

Her eyes were brown, with a slight squint that was not unattractive, and he knew at any other time she would make him a perfect companion for an hour or two's entertainment. She would know her place and never disturb his peace of mind.

Unlike Olivia Monteith.

Nic glanced about, realizing he'd lost sight of her again. To his horror, he saw that she was climbing up onto the dais, with the dancers, and preparing to join them. Her admirers—she seemed to have gathered a dozen or so by now—were clapping their hands and stamping their feet and calling for her to dance. She looked down at them with a fond and slightly lopsided smile. The black dress was slipping again, but she probably didn't notice, and probably didn't realize she was showing far more of herself than was proper.

Proper. He snorted. It was not a word Nic had used for a long time. And yet here he was, like some sort of puritan knight, guarding his property from the lechery of men who were behaving just as he himself had behaved in years past.

He couldn't stand it. He couldn't stand what she was doing to him. It was time he reminded her, and himself, that he was no tame pussycat. Nic shook off the surprised brunette and began to fight his way through the crowd until he reached the dais.

By now Olivia was kicking up her feet, her black dress lifting to show quite a lot of slim stockinged leg. One of her slippers came off, sailing into the crowd, and there was a mad scramble to souvenir it. Olivia stumbled, doubled over with laughter, and Nic took his chance to jump onto the dais and swing her up into his arms. Running down the steps at the side, he made off with her to shouts of protest, cries of "Foul" and "Unfair," and "Let the doxy make her own choice, Lacey!" He ignored them all, as well as Olivia's breathless squeaks and wriggles.

He was still carrying her, out into the hall and up the curving flight of stairs, right to the top, without even taking time to catch his breath. He felt like a warrior of old, claiming his prize of war, as he strode boldly along the wide, opulent corridor. Several of the bedchambers were already engaged, but he finally found one that was empty. With the door closed and locked, he set her free.

She backed away from him, looking cross and disheveled, and he saw that her neckline had slipped again. She noticed his interest and tugged it up, watching him suspiciously, her eyes overbright from champagne, while her fair hair tumbled around her shoulders. She looked, he thought, completely adorable. But that didn't make him any less furious with her for spoiling his night and turning him into some kind of unwilling fairy godfather.

"You don't have to do this," she said, her words running into each other. "Pr-protect me, I mean. I am p-perfectly capable of looking after myself."

"Yes, I can see that," he sneered.

"I—I never realized before what a boring old pr-prude you are, Nic."

Nic knew then that he'd reached his breaking point. He had tried to be good and do the right thing, and where had it got him? No more Nic the gentleman. It might be reprehensible, but now he was going to do what he'd wanted to from the first moment he set eyes on her on the ballroom floor.

Slowly he prowled toward her, watching her, a hard smile flicking at his lips. "Is that what you think I'm doing, Olivia? Protecting you?"

"Yes. Because you think I—I can't look after myself." But despite her air of self-righteous certainty, her glance slid nervously from his.

"Well, can you?"

"Absolutely." Her dress began to slip again as she turned to keep him in sight as he circled her.

"Do you know why I attend the demimonde ball, Olivia?"

"To enjoy yourself as gentlemen are wont to do, I i-imagine."

"To find a woman I can tutor in my likes and dislikes."

"Tutor?" she said, doubtfully. "In conversation, do you mean?"

"In bed," he corrected her, moving closer still.

Her eyes widened, her lips opened, but no sound came out. She cleared her throat. "Do gentlemen have likes and dislikes in bed? Well, I suppose they do. It makes perfect sense that—"

He cut her short. "I think, seeing you've succeeded in ruining my chances of finding a companion I can tutor, you should offer yourself up in her place."

Now he had her full attention. "Oh you do, do you? I offered you the chance to show me the pl-pleasures of the fl-flesh before, and you refused. I don't think you should get a second chance."

"I deserve a second chance, Olivia."

He looked down at her breasts, and with one finger reached out to trace the pink half circle of her areola, peeking above the black velvet and lace. She began to speak, but when he delved beneath the cloth and stroked her nipple, whatever she'd meant to say ended as a gurgle.

"I've been wanting to do that all night," he said in a deep, rough voice. "But you knew that, didn't you, minx? You've known it all along. Well, I hope you're satisfied."

She shook her head as if to deny his words, but when he put his arm around her, she swayed into its curve, her eyes fluttering closed. He bent his head and took her nipple delicately between his lips, using his tongue to touch and tease. She tasted like raspberries.

"Is that one of your likes?" she gasped.

"Oh definitely," he growled, and pulled her further into his arms, until her body was crushed so hard to his it was difficult to tell where one began and the other ended.

The desire in him erupted. He'd been fighting this ever since she called on him and proposed to him, and he was going to fight no more.

Her remaining slipper arced across the room as he swung her into his arms, her breasts bare to his gaze and his mouth. He proceeded to lavish attention on them as he carried her to the bed. She clung to his neck, her voice a meaningless low murmur, but he was on fire and the time for talking was over.

He tossed her onto the bed and stripped off his jacket and pulled the shirt over his head, careless of torn seams. She'd rolled onto her back and was propped up on her elbows, watching him, her hair tangled about her, her eyes heavy-lidded, her lips partly open.

He began to unfasten his trousers, watching her, waiting for her to grow shocked and coy, perhaps hide her face in her hands. She didn't. Her gaze took in his body as it was revealed, only widening when his cock sprang free.

"G-goodness," she managed. "Does it always do that?"

"Only when I'm aroused," he said, "and believe me, I am very aroused right now."

"I can see you are." She brushed her hair from her eyes for a better view. "How can you tell if a woman is, eh, aroused?"

Nic couldn't remember ever having a conversation like this one, but then Olivia Monteith wasn't like other women.

"Your breasts. See how your nipples are peaked. Hard."

She looked down at herself and then reached to touch a pink bud with her fingertip, her face flushed and rapt. Nic tried not to groan aloud. He climbed onto the bed and moved closer, his heavy erection swaying between his legs.

"I see," she whispered, touching herself again. "And there's an ache . . ." Her bright eyes lifted to his.

"An ache?" he rasped, running his hand up her stockinged leg, bunching up her skirts as he went. "Where does it ache?"

"I can't say . . ."

Or she wouldn't.

Nic smiled to himself as he carefully lowered his body onto hers. She made a sound, falling back into the soft mattress, and he propped himself up on his arms so that he could see her glorious face.

"The ache means you're getting ready for me," he said. "Growing warm and moist and soft, so that I can slide all the way inside you. Deep inside you."

"How deep?" she whispered.

He bent his head to hers, anticipating the kiss. "Deep enough to make you mine," he told her.

Her lashes lowered. She smiled. "I think I would like that."

Her lips were soft and eager, and he slid his tongue inside her mouth, aware of her thighs beneath his, the hard nubs of her breasts against his naked chest. Desire, the need to possess, had overcome all his scruples. He'd have her, and the consequences be damned.

Nic reached down and closed his fingers over her hip, caressing the satiny flesh, moving lower. She was wearing something silky in place of the usual hideous drawers that women tended to wear under their pretty skirts, but the fact that she was wearing anything at all made her unique at this gathering. Still, there was a slit into which he could slip his hand. His fingers touched soft hair and slick flesh, and he felt her instinctive withdrawal. He began to murmur soothing words as he continued to stroke her, feeling her respond. Her nectar coated his fingers as he pressed them inside her, preparing the way.

Knowing he was the first had a peculiar effect on him. Before tonight he'd never thought of himself as possessive, but now the need to hold on to her, to own her completely, gripped him with an unstoppable urgency. Nic told himself not to be ridiculous, but the feeling remained. Was it some fundamental male urge left over from the days of the cavemen, who had to fight for everything they wanted and then fight to keep it?

But what right have I to keep Olivia Monteith? This will only lead to trouble. Remember Sarah . . .

"Nic?" Her soft voice pierced his distraction. She was touching his cheek, and then she began to nuzzle her lips against his jaw. "Nic, don't stop," she breathed. "I don't want you to stop. I like what you're doing to me."

But it was too late. The intrusive voice in his head had acted as a brake. Nic had come to his senses with the realization that he was about to deflower Miss Olivia Monteith. Remember Sarah? How in God's name could he forget her and the tragedy that had ripped his family apart, a tragedy Olivia knew absolutely nothing about? Why the bloody hell did everything have to be so complicated?

He lifted his head and met her eyes. "Olivia . . ."

She stared at him, reading his words before he could utter them, and the desire in her face drained away, leaving her white and tired, and suddenly very vulnerable.

Chapter 11

She couldn't believe it. Well, she could, but she didn't want to. To suddenly develop scruples now, at the last possible moment! Her body was humming from his touch, aching for more, and he was going to tell her that stopping was for her own good. It really was too much.

"I'm taking you home," he said gravely, and sitting down on the edge of the bed, began to pull on his black evening trousers. The silky cloth slid over his thighs and his shaft, still erect, but when he saw her watching he turned prudishly away.

Olivia felt like screaming. Where had the rake gone? He'd disappeared, along with the Nic who had stood before her, naked and unabashed, talking of tutoring her in the ways of the demimondaine and making her feel weak at the knees. Now in his place stood a puritanical prude who seemed determined to spoil everything while telling her it was for her own good.

Olivia could weep with frustration, but she wouldn't let him see how much she was affected. He'd probably offer her his handkerchief and tell her she'd have forgotten all about him by morning. She'd had such hopes for tonight, such certainty that he would finally wake up to the truth, and instead she was right back where she'd started.

"There's no need for you to take me home. I'm staying at the inn," she informed him coldly. "Besides, I might remain at the ball for a little longer. I was enjoying myself before you—"

"Spoiled it?" he mocked, and began to pull on his white shirt, covering the broad expanse of his wonderful chest.

"Exactly."

"Believe me, Olivia, you'd be sorry if I left you here. These people don't have your best interests in mind."

"I thought they were your friends!"

"They are acquaintances, and I hold no illusions about their reasons for being here."

"How do you know I'd feel sorry if you left me here? You don't know me at all. I might be glad!"

He didn't seem repentant, and the look he gave her was totally unmoved. "You are coming home. That inn is no place for you. I will have someone collect your belongings and then we will leave."

Olivia opened her mouth to argue, and then paused as the meaning of his words sank in. "But I thought you were going to Paris?"

"I thought I was, too," he muttered, stooping to pull on his shoes.

He wasn't going. He was changing his plans. For her. Olivia tried hard not to let a triumphant smile slip out. She'd won! Not in the way she expected, but nevertheless she had won this bout.

Slowly, as though unwilling, she climbed off the bed and began to straighten her clothing. Now that her head was clearing she couldn't help but notice her surroundings. The bedchamber was shabby and none too clean, and there was an odd smell coming from the empty fireplace, as if something had died in the chimney. This was not the sort of place she would have chosen to be initiated by Nic into the pleasures of the flesh. She gave a shiver, and then started as his arm came around her shoulders.

"You're cold," he said, his deep voice sending more chills up her back. "Did you bring a cloak, Olivia?"

"Yes."

"We'll fetch it on our way out. Are you ready? Can you walk in your stockings, or would you rather I carried you?" His eyes slid down, and for a moment he seemed to lose his train of thought, before his gaze skittered away.

Olivia looked down at herself. The décolletage had slipped again, and once more she tugged it up to a respectable height. "I will walk, thank you," she said. As they went toward the stairs, she noticed Nic was limping quite badly, and she was glad she hadn't asked to be carried. He'd already carried her from the ballroom, she remembered, and he'd only just recovered from his fall. Had he injured himself further? She thought about asking him, but knew it would only make him cross to draw attention to his infirmity—he seemed to consider his lame leg a weakness of character rather than a physical affliction.

Downstairs, her cloak was fetched, and Nic sent for his coach. When it arrived, Olivia was surprised to see Abbot with it. "Miss Monteith!" he said, obviously as surprised to see her. "How . . . how extraordinary!"

Nic gave his manservant a cool glance. "'Extraordinary' is one word for Miss Monteith's appearance at the demimonde ball, Abbot, but I can think of others. I'm wondering exactly how she managed to get here all by herself."

Immediately Abbot's face assumed a blank expression.

"I am very glad to see you, Abbot," Olivia said, with a reproving frown at Nic. "I did not realize you were attending the ball, too. What do you do while Lord Lacey perambulates?"

Abbot's mouth twitched. "I wait, Miss Monteith. This ball is not for the likes of me."

"When you are both quite finished passing the time of day . . ." Nic interrupted with quiet menace.

Abbot hastily resumed his blank servant face. "I'm sorry, my lord. May I inquire if we are still going to Paris now that Miss Monteith is here? You are not thinking of taking her with us, surely?"

"Do I hear a note of censure in your voice,

Abbot?" Nic asked in a silky voice. "I don't expect my morals to be questioned by my inferiors."

Abbot stiffened. "I am not questioning your morals, Lord Lacey. I am simply asking whether your plans have altered."

"As a matter of fact my plans *have* altered. We're not going to Paris after all . . . at least not today. We are going to Miss Monteith's inn so that you can collect her belongings and find her some slippers, and then we are taking her home to Bassingthorpe."

Taken off guard, Abbot forgot himself. "Well, I am relieved!"

Nic's eyes narrowed even more dangerously. "Did you say relieved?"

Abbot hesitated and then appeared to decide that if he was already in trouble, he might as well go ahead and express his true feelings. "We are neither of us getting any younger, my lord. Speaking for myself, I would much rather go home to Bassingthorpe than argue with French domestics when the housekeeping in Paris does not please you."

Olivia held her breath, prepared for Nic to give his manservant a severe set-down. So it came as a surprise when instead he sighed and said, quite mildly, "You are becoming a bore, Abbot. Especially when you are right. Now if we are quite finished with the nonsense, we must get going, or it will be dawn before we start."

Abbot apologized, although Olivia didn't think it necessarily his fault, but as he opened the coach door for Olivia, she caught the hint of a smile in his eyes. Perhaps she had things all wrong, she thought, and what had seemed like an argument to her was simply Nic and Abbot's way of sorting out their differences.

"Are you comfortable?" Nic was watching her from his corner.

"Thank you, yes."

The Lacey coach might be an antique, old and heavy, but the interior was sumptuous. There was even a monogram etched into the glass windows, an M and a W entwined.

"Who are M and W?" she said, touching the cold glass.

"My parents. It was a love match. You'll find M and W all over the castle."

Remembering Nic's mother and her harsh, unsmiling countenance, Olivia found it difficult to believe she was ever young and in love. She wondered what sort of childhood Nic might have had, and whether love had much to do with it.

Things would be very different when she became the next Lady Lacey, she told herself. Their children would be welcomed and loved, and Castle Lacey would ring with laughter rather than tears. Her thoughts were full of the blind determination that had carried her this far, and if there was a hint of doubt in her heart, then she refused to listen to it. Olivia knew she'd come too far to turn back.

But just for a moment she stared at the entwined letters on the coach window, thinking that not all dreams came true, and not everyone ended up happily ever after, and it was like staring into a cold, deep chasm that had opened unexpectedly in front of her feet.

Nic was trying to sleep. He was tired but not tired enough to stop the brooding thoughts whirling around in his head. After Abbot had collected Olivia's belongings from the inn and paid her bill, she'd cuddled up in her cloak and a lap rug provided by the ever-reliable Abbot, and promptly fallen asleep. In repose her face held an innocence that made him feel even more ashamed of his lack of self-control.

In the past he'd always assured himself that the women with whom he consorted knew the rules of the game. They were professionals. He did not pursue innocents, and he did not seduce respectable women. The one time he'd become involved with the seduction of a respectable woman, disaster had come crashing down on his family. His father had died as a consequence, and his mother blamed him for his father's death. Nine years later, Nic was still entangled in that web of deceit and lies.

Why then was he about to make the same mistake? Pursuing and seducing an innocent, no matter that she seemed to want to be pursued and seduced, would have serious repercussions for them both. He'd be setting a marriage trap for himself and dragging Olivia Monteith into the mire of scandal and disgrace.

She didn't deserve that and he didn't need the complication.

Eyes closed, Nic toyed with the thought that perhaps he should let Theodore have her. The man was clearly in love with her, and although in Nic's opinion he wasn't nearly good enough, Nic had to grudgingly admit that Theodore would do his utmost to look after her. Olivia would be comfortably off, cared for, and treated as she deserved—like a queen.

And with Olivia safe, Nic could then travel to Paris with a clear conscience, despite what Abbot said about being too old.

Blast the man!

He reminded himself that there was a time when Abbot would never have dared to speak to him like that. It was just that after so many years together they had become as familiar with each other as . . . as, well, friends. The word startled him. He could hear Abbot and the coach driver now, their voices rising and falling over the rattle and rumble of the wheels. He remembered how overjoyed Abbot had seemed when he found out they were taking Olivia home, and how concerned he'd appeared to be that some harm might come to her.

No, Nic admitted uneasily, that wasn't quite right. Abbot had been concerned that *Nic* might harm her.

He shifted in his seat, easing his leg into a more comfortable position. Surely Abbot didn't believe that Nic would really harm Olivia? He might have seen his master do some things they would both rather forget, but Abbot also knew Nic had his own moral code. Nic Lacey had been brought up as a gentleman, and at heart that was what he still was.

What the devil did Abbot want him to do? But he thought he knew. Abbot wanted Nic to marry her. He hankered for the quiet domestic life, wearing slippers and putting his feet up in the evenings, wearing a nightcap and drinking a glass of hot milk. Well, Nic thought irritably, Abbot might be ready to retire but *he* wasn't. And why the hell, he asked himself angrily, should he care what Abbot thought anyway!

Nic sank into brooding, his thoughts going around and around, as the coach rumbled onward.

Olivia woke off and on throughout the journey. She was warm and relaxed, and the movement of the coach was soothing. As well as refurbishing the interior, Nic must have had the springs replaced. She could see him across from her, head back against the velvet squabs, eyes closed, his mouth slightly open. Now and again he would give a soft snore.

She felt easy and comfortable in his company, and she couldn't help but wonder how she might have felt if Nic had done as she wanted him to, and slid deep into her body and made her his own. Surely such intimacy would have brought them even closer, created a bond between them, for how could it not?

The memory brought a smile to her lips. The moments with Nic, brief as they had been, boded well for their future happiness. Olivia was no shrinking violet, and she looked forward to spending many nights in Nic's bed. And he was obviously physically attracted to her. She imagined them together, enjoying the pleasures of the flesh, as he tutored her in all he knew. And because he was a rake and knew so much, it would take him a long time to teach her everything.

And then what?

Olivia admitted to herself that if she did have a worry about their future, it was that he might grow bored with her. Once they were used to each other, once they had discovered all their secrets, would he return to his old ways? There was that old cynical saying, "Familiarity breeds contempt," and unfortunately in Olivia's experience there was some truth to it. She pictured herself in a year's time, alone in the drafty castle, while Nic rode off in splendor to the demimonde ball . . .

"No!"

Olivia heard her own voice with a shock, and held her breath as Nic stirred, a frown creasing his brow, before settling into sleep again.

No, I won't let him go off alone. If he insists on going to the demimonde ball, then I will insist on going with him!

Chapter 12

When at last Nic opened his eyes, he found they were on the outskirts of Bassingthorpe. Surprisingly, in the circumstances, he had slept deeply and well, better than he'd slept for a long time. On the few occasions during the journey when he'd awoken, he'd only had to look across at Olivia's beautiful, calm face, and he'd drifted off again, perfectly content.

He yawned and stretched, sitting up straight. Olivia was also awake, watching him sleepily, the hood of her cloak drawn over her head so that only the pale oval of her face was visible.

"You were snoring," she announced.

He raised an eyebrow at her. "Is that a problem?"

"No, I am a very sound sleeper." She smiled, and then turned to the window. "We're home," she announced, and sighed, as if the fact was a disappointment to her rather than the relief it was to him.

"Yes, we are."

She looked down at herself, at the black velvet

visible beneath her cloak. "I can't let anyone see me in this."

He was tempted to frighten her into thinking he was going to drop her at her gate and leave her to explain herself, just to teach her a lesson. But she looked so woebegone he didn't have the heart.

"We're going to Castle Lacey first. You can change your clothing there."

"Thank you. I am grateful."

"I'll wager you are, you minx. How on earth did you manage to get to the demimonde ball in the first place without Mrs. Monteith finding out what you were up to?"

"I told her I'd been invited to one of my friend's homes outside London, to celebrate her birthday. My friend—her name is Marissa—agreed to help me and arranged for a coach to collect me and take me to the ball."

"So you and your friend are both complicit in the lie. Who is this Marissa and why should she help you to ruin yourself?"

"Marissa is . . . never mind." Olivia pulled a face. "Yes, you're right, I did lie. But it was either that or be locked in my room and married off immediately to Mr. Garsed."

"Perhaps being married off to Mr. Garsed would be the best thing for you, Olivia."

"You were warning me against him before!"

"Yes, but I've had a chance to reconsider the matter. If you married Theodore you'd certainly have far more freedom than you have now."

Her eyes narrowed. "Freedom?"

"Yes. The man's besotted with you. If you were so inclined you could twist him around your little finger."

Olivia shook her head at him pityingly. "Is that all you think I want? A man I can run rings around by pretending an affection I don't feel? I don't think either of us would be very happy in those circumstances, do you?"

Nic shrugged, assuming a bored expression. "Is marriage meant to be happy? Perhaps you've wasted your time reading too many romantic novels."

"Perhaps *you* haven't read enough," she snapped.

Despite himself, Nic grinned. "I have read quite a few warm books, do they count?"

"You're avoiding the question. You've decided it would be best if I marry Mr. Garsed so that you won't have to bother about me anymore. That's it, isn't it, Nic? You want to go back to your cozy life where you don't have to care about anyone, and if you start to care, well, you can just pay them off."

Nic felt a tingle of shock as her words sank in. Was that true, was he such a cold and heartless bastard? He tightened his mouth. Well, even if it was true, she had no right to judge him.

"I refuse to be miserable just so that you can lead an easy life." She folded her arms and stared from the window, refusing to look at him.

"Am I spoiling your rosy dreams of love?" he mocked. "Better you learn the cold realities now than be disappointed later. In my experience love is merely a fantasy, a biological trick to lead naïve couples into the sort of illogical behavior that usually ends in disaster."

Now she was looking at him, her blue eyes narrowed as if she was seeing inside him and didn't like what she saw. "What a horribly bleak way of looking at things!"

He shrugged. He supposed it was a bleak outlook, but he'd been shaped by his past, and he wasn't going to change his mind now. If Olivia was seeking a husband with bright and shiny dreams of a future together, then it was just as well for her sake, and his, that Nic had not the slightest intention of marrying her.

"You didn't used to talk like this."

"Perhaps I didn't want to spoil your childish dreams."

"And then I grew so boring you dropped me."

He met her quizzical gaze and forced a bland smile. "Exactly."

"Nic, if you'd only let me, I could—"

"No!" He took a deep breath, moderating his tone. "Olivia, please. Enough. Let's just get this over with as painlessly as possible. Then you can go home and I can go to bed, and we can forget this ever happened."

She gave him one last glare and turned back to the window.

They were still not speaking—and Nic thanked God for it—when they trundled up the driveway to Castle Lacey. His mother's house was in darkness, and there were no lights from the castle. Although the dawn light was creeping across the park and gardens, reflecting in the mullioned windows, the buildings themselves looked forbidding. Not the cheeriest of homecomings, especially when he'd left so recently believing he wouldn't be back for several months.

It wasn't always like this. Nic had to admit that when his father was alive and his mother was speaking to him, the atmosphere had been different. His childhood hadn't been unpleasant, not at all. As an only child he'd been spoiled, and he knew at school he'd caused his parents quite a bit of worry and despair, but they'd sorted through that. The day he saved the child Olivia from drowning he'd realized what a fool he was being, and he'd made a vow to do better. Eventually he would have grown into the man they expected him to be and everything would have been all right. If only . . .

"Nic?"

Olivia's voice startled him out of his gloomy thoughts. She was watching him, a worried crease between her brows.

"Hmm?"

"Won't Lady Lacey be wondering who is arriving so early?"

"My mother occupies the gatehouse these days. She doesn't interfere in my life, nor I in hers. Don't fret, Olivia, she won't come poking her nose in where it isn't wanted."

"Is it true—" she began, but whatever she meant to ask was never finished. The coach drew to a halt before the castle, and the next moment Abbot was busy opening the door. Olivia gave him a smile as she was assisted out into the chilly morning.

"I'll get rid of any of the servants who may be up," Abbot said to his master. "Then Miss Monteith can be comfortable."

"By all means let's make sure that Miss Monteith is comfortable," Nic replied dryly.

"It may take me some little while," Abbot went on, pointedly ignoring his tone. "I suggest you take your time, my lord. Admire the roses. I have been told they are at their best in the dawn dew."

Nic groaned, but Olivia was already smiling and declaring, "What a good idea, Abbot!"

It wasn't until Abbot had gone and they were alone that she seemed to recall his lame leg. He blamed himself for stumbling, slightly, as he opened the gate into the walled garden. Olivia opened her mouth, met his gaze, and closed it again. He was grateful she had the wit to realize he wouldn't appreciate her drawing attention to his status as a cripple.

But Olivia could never be kept down for long. Now, smiling, she took his arm in hers, surreptitiously supporting him. "Isn't this lovely," she murmured, breathing deeply of the cold, clear air. "So—so bracing."

Knowing very well what she was about, Nic shot her a mocking glance. "Extremely bracing," he added. "In fact, I don't think I've ever felt quite so braced."

Her smile wavered. "I am trying to be polite,"

she said quietly. "I know it is difficult, considering it is barely light, we are hiding from the servants, you are in a foul mood, and my feet hurt from dancing most of the night. But I am trying."

Blast it! Nic wished she wouldn't do that—make him feel like a cruel monster. Now he would have to make it up to her, he thought, as they made their way into the rose garden.

"I call this one Mildred's Rose," he said, pausing by a particularly enormous bloom. "The scent reminds me of an old aunt who has long since died. She reeked of a perfume just like this."

Olivia bent and breathed in the scent. "Oh. It is a little peculiar."

"She was a peculiar woman."

She smiled uncertainly, and they moved on, and he pointed out another rose, smaller and darker, with yellow stamens.

"This one makes me think of a woman I met in Brighton. I don't know why."

"Or you won't tell me," she retorted.

"Probably," he said, with a twitch of his lips.

But Olivia had found something more to her taste, and she exclaimed over the full and exquisite bloom, before burying her nose in the huge cup of purple-pink petals. "Oh, heavenly," she sighed. "So romantic."

When she lifted her head Nic noticed she had some pollen on the tip of her nose.

"Do you know the name of this one?" she said, glancing at him cautiously as he continued to stare. "Nic?"

"No. I'm sorry, but I don't. My mother will know. I'll see if I can find out."

"You'll ask her for me?" There was something in the question that made him think she wanted him to confide in her, and when he didn't immediately answer, she answered it herself. "It's true, isn't it, what the gossips in the village say? You and your mother don't speak, do you?"

Nic gave her a sideways glance. "Yes, it's true. My mother and I do not speak. We have not spoken for a very long time."

"I wish I knew why, Nic."

He could see her thoughts in her eyes. What had he done that was so terrible that his mother no longer had contact with him? What was the dark and desperate secret of Castle Lacey? He wondered what would happen if he told her the truth, but he didn't really have to wonder. He knew.

"Nic?"

Instead of answering her, Nic reached out and brushed his fingertip down her nose, holding it up for her to see the smear of bright yellow pollen.

"Oh." She blushed. "Thank you."

He smiled down at her, and their gazes met and tangled, and at that moment he knew he was going to kiss her. He was saved from making another mistake by the sound of a voice drifting from the direction of the castle.

"Is that Abbot?" Olivia said, turning to look.

It was indeed Abbot, waving at them from the steps on the terrace.

"Come on," Nic said, sounding relieved. They

made their way back through the rose garden to the gate, and he strove to walk without limping as they hurried toward the terrace. His leg still hadn't mended from his fall and the cold air wasn't helping, but he was eager to get Olivia home.

Nic didn't trust himself, and it was getting more and more difficult to remember why he couldn't have her.

Olivia followed Abbot as he led them to a small room off the salon, where a fire was warming the room, and two chairs were drawn up before it. Nic moved to hold his hands out to the flames, leaning against the mantelpiece, so that he could ease the weight on his painful leg. Olivia slipped off her cloak and sat down, surreptitiously checking to see whether her dress was decent.

A moment later Abbot returned with a tray of food, bits and pieces from the pantry, and a jug of red wine and two goblets. Nic splashed the liquid carelessly into the goblets and swallowed down his own.

"You may as well go to bed, Abbot," he said, refilling his goblet.

Abbot looked at Olivia, an uneasy expression in his eyes. "What about Miss Monteith?" he protested.

Nic met his gaze and held it. "Don't you trust me to deal with Miss Monteith, Abbot?" he said lightly, but there was an underlying note of something more serious in his voice.

"I thought you might prefer to go to bed and let

me deal with Miss Monteith, my lord. Your leg has not yet healed and—"

"I am not quite a cripple yet, thank you, Abbot. I will do what is necessary to see Miss Monteith is safe."

Abbot hovered in the room, clearly not wanting to obey, but Nic was having none of it.

"Go, Abbot. Unless you don't trust me. Is that it? Don't you trust me to behave like a gentleman?"

Abbot knew when he was beaten. "Nothing of the kind, sir. Good night." His manservant bowed low, and closed the door carefully behind him.

There was an awkward silence.

Nic rubbed his hand across his eyes. "Blast it," he muttered. "Why does he have to put my back up? He should know by now what is and isn't acceptable in a servant. In *my* servant."

"He was only trying to be thoughtful," Olivia replied soothingly.

"So was I," he retorted. He took another swallow of the wine and nodded at the platter. "Are you hungry?"

In truth, Olivia felt light-headed from the late night and now the red wine she was sipping. She took a piece of cold meat and popped it into her mouth, adding a slice of cheese and a crust of bread. There was nothing sophisticated about the meal—Theodore Garsed would be appalled—but she thought it tasted delicious. It was a moment before she noticed that Nic wasn't eating, although he'd poured himself yet another goblet of wine.

His face was wearing that dark, brooding expression that never seemed to bode well.

Not that she was afraid of him, she told herself. How could she be afraid of Lord Lacey when she had set her heart on making him her husband? Anxiously she slid another piece of food from the platter into her mouth, only realizing as she bit down that she'd inadvertently taken a pickled onion.

The vinegary taste took her breath away. Olivia coughed, trying to stifle it, but that only made things worse. She coughed again, and then as the stinging fumes reached her nose and eyes, sneezed violently. A large handkerchief appeared in front of her and she took it gratefully. When she finished mopping her face, she cleared her throat and tried for a calm smile.

Nic was watching her with concern. "Olivia?"

Her calm smile trembled at the edges. "Pickled onion," she whispered shakily.

He glanced at the tray, then glanced at her, and his expression cleared. He began to laugh. Olivia found herself joining in. It wasn't really funny, but it gave them the chance to release the tension, and she was delighted to see the brooding, haunted look had vanished from Nic's face. He took one of the onions himself, pulling a face as he crunched into it.

"Cook has overdone herself with these," he admitted.

"You should try the cheese," she suggested.

He did, and suddenly he seemed to realize he

was hungry, wolfing down meat and bread as well.

"I am quite certain Mr. Garsed doesn't offer his guests pickled onions," she said, sipping her wine.

"You're probably right. I apologize for my lack of taste."

"I can honestly say that if it came to a choice I'd much rather be sitting here with you than at a banquet with him."

He began to answer, and then his gaze slid down and he froze. Olivia froze, too, because she knew what he was looking at. Her sneezing had caused her wretched dress to slip again.

"Olivia," he said, although it was more of a groan.

Instinctively she reached to tug up her dress, but something far more fundamental made her stop. The heat in his eyes had lit an answering fire in her, and already she could feel it burning deep inside. "Nic," she whispered.

He seemed to be struggling with himself, but either he didn't struggle very hard or his need to do what he wanted was too powerful to be stopped. A heartbeat later he was kneeling on the patterned rug before her, his mouth on hers.

Chapter 13

Nic forgot his resolutions. He forgot his latest plan, to place her safely in Theodore's hands, before setting off for Paris. He even forgot the abominable ache in his leg, although it did give a nasty twinge when he dropped to his knees before her chair. All he cared about was the touch, the feel, the scent of Olivia Monteith. His world was full of her and only her, and as her soft mouth clung to his, his practiced fingers were busy unhooking her dress and letting it fall to her waist, so that he could release her glorious breasts into his hands.

Olivia clutched his shoulders, then her arms slid around his neck, clinging to him as if she thought she might fall. Gently he began to taste her, his tongue laving the curves and circling the peaks. While he worked on one breast with his mouth, he held the other in his hand, his thumb brushing back and forth over her turgid nipple. Her fingers tangled in his hair, and she made little sounds of enjoyment.

Nic glanced up at her through his lashes. Her

eyes were closed, her cheeks flushed, and her mouth reddened from his kisses. She wanted him as much as he wanted her, and this time he wasn't going to let some foolish idea of gentlemanly conduct or past history stop him. She was his for the taking and he'd bloody well take her.

He planned to lift her down onto the rug beside him, but as he began to ease her from the chair, she seemed to know what he was about, and slid down herself, so quickly that she landed on the floor with a bump. Nic caught her in his arms, and they tumbled to one side, landing amid a tangle of legs and a flurry of her skirts. Her face was resting so close to his he could see the faint sprinkling of freckles on her nose, and the thick frame of her dark lashes about her bright blue eyes.

Olivia smiled.

Nic, the hardened rake, who thought he could never be emotionally touched by a woman, knew he'd been wrong.

Reaching out, he cupped her cheek and leaned forward to kiss her, tilting his head so that he could make the most of her lush mouth. She responded eagerly, without a hint of coyness or doubt, wrapping her arms about his neck and wriggling against him. He slid his tongue between her teeth, teasing her. He was aware that his cock was painfully hard, but he was trying to hang on to some vestige of his famous technique, when all he wanted to do was plunder her.

Physical pleasure, he reminded himself feverishly, trying to focus, was a matter of balancing control with passion, using technique to increase excitement by stepping back from the brink, over and over again, so as to intensify the final climax. There was a certain pragmatic quality about making love, and usually he had no trouble in remembering that.

Olivia gave a little groan, throwing her foot over his legs, sliding her calf along his thigh, as if she wanted to climb inside his flesh. He rolled over onto his back and pulled her along with him, so that she sprawled across him, all soft curves and heated womanhood. Her hair, hanging from its pins in loose strands, tickled his nose. He nuzzled against her arched throat, working his way up to her mouth, and then nipping at her lips.

She squeaked. He felt her breath in his ear, and her fingers tugging at his starched and ironed neck cloth. Abbot would be appalled at such cavalier treatment of his creation, but neither of them cared. She pulled the crisp linen away and pressed her nose into the hollow of his throat. He drew up her skirts, feeling her stockings and her garters, and then the warm, bare flesh of her thighs. She gave a gasp and wriggled against him, eager for more contact. Nic was happy to oblige.

As she fumbled at the fastenings of his shirt, Nic revisited the familiar territory of her silky bloomers, cupping the full globes of her bottom in his palms, arching his hips against her. She groaned, her mouth open. She'd given up on the fastenings of his shirt, and instead she'd pulled the cloth up to his shoulders, exposing his bare chest to her gaze. Now she began to kiss him, nuzzling the dark hair that grew there; her breasts rested against him, the peaks brushing his skin.

She was so sensitive that even that brief contact must have affected her, because she looked up at him, her eyes heavy and bright beneath her lashes. Slowly, daringly, she bent low and allowed her nipples to brush against him again. He took them in his fingers, tugging at the hard little nubs, and she gasped. Her body was still resting on his, and her thighs opened and slipped down, so that her knees were anchored on either side of his slim hips.

Olivia pressed her palms against his chest and sat up, gazing down at him through the tangle of her hair, watching as he stroked her breasts, lost in sensation. Nic was watching her. Each time he stroked her, a tremor seemed to run over her soft skin, and he could feel the heat from her. She was ready, more than ready, but there was still a long way to go.

He stretched up to take her nipple in his mouth once more, and at the same time slipped his hand inside her bloomers and began to stroke her warm, slick flesh. She moved against him, her eyes closed, her entire being focused on the sensations he was creating within her. The flush beneath her skin, the hard peaks of her breasts, the little sounds coming from her, all told him that she was very close to her climax.

He slid his fingers inside her, using his palm to press down on her sensitive bud. Olivia bucked against him, nails digging into his chest. "Nic," she wailed. He began to tug at her nipples with his mouth, rough, his fingers slipping in and out of her, bringing her closer and closer to her peak. And then she was there, gasping and crying out, her body clenching on him as wave after wave of pleasure washed over her.

Nic gave her only a few moments to recover. Suddenly he was feeling selfish. He didn't want to wait. He needed to be inside her, possessing her, while she moaned into his mouth.

He sat up, lifting her in his arms so that she was still cuddled against him, her legs straddling his, her skirts bunched around them. Her body was open and ready; she was as relaxed as a virgin could be. Nic reached down, unbuttoning his trousers, freeing his rigid cock.

"Put your arms around my neck," he commanded her in a deep rasp.

She complied, still dazed from her first climax.

He cupped her face in his palms, forcing her to look into his eyes. For a moment he simply gazed at her, enjoying the disheveled picture she made, and the fact that she was his. "Now," he groaned, and thrust forward, bringing her hips against him at the same time, and breached her maidenhead in one strong, smooth motion.

She hardly had time to cry out before he was kissing her, caressing her lips with his, sucking on them, and murmuring soothing words. Soon she was returning his kisses, winding her arms about his neck and opening her mouth in her growing passion. He cupped her breast, gently squeezing the full flesh, taking his time although his cock was threatening to explode where it was lodged deep inside her. But he held his hips still, and forced himself to retain control.

It was Olivia who moved first, rocking her hips against him, tentatively at first, and then with growing confidence. The stem of his shaft was rubbing against her sensitive bud, giving her pleasure, and she bit her lip as the excitement began to tighten inside her. He began to move with her, sliding slowly out, and then slowly back inside again. He was wondering if there was a place in rake heaven for men who could show such patience as he, when all he really wanted to do was be a caveman.

But that wouldn't gain him the result he desired. Gentle patience now would be time well spent in the future. It would repay him well as Olivia became more experienced and they could enjoy more varied pursuits together . . .

His mind froze as he realized what he was thinking, what he was considering. The future, what future? But before he could do anything about it, Olivia reached down between their bodies and wrapped her fingers around the base of his thick shaft, holding him firmly. He tried not to wince as his sensitive flesh ached for more.

"Nic," she whispered, her breath warm and sweet against his throat. "You're inside me. Deep inside me. You've made me yours."

"Not yet," he said.

"When then?" she demanded, leaning back to look into his face. "I don't think I can wait much longer."

She was right; it was time. Cupping her bottom, Nic lifted her, and laid her down on her back on the rug. Her legs were apart, her body wide open to his perusal. He ran his fingers down the slick cleft, and then back again, circling her bud with one fingertip.

"Nic," she groaned, and he knew she was going to come again, and this time he wanted to be inside her when it happened. He set his cock at her entrance and paused. The anticipation was beyond anything he could ever remember, and he'd felt a great deal over the years. He gave himself a moment to revel in it, and then he thrust into her.

Her body was tight, enveloping him, rippling as he moved with increasing momentum. The ache inside him was building to beyond anything he'd known before.

"Nic, please . . ." she gasped.

"A little more," he said, driving hard now, and pressing deep. He forgot to be gentle, he forgot it was her first time. She whimpered, her hips moving beneath him, and he shifted slightly, so that his shaft rubbed against the little nub, ensuring her ultimate pleasure. She cried out, and her inner muscles clenched about him. Her body was wracked with shudders, and she arched up against him, as if to gain the last drop of ecstasy. At the same time he felt himself release inside her, his body going rigid. He shouted out her name, feeling the tremendous wave of pleasure roar through him.

I've given her this, Nic told himself feverishly. *Whatever happens from now on, I've shown her the pleasure to be found between a woman and a man.* He believed, arrogantly perhaps, that any further experience she might have would be measured against this one.

For a time they lay still, but Nic was already becoming aware that he was heavy and he lifted himself up, taking his weight from her. She made a little sound of protest, as if she liked to be squashed. He bent to run his tongue lazily over her breasts, and felt her shiver in response.

She turned her head and smiled at him, and he knew then that it was true—she was his. She was completely and totally his.

Chapter 14

Olivia had never felt so close to anyone in her life. She'd said things to him she'd never said before, she'd been naked in his arms, exchanged deep kisses, and been intimate in so many ways. Never before had she experienced this heat and passion in a man's arms, Nic's arms, and she knew that it had changed her. It would be impossible for her to be the same again.

She didn't want to be the same again.

Slowly, savoring every moment, she opened her eyes. Nic was leaning back in an armchair, with his arm wrapped around her as she sat curled on his lap. Her dress was now decently covering her breasts, and Nic had poured himself a brandy from the decanter beside him. She blinked—the room was different. Vaguely, she remembered being carried through the silent house and up the stairs, and into a darkened chamber. The fire was lit and the room was warm, and as she looked about her she saw a bed with tapestry curtains.

This was Nic's bedchamber.

He smiled at her over the rim of his glass.

"Good morning," he said, gesturing toward the window. She followed his glance and saw that it was truly morning now, the sun outside setting the undrawn curtains aglow.

Her body ached in places that were new to her, and she felt sleepy and wildly alive at the same time. She reached up to touch his jaw, feeling the rasp of the beard that was a dark shadow against his skin. He was still wearing his evening clothes, and despite the circles under his eyes and his slightly rumpled appearance, he was the most handsome man she'd ever seen.

"Good morning," she whispered.

He lifted the glass to her lips and she sipped, some brandy trickling down her chin. He set the glass down, and got busy with the tip of his tongue, lapping up the liquid. When he was done, he smiled and began to kiss her, slowly, intensely.

Olivia knew there were so many things to say, so many things to do—the most important being to get home without causing a shocking scandal—but right now nothing seemed to matter but returning Nic's kisses and the growing warm rush of returning desire.

Rakes definitely made the best lovers.

"Nic . . ."

"Mmm?"

He was exploring the curve of her ear, and she felt the rasp of his teeth against her earlobe, sending a shiver down her backbone. He cupped her breast through the black dress, and the sight of his long fingers doing something so intimate was enough to make her gasp and squirm into his arms.

It occurred to her that he had spent a great deal of time touching her, undressing her, and she wanted to do the same to him. Was she brave enough, did she dare? Olivia ran her fingers across his broad shoulder, until she reached his neck. He hadn't put his neck cloth back on after she all but tore it from him, and now she stroked his warm skin. His shirt was open at the top, and she could see a tantalizing strand or two of hair from the thick mat across his chest. There was a pulse in his throat and she pressed her lips to it, and the scent of him, the feel of him, ignited a spark inside her.

Olivia knew she could do this; she would.

"Take off your jacket," she said, reaching to help him slip his arms from the sleeves, tugging the garment from him and dropping it to the floor. Next came his shirt, and he raised his arms as she pulled it over his head, and also discarded it. His naked chest was right there in all its masculine glory, and she ran her palms over it, enjoying the different textures of skin and muscle and hair. She traced a circle around his left nipple with her fingertip, fascinated by the flat, dark shape and the desire-hardened nub in the center. When she bent to close her lips over him, he made a murmur of approval, and the knowledge that he was enjoying what she was doing as much as she was enjoying doing it gave her even more confidence. It urged her on.

Olivia found his other nipple, and spent some time there. The sensation was intensely erotic for her, the realization that she was in control of him and he was submitting to her. Next she explored his stomach, and the dark line of hair running down to his navel and on to the fastening of his trousers. Suddenly it seemed very important she follow that line. She ran her tongue as far as she could, feeling him shudder, and then her fingers began to work on the buttons.

Her heart was beating hard. She was seducing him, and he was allowing it. In fact—she glanced up at him—he was enjoying it. Nic was watching her beneath half-lowered lids, his chest rising and falling heavily with each breath he took. She thought he might tell her what to do, after all he'd made her believe he preferred his lovers to be well tutored in his likes and dislikes, but he said nothing.

This sense of power, of being in control, was something Olivia had never imagined she'd feel in such a situation. All her life she'd been told that the man was to be deferred to in such matters, that the woman must be compliant, bearing it as best she could. But here she was, doing exactly as she wished, and Nic was allowing it.

Olivia slipped her hand inside his trousers and found him, hard and ready. She took him in her hand, exploring this part of him with a sense of wonder. Steel and velvet, she decided, but there was nothing inanimate about him. He was so alive. She bent closer, and then ran her tongue along his stem.

He groaned. "Yes."

Olivia pushed her hair out of her eyes and looked up at him. He was sprawled back in the chair, hands clenched on the carved wooden arms, his face a taut mask of pleasure. He was hers, she thought in wonder. Who would have thought that an inexperienced young lady could have a rake at her mercy like this?

Emboldened, Olivia bent over him again, and this time she took him into her mouth.

He jerked, catching her head, holding her still while he thrust gently. The experience was new and exciting, and she was prepared to go further, but he had other plans. Nic stood up. Half naked, he stared down at her, like some magnificent and savage idol, with his shaft rising up toward his belly, and his skin gleaming in the firelight. Beneath his hooded lids his dark eyes glittered with an inner fire of their own, and he reached down to her, fingers outstretched.

"Come to bed," he said.

"Yes," she whispered, taking his hand and rising to her feet.

The bed was old and grand, with four posts and the tapestry hangings. It looked like something that was befitting Lord Lacey of Castle Lacey. A little voice murmured in her head: *How many women have lain here?* But she ignored it. The past didn't matter, she told herself firmly. It was now, the present, that was important.

Perhaps he read something of her thoughts, because he spoke in a low, deep voice. "Do you think a Lacey and a Monteith have ever stood here before now? The first Lord de Lacey held droit du seigneur over his tenants. My wicked ancestor had only to see a girl in the fields and fancy her, and he could have her brought to his bed."

Olivia had been struggling with her dress fastenings, and now the black silk and velvet pooled at her feet. She began to take out her few remaining pins, letting her hair fall. "Your ancestor doesn't sound very nice," she said.

He came and stood before her, a strange smile on his face. "He wasn't."

She eyed him doubtfully. "Nic?"

"It's said he had a way of transfixing the girls, forcing them to his will by the sheer power of his personality."

She stepped back now, frowning at him, wondering where this was going. "I find that difficult to believe."

He reached out and caught her chin in his fingers, holding her almost painfully. "Let's put it to the test, shall we?"

Her heart gave an uneasy jolt. He was playing games with her, perhaps even trying to frighten her away, and she was frightened—a little bit. But she was also excited, and it was the excitement that made her nod her head in acquiescence.

"Lie down on your back, demoiselle," he murmured.

The bed was far bigger than she was used to, and the mattress softer. An avalanche of pillows and bolsters was scattered about them, as Olivia lay down, wriggling to get comfortable. Nic climbed over her, his hands catching her wrists and holding them above her head.

"Open your legs," he commanded.

She could feel his cock against the apex of her thighs, seeking entrance. Slowly she opened her legs, and felt him settle between them. The only part of their bodies touching was from the waist down—he held himself up from her chest. He wouldn't hurt her, she was certain of that. She trusted him; she wouldn't be here if she didn't.

"Can you feel me?" he growled.

"Yes . . ."

He drove deep inside her, all the time watching her face. She strained against him, trying to initiate the caresses and kisses she enjoyed so much, but he held himself away.

"Can you feel me?" he asked again.

"I . . . I don't understand. Nic?"

"Pretend I am my wicked ancestor, Olivia, and you my unwilling bedmate. Are you still unwilling?"

"If you have dragged me in from the fields then I am sure I am," she said breathlessly.

He was moving inside her, first from side to side, then rotating in a way that seemed to touch every inch of her. And then he paused and his lips curled in a wicked smile.

"Are you sure you're unwilling?" he said, and moved with a single deep thrust.

"Very unwilling," she groaned, trying to nuzzle against his throat.

"Wait," he commanded. "I want you totally mine."

He narrowed his eyes and shifted again. And then he thrust inside her once more, and it was as if she took flight. Whatever he'd done, Olivia was beyond thought. She cried out, and her body convulsed with a bolt of such ecstasy she wondered if she was going to faint.

"Ah," he growled, "you can feel me now."

He thrust again, and pushed her over the edge before she even knew she was there. Her body clenched so hard around him that he lost his control, too, and gave a hoarse shout as he shattered.

They lay, trembling, unable to do more than breathe, until slowly the bedchamber came back into focus.

If this was what his wicked ancestor had done to the girls from the fields, Olivia thought, then she couldn't understand why they were unwilling. No one could fight pleasure like that.

"Nic . . ." she tried to speak, but he wouldn't let her.

"Sleep," he said, drawing the covers over them both. He pulled her into his warm arms, kissing her temple. "Sleep, Olivia."

So she did.

Chapter 15

Sleep for Nic wasn't as easy as it seemed to be for Olivia. He'd thought to frighten her, he admitted it now. In some perverse way, by play-acting as his wicked ancestor, he'd considered driving her away. But it hadn't worked. She'd thrown herself into the playacting with him, losing any inhibitions she had left and thoroughly enjoying herself. Besides, he knew that if she had been frightened he wouldn't have gone through with it.

His body was drained, totally relaxed, in a way he couldn't remember feeling before. Who'd have thought an inexperienced girl could do this to him, the wicked rake? Remembering the way she'd touched him, the wet lick of her tongue, he almost groaned again. The sight of her lying under him, naked and wild with delight, was something he'd never forget.

He considered all his years of sexual excess, wondering if at moments like this he was meant to regret them. But he couldn't. He'd learned a great deal, and now Olivia was the beneficiary.

Was Abbot right? Was he growing old? Because instead of dreaming of catching the ferryboat to Paris, all he really wanted to do was lie here in his bed in his castle with his woman in his arms.

Domesticated Nic? The idea made him uncomfortable, but he forced himself to stop and look at it. He smiled wryly. Could Wicked Nic really live a life of cozy nights dining in and cozy mornings making love to his wife? Or watching her tending to their child? No, *children*, he corrected himself. He'd been an only child, and he was strongly of the opinion that he'd have done much better with at least one brother or sister.

He'd sworn never to marry. Was he changing his mind? After one night? It was ridiculous, insane, but he couldn't seem to help himself. The rake wasn't tamed, no never that, but maybe, just maybe, he had met his match.

There was a soft knock on his door. Before he could tell whoever it was to go to the devil, it opened, and Abbot stepped inside.

"My lord?" he said quietly. "I was just . . ." His voice trailed off.

Nic saw him peer toward the bed, and something in the stiffness of his bearing told him that his manservant knew very well who it was sleeping beside him. A wave of guilt washed over Nic as he remembered his assurances that no harm would come to Olivia, but almost immediately he replaced it with anger.

He'd damned if he'd be dictated to by a servant!

Nic sat up and swung his legs over the side of the bed. Abbot took a step back—perhaps he was planning to run for it—but Nic stopped him with a single word.

"Stay."

He pulled on his trousers, leaving his chest bare, and reached for the half-full glass as he passed, drinking the brandy down in one gulp. His leg ached, twinging with every step, but he ignored it, just as he'd been ignoring it for the past nine years. He shoved Abbot outside the door into the corridor, closing it securely behind them.

Abbot didn't even draw breath.

"You swore to me you would return Miss Monteith to her home. I would never have—" His voice was low and harsh, as if he was having trouble keeping the emotion from it, and his face was even more creased than usual.

"What time is it?" Nic interrupted.

With difficulty Abbot swallowed down his ire. "Nearly time for luncheon."

"Hmm. Better wait until nightfall then, before you take her home. Bring some food up, Abbot. I'm famished."

"Lord Lacey." Abbot took a deep breath. "My lord, I don't think you understand the seriousness of the situa—"

"You think not?" Nic mocked. "Let me see. I've seduced a woman of impeccable breeding and respectable family, and ruined her utterly."

Abbot was struggling to hold his tongue.

"Actually, I think I've done her a favor, Abbot. At least she'll have something to remember when she marries that bore Theodore."

He sounded cruel. He was angry and disturbed and he hardly knew what he was saying. He didn't want Abbot's disapproval, he didn't need it. He knew what he'd done.

"I cannot begin to imagine what repercussions this will—"

"What if I marry her?"

Abbot stared at him as if he'd lost his mind, then made a snorting noise and turned down the corridor, his back stiff as a poker.

Nic gave an impatient sigh and went after him. "Abbot, wait," he began, but when his manservant turned troubled gray eyes on him, he hardly knew what he was going to say. "I never intended it to happen," he said, rubbing a hand over his own eyes, feeling weary and depressed. "I tried very hard not to let it happen."

"She's a respectable young lady. You always said you would never make it your business to—to consort with respectable young ladies. Not after—"

"I did say that, and I meant it."

Abbot considered him in silence. "If we can get her away tonight with no one the wiser then all will be well, my lord."

"Will it, Abbot? You don't think I need to go down on my knees then and pop the question?" He laughed, but it had an odd forced sound.

"Not unless you want to," Abbot said, with a

lift of an eyebrow. "Are you telling me you want to marry Miss Monteith?" he added, for good measure.

"No! Yes . . . Blast it, how should I know?" Nic turned away. "Fetch us something to eat and drink, man."

He could feel Abbot's eyes on him, boring a disapproving hole into his back. The manservant hadn't believed him when he said he'd marry Olivia. He thought it was a stupid idea. Before now Nic had thought it a stupid idea, too. Had he really changed his mind?

Nic slipped back inside the bedchamber. Olivia was still sleeping, her yellow hair a bright splash on the pillows, and Nic stood a moment, watching her. He let himself imagine what it would be like if she were here every day of his life, just for a single, brief moment, and then he shut his mind down.

Olivia stretched and opened her eyes. She could smell food, delicious food. She rolled over and saw that someone had brought a banquet. There were steaming dishes, bowls of fruit, champagne sitting in ice, and a delicious-looking cake decorated with cream and strawberries.

"Oh," she groaned.

Nic chuckled. He was standing by the window, bare-chested, his trousers low about his hips, his hair tousled, with the light slanting across his face.

"Nic, I am so hungry . . ."

She climbed from the bed, peering into the dishes and under the plate warmers, dipping her finger into a bowl of syllabub, and plucking one of the strawberries from the cake.

"What will we have first?" she said, glancing up at him as he came to join her.

"Whatever you want."

It felt decadent, exciting, and all the other things she'd been longing to bring into her life.

Nic began to load a plate. They ended up sprawled on the bed, eating and drinking. Afterward they made love, slowly and thoroughly, and went back to sleep in each other's arms. Olivia couldn't remember the last time she'd felt so alive, her mind and body humming, and it was like a dash of cold water when it ended.

There were more respectable clothes to change into, and she left the black velvet and silk dress lying forlorn on the bed. Nic left her alone to wash and dress, and she was just finishing pinning up her hair when he returned with her cloak.

"You have to go," Nic said, drawing the warm garment about her. "Abbot has arranged everything."

"Of course," she agreed, while in her heart Olivia wanted to stay forever. "When will I see you again?"

He avoided her eyes. "Who can say?"

She'd wanted him to say, *Come again soon*, or better still, *I can't live without you*, but it was clear to her now he would say neither. She had won the battle but the war still hung in the balance, and as she stood before him she wondered whether she'd ever bring it to a satisfactory conclusion.

He pulled her hood up over her hair and bent to kiss her lips, gently and without passion, and she sensed him withdrawing from her. Was that what he did with all those other women, once the liaison was over? Remove himself emotionally as well as physically, as if they'd never existed as a couple?

Olivia told herself, a little desperately, that it wasn't going to happen with her. If necessary she'd camp on his front steps.

"Come on," he said, moving to the door. "Abbot will meet us at the coach. He believes in punctuality."

In no time, they were outside and following the winding path that led through the shrubbery.

"Where are we going?" she asked him, feeling the dew-damp grass soaking through her thin slippers. "I thought there was a coach waiting."

"There is. Abbot arranged for it to collect you some way along the road beyond the village. If we cut across the garden and the park, then beside the gatehouse, we will be able to reach it without being seen."

"Abbot has gone to a great deal of trouble."

"Yes. The coach," he explained, "was even hired under a false name. If he is asked, the driver is under instructions to say he has driven you from London and your friend's house. Abbot is doing his best to protect your reputation, Olivia."

"Yes, I see Abbot is very thorough. Perhaps

he's had a great deal of practice?" she suggested evenly, casting him a sideways glance.

"Perhaps he has," Nic said dryly, "and he never fails to let me know he disapproves of the necessity. Sometimes he's like an old nursery maid."

Olivia drew her skirts aside to avoid catching them on a hedge. "He thinks you could do better with your life. He knows that you are a good man, Nic, just as I do."

He turned to look at her, and even in the darkness she thought she saw pity in his eyes. "Olivia, you don't know me."

Olivia gave a smile. "But I do know you."

"If I was like Theodore Garsed, with nothing to talk about but my last meal, would you be here with me now?" he mocked. "I don't think so. My reputation makes me interesting, Olivia. The half-whispered secrets and the shocking gossip. I know what they say. If I became just another ordinary man no one would give me a second glance."

Olivia laughed, but stopped when she realized he was being serious. She shook her head at him. "Oh Nic, that's not true. Whatever you did, whatever you were, you would never be ordinary."

They walked in silence, entering the park, and making their way along the edge of the long driveway. After a time they crossed to the other side, following a path through the thickening trees, as the park turned into a wood. Olivia saw the dark bulk of the gatehouse rearing up ahead of them, with only one or two lights showing.

"This is the quickest way to the road," Nic said,

seeing her looking doubtful. "Don't concern yourself. No one will see us. My mother keeps early hours. We are quite safe."

Olivia trailed after him through the trees, and eventually they reached a mown stretch of grass that bordered one side of the building.

"The coach should be waiting just beyond the gates that open from the road to the driveway," Nic said. "Not far now."

The words were hardly out of his mouth when there was a shout behind them. Branches snapped as someone crashed through the undergrowth. They both froze. The shout came again, and now there was the dull gleam of a lantern, getting nearer, the light wavering and shaking because whoever held it was running.

"Devil take it," Nic said, releasing his breath. "Wilson, the gamekeeper. The bloody fool thinks we're poachers."

Olivia knew it wasn't funny but she felt a terrible urge to giggle, and put her hand up to her mouth to stifle it.

"I don't want him to recognize you," Nic went on, lowering his voice. "Go over to the gatehouse and wait for me in the shadows. I'll get rid of him."

He didn't wait for an answer, hurrying to meet his overzealous gamekeeper, calling out his name in warning. Olivia did as she was told, moving closer to the gatehouse. There was a terrace flanking this part of the building, and she climbed the stone steps that led up to it. There were rows of

pale blossoms, and a fountain splashing, catching
the moonlight in ripples of silver. She leaned over
to peer into the pool that collected the water, but if
there were fish they were well hidden among the
reeds and lily pads.

A shiver ran up her back, the hairs standing up
on her nape. Even before the voice spoke, Olivia
knew she was no longer alone.

Chapter 16

"**W**ho is there?"

Haughty and used to being obeyed, the tone was instantly recognizable. It was like a repeat of their first meeting, in the castle garden by the Pan fountain. Olivia tried to breathe calmly, wondering if it was possible for her to turn and run. If she reached the stairs she could reach the safety of the trees. But Nic and the gamekeeper were over there, she reminded herself. What if Wilson recognized her? What if he thought she was a poacher and shot her?

But she had dilly-dallied too long and it was already too late. Lady Lacey moved from the shadows and stopped directly behind her, trapping her against the wall of the pool and preventing her from going anywhere.

"You are trespassing. Who are you? Turn and face me, I say, or are you a coward?"

Olivia was no coward, and she turned, keeping her face deep in her hood. She was surprised to see that Lady Lacey was holding a thin cigar in her fingers, the pungent smoke mingling with

the strong perfume of night-scented stocks. She
knew that there were women who had taken up
the masculine habit of smoking, but Lady Lacey
seemed like the very last person she could imagine joining their ranks.

"I-I'm sorry to have startled you, my lady," she
said, in a low, husky voice, disguising her usual
calm tones as best she could. "I didn't realize you
were still awake."

Suspicious, Lady Lacey peered at her, but Olivia
only lowered her face further into the folds of her
hood. Just then the voices of Nic and his gamekeeper drifted toward them from the woods,
rising and falling over the distance. Lady Lacey
looked in their direction with a frown.

"What on earth is going on? Who is out there? I
am going to call my servants—"

She turned away, taking a step toward the
house, but Olivia reached out and caught her
wrist, holding it tight. It was the hand holding the
cigar and it dropped from her shocked fingers.

"No, you must not, Lady Lacey."

Lady Lacey stared at her in amazement, as if
no one had ever dared to tell her no before. "How
dare you! Release me at once. I will not—"

The glow of the lantern shone out, then faded
into the trees, and a moment later Olivia could
hear someone coming quickly up the stone steps.
She recognized Nic's tall figure as he reached the
terrace, and was silhouetted against the night sky.
He saw them at the same time and slowed, taking
in the situation, before he approached them.

"That is my son," Lady Lacey said, her voice heavy, as if the weight of the words was actually causing her pain. Her gaze slid back to Olivia, sharpening. "You must be one of Dominic's unmentionables."

That was when Olivia made her decision to run for it. As if she'd read her mind, Lady Lacey's bony wrist twisted in her hand, and the woman's fingers fastened painfully about hers, holding her prisoner.

Nic's tall figure stopped in front of them, and Olivia could feel the agonizing tension between mother and son. She didn't understand it.

"I hope for your sake my son paid you well," Lady Lacey said with a dry bitterness, speaking to Olivia but looking at Nic. "He prefers to pay. You see, that way he doesn't feel he needs to engage himself, emotionally. My son doesn't feel, he doesn't care. He's selfish and immune to the suffering he causes those around him. Heed my words, girl, or you'll end up as one of his victims."

The words must have stung, although Nic said nothing. But Olivia wasn't going to be silent—if he would not stand up for himself then she would do it for him.

"You're very wrong."

"Oh, am I!" Lady Lacey spoke angrily. "Well, then, speak up, girl. Tell me why I am wrong about my own son."

"Olivia," Nic murmured, "don't."

"It's not true," Olivia said boldly. "Nic isn't like

that. You may be his mother but you don't know him at all."

Lady Lacey peered more closely at the dark formless shape of Olivia in her cloak, with her face hidden inside the shadows of the hood. In response Olivia tried to make herself smaller.

"Who are you? Answer me, girl! I will not be ignored."

For a brief moment Olivia considered playing at being one of the women she'd met at the demi-monde ball, but it seemed a poor trick to play on Nic's mother, no matter how wrong she was about her son.

"I am no one important. A friend. Someone who has known Lord Lacey all her life and who trusts him. I know he would never hurt me."

Nic groaned softly in despair.

Lady Lacey was silent. Olivia had expected her to be furious. No one liked to be told she was wrong, and Her Ladyship seemed like the sort of woman who was used to being deferred to rather than challenged. But when Olivia dared to lift her head and glance up at the other woman, she saw that Lady Lacey wasn't angry after all, but pensive and sad. Lady Lacey's haughty face was old and wan and tired, and for the first time Olivia found herself pitying her.

"My son lives his own life. He does what he does, and although I don't approve of it, I don't try to stop him. I decided a long time ago that my son must go to hell in his own way."

"Very wise of you, Mother," Nic said dryly.

"Never allow yourself to have unrealistic expectations about me, then you can never again feel disappointed."

There was a silence. Olivia tried to pull away from Lady Lacey's grip, but the older woman only tightened it further. It was a mistake because it drew her attention back. "Who are you, girl?" she demanded yet again. "I know your voice."

"I told you, my lady. I am no one."

"Then take off your hood and show me what 'no one' looks like."

Olivia looked at Nic, caught in a trap. They really had no choice, and he gave a nod, looking resigned. She reached up and slowly slid back her hood, letting it fall about her shoulders. Her hair was pale gold in the moonlight, and as Lady Lacey stood, peering into Olivia's face, there was no doubting the appalled recognition gathering in her eyes.

"Miss Monteith!" She gaped. "It is Miss Monteith from the village, isn't it? Oh dear Lord, another one."

"Lady Lacey, please, I must go," Olivia said breathlessly, her fingers beginning to ache. "I really must go. Please. "

But Lady Lacey had no intention of letting her go. She was so distraught she didn't even appear to realize she was still holding her. "Miss Monteith, have you no care for your reputation? Are you so lacking in good sense that you would risk everything? I can hardly believe what I am seeing."

"Lady Lacey—"

"How could you?" She was glaring at Nic. Her voice dropped, and there was a tremor in it, as if she could no longer contain her emotions. "Have you forgotten what you did last time? Have you forgotten your promise? Despite myself I believed you when you said you would never harm an innocent girl again. I believed Abbot when he said you only indulged yourself with trollops and trulls. And yet here . . . here is Miss Monteith, as large as life . . ." She put a hand to her chest, as if she was finding it difficult to breathe.

"Mother." Nic moved as if to touch her, but she stumbled back, away from his hand.

"I cannot let this pass," she whispered. "This time I cannot look the other way. There will be a price to pay, Dominic."

And with that she turned and half ran across the terrace toward the house, her skirts rustling furiously. A door slammed, and afterward the silence seemed twice as loud.

Olivia was shaking. She wrapped her arms about herself, tucking her hands inside the cloak. "What will she do?"

Nic's face was bleak. "I don't know."

"Should I speak to her?" Olivia offered. "Perhaps I can make her understand."

"I doubt that." He put his hand on her waist, urging her toward the terrace steps. "Come. The coach is waiting. When you are home, tell your family you had a fine time at your friend's birthday. Say nothing of this, Olivia."

"Of course not."

"I'll try and smooth things over. When my mother understands that your reputation is safe, she will agree to leave the matter lie."

Olivia doubted it. Lady Lacey had been so fired up with self-righteous anger, Olivia wondered if anyone could stop her from carrying out her threat.

"What did she mean, Nic? About last time? About the other one? And what promise did you make?" Olivia hurried after him as Nic increased his long strides.

He didn't answer her.

"Nic," Olivia murmured, "do you really think everything will be all right?"

But if he heard her, again Nic didn't answer.

Abbot was beside himself by the time Olivia and Nic finally arrived at the coach. It was pulled up by the side of the road, half hidden among some elm trees. He didn't give them a chance to explain or say good-bye, before bundling Olivia inside and banging his hand on the door as a signal to the driver to move. Then he and Nic stood and watched as the heavy vehicle trundled away toward the village.

"No one will know," Abbot said, eyeing his master, who seemed very quiet. "The girl's reputation is safe."

Nic gave a strange breathless laugh. "Oh, do you think so, Abbot?"

"Yes, of course. Why not?" he asked curiously. "Have I forgotten something?"

Briefly, unemotionally, Nic told him what had happened.

After he was finished, Abbot stared at him for several long, horrified seconds. "But what will Lady Lacey do?" he said at last, trying to take an optimistic view of what was a catastrophic turn of events. "What can she do?"

"Don't be deceived, Abbot. My mother may be old, she may be a recluse, but she has a great deal of power. The Laceys once owned this village and everyone knows it. She can do me, and Miss Monteith, a great deal of damage."

"Would she be so vindictive, my lord?"

Nic turned to look at him, his eyes full of pain. "I think she would. I didn't realize just how much she hated me until tonight. Stupid of me, perhaps, but I thought that, one day, she might forgive me. Now I know she never will."

Abbot wanted to reassure him, but for once he could find no words to say. He felt drained and exhausted. Even when Nic began to walk back to the castle, and Abbot knew he should follow like the good servant he was—the good friend—he didn't.

For years he'd protected Nic, tidied up after him, smoothed over his problems. Well, he was sick of it. Nic was old enough to look after himself. It was time he and his mother actually spoke to each other, face-to-face, instead of exchanging notes through him. Perhaps if they'd spoken to each other before, this situation would never have occurred.

Abbot began to walk in the direction of Bassingthorpe. He didn't see the shadow against the window of the cottage on the opposite side of the road—he was too deep in his own thoughts. And even if he had, he would have thought nothing of it. Mrs. Brown lived in the cottage and she was almost blind, and her maid, Jenny, came in only during the day, returning to her home and family at night.

As far as Abbot was concerned they could not have been seen, and besides, he had other things on his mind.

Estelle opened her eyes, sitting up in her warm bed, and wondering what had woken her. And then she heard the sounds outside—a vehicle and horses. Voices. She knew one of them belonged to Miss Olivia. She had come home safe and sound from her risqué adventure. Estelle was glad about that—she was fond of Miss Olivia—and hopefully she had won Nic Lacey over, or at least forced him into making her a proposal of marriage. Estelle smiled to herself, imagining Abbot's face when she told him they could finally live together as man and wife.

Her smile faded as she contemplated what he would say to her when he knew she'd been behind Olivia's attendance at such a scandalous gathering as the demimonde ball. Abbot was far too straitlaced, but conversely that was one of the traits about him she loved the most. She accepted that it was up to her to take the risks and dodge around the obstacles, so that they could get the conclusion they both wanted. Surely the end justified the means? Well, it did in her book, anyway.

"Estelle!"

The hissing whisper had her out of her bed and reaching for the latch on her window. When she leaned out and looked down she saw Abbot standing below, his face a pale blur as he gazed up at her. Never before had he visited her like this, in the middle of the night. For one brief, excited moment she thought he must be so full of love for her that he couldn't keep away, and then common sense reasserted itself.

If Abbot was there, then there was a practical reason.

"Wait there," she called out softly, and hurried to the door, slipping on her robe and shoes as she peered out into the narrow corridor. No one else was about, and she was soon creeping down the back stairs. When she opened the tradesmen's door, Abbot was waiting right outside.

He put his arms around her, drawing her against his body, and held on tight.

Surprised, but pleased all the same, she hugged him back. But this was so unlike him that she couldn't help but worry that something was wrong.

"What is it?" she murmured, pressing her lips to his chin, which was the only part of his face she could reach. "Abbot, what's happened?"

"I need you," he groaned, with such longing in his voice that tears stung her eyes.

"Something's happened," she declared sharply, drawing away so that she could see his face in the moonlight. "Abbot, you must tell me what's happened or I'll go mad."

His mouth was a grim line, and the heavy crease between his brows looked as deep as a valley. "Lord Lacey has ruined Miss Monteith. He told me he wouldn't, but he did it anyway. I trusted him, Estelle. After all these years, I thought I knew him. I never thought he'd do something so unpardonable again, not after what happened the last time."

Estelle hardly heard him in her mounting excitement. Wicked Nic and Olivia were lovers; he'd have to marry her now.

"You're glad, aren't you?" Abbot accused her, correctly reading her expression. "You think it's a good thing."

"I . . . yes, I suppose I do. But what did you mean, 'after what happened'? I don't understand."

Abbot shook his head, turning stubbornly away.

She reached up to cup his cold face in her warm hands, forcing him to look at her. "I'm sorry if I'm not as upset as you. I'm glad because I love you and I want to marry you and live beside you. Is that so terrible?"

He shook his head, the grim line softening. "No, it isn't so terrible."

"Then tell me what you meant. What has Lord Lacey done that makes his compromising Olivia so much worse?"

He bent over her, urgency in his voice. "You must swear to me to tell no one else. Swear to me, Estelle."

"Yes, yes, I swear."

He took a breath, and she could see what a struggle it was for him, the loyal manservant, to break a confidence. "Before Nic's father died there was a woman, a—a respectable young woman. Her parents were well-to-do, but that didn't stop Nic. He seduced her . . . ruined her. Her parents hid her away, but one day she returned to Castle Lacey. She was carrying a child—a mere babe in arms."

"Oh dear," Estelle murmured, her spirits falling.

"Lady Lacey was out calling on friends, so the girl was taken to the library, to speak with the late Lord Lacey, Nic's father. Nic arrived, and soon afterward the girl and the baby were taken away in the coach, to London. Nic and his father remained in the library—they had a dreadful argument. It could be heard all over the castle. His father kept shouting: 'Swear to me. You must swear to me.' It went on for a long time, and then Nic slammed out of the library and went to saddle his horse. He rode off across the park. When he came back, he seemed calmer, though he still looked dreadful. He went back to the library, but when he opened the door he found his father lying on the floor. He'd taken a turn and was close to death. In fact, he died moments later."

"The shock killed him," Estelle breathed.

"When Lady Lacey returned and discovered

what had happened . . . well, I don't think she has ever recovered from the shock of it. She blamed Nic entirely for what happened, which is why she's never spoken to him since."

"What happened to the woman and the child?" Estelle said, after a moment's respectful silence.

"They live in London, and Nic visits them whenever he is there. He pays for their home and all their expenses."

Estelle chose her words carefully. "This isn't unique, Abbot. There are a great many gentlemen with bastards, and not all of them treated as well as this one. I'd be more shocked if Nic had abandoned the child into squalor."

"I heard him swear to his father it would never happen again," Abbot said stubbornly. "After his father's death he was so consumed with guilt and grief, he got drunk and climbed the old wall. He fell and broke his leg, badly. When his mother regained her senses, she came to his bedside, and she made him promise he would never prey upon a respectable young woman again. It was the last thing she said to him for nine years."

"You heard him swear?" Estelle said after a moment.

Abbot nodded. "I was in the room."

"So he has broken his word." Estelle shrugged. "I'm sorry, Abbot, but sometimes it is necessary to break your word. A promise is only good as long as it makes sense. Olivia Monteith is set on capturing Nic Lacey, and no promise was going to stop her, especially when he is wild for her, too."

Suddenly Abbot looked exhausted. "Is that what you really think?" he said. "That promises are worthless?"

Estelle wrapped her arms about him and held him, cradling him against her. "I didn't say that, not exactly. Besides, what are the Laceys to you? This isn't your fault. Let them sort it out among themselves."

His voice was muffled against her hair. "What was Miss Monteith doing at the demimonde ball, Estelle?"

Estelle felt a moment of panic, but it was brief and she pushed it firmly aside. She convinced herself that her interfering had not jeopardized anyone's happiness, or harmed the man she loved.

"Never mind about the ball. You have more important things to think about. You're going to be a father, Abbot. We're your family now, and we love you. You need to take care of us."

"Yes," he murmured. "Yes, I need to take care of you and the babe."

Estelle longed to take him upstairs, but she knew she didn't dare. The Monteiths were very strict about such matters, and if she was caught she would be instantly dismissed. It made her angry that she couldn't lie down with the man she loved when he so desperately needed her. They must marry, and soon.

Chapter 17

Nic didn't know where his manservant had gone and he told himself he didn't care. Abbot would only give him one of his disappointed looks, and Nic didn't need to be reminded of what he'd done. And he certainly didn't want to think about why he'd done it. He bathed and donned his silk dressing gown and removed himself to the sanctuary of the library. There was much to think about and consider, and he preferred to do it alone and uninterrupted.

The scene on the terrace had been appalling. His mother, white-faced and shocked, and Olivia standing there, seeing it all. He could imagine how it had looked to her. What must she have thought? He admitted to himself now that he'd had an overwhelming impulse to spill everything into her sympathetic ears, all his secrets, all his lies. Olivia was so easy to talk to, so comfortable to be with. But how could he do that to her? How could he begin to explain?

Besides, she would never forgive him.

Suddenly he wanted to see her again. Her cool

beauty had drawn him from the first, and when he discovered the hot and passionate woman beneath, Nic knew he'd already been more than half in lust with her. But love . . . well, that was another matter. He didn't think he'd ever been in love.

There was a time he'd come close to it, when he was a callow youth at Cambridge. He'd been visiting with friends and set eyes on the sister of one of them. She was called Miriam, and although she was a "lady," she was already a practiced flirt and more—she'd introduced him to the pleasures to be found in a woman's body—and he'd dreamed of making an honest woman of her. But Miriam had other plans and soon lost interest in him, moving on to other conquests. It had been painful and for a time he'd been a mess—that was early in the summer when he'd pulled ten-year-old Olivia from the stream.

Nic remembered he'd taken a bottle of his father's best brandy up to his room and drunk most of it. He was still tipsy when he wandered down to the stepping stones, but luckily not so far gone that he couldn't play the hero and save Olivia Monteith. That afternoon, as he sat with her, basking in her admiration, Nic had come to the realization that there were more important things in life than Miriam, and he'd determined to be the son and heir his father wanted him to be.

Now he sat, alone, in the chair that was once his father's, surrounded by the books his father had spent a lifetime collecting, and the past rushed in on him, try though he might to stem the tide.

There was his father, red-faced, furious, his mouth wide as he said things Nic had never heard him say before. It was like looking at a stranger, and the shock and shame Nic felt rendered him a stranger, too. They were father and son, how could this be? He heard his own voice shouting back, saying things he now regretted, intensely regretted. But how was he to know that his father would be dead before nightfall?

If one good thing had come out of it all, then it was the child: Jonah.

He hated the name. The child's mother had named him, claiming it was a suitable punishment for them all. She had always been dramatic, nothing was ever simple when it came to dealing with her. The reason she gave for naming the boy was that they had flouted the laws of the church and man, and been punished for it, and Jonah would remind them of that, always. But Jonah himself was an intelligent, bright boy with Nic's dark eyes and a laugh that was delightfully infectious. Nic preferred to think of him as a blessing rather than a curse.

Over the years he'd made certain Jonah wanted for nothing. The boy lived a quiet life, that was a necessary requirement, but it was a full one, a rich one in many ways. Jonah's mother had been obedient to Nic's wishes, well most of them, although lately she had begun to grow more diffi-cult. Her family had long ago cast her off, but they still lived in the village. Nic saw them occasionally, when their paths crossed, but nothing was ever said about the past.

It was as if the seas had closed over the truth, leaving little trace. If you didn't look closely you wouldn't have known it had happened.

And now Olivia had come into his life.

In other circumstances he would have thought her the perfect companion—intelligent, beautiful, educated, knowledgeable in the ways of society, and eager for him to tutor her in the pleasures of the flesh. But how could he think of making a life with her, in the circumstances? And yet that was exactly what he was doing.

He'd known that to touch her was to ruin her, and still he'd done it. Almost as if he'd planned to surrender his principles so that he could have her, despite what her parents, his mother, Abbot, Theodore Garsed, and anyone else might say. Was that why he'd taken her over and over again? So there could be no doubt that she belonged to him?

Nic's musings were interrupted by a commotion in the hall. He could hear voices—for a moment he thought it was his mother, but of course he knew he must be mistaken. His mother hadn't set foot in Castle Lacey for years, and after what had happened tonight he didn't expect her to change her mind. But then he heard the voices again, and this time he was certain.

He rose to his feet, but before he could open the door, a wide-eyed servant burst in. "Lady Lacey is here to see you, my lord," she said, as if she could hardly believe her own words, before scuttling away again.

And then there she was standing in the doorway—his mother.

Her face was flushed and her dark eyes snapping with anger, and in that moment he was thrust back into the past again, to that time after his father died and she blamed him.

Nic took a shaky breath. No, he wouldn't let himself be drawn into those bitter, murky waters. He was older and wiser now, and he knew what he wanted and what was important. He forced his voice to be calm.

"Will you sit down, Mother?"

Her hand trembled as she rested it on the back of a leather chair, and he wondered if she was seeing his father sitting there. But like him she rallied, and when she answered, her voice was as calm as his.

"Thank you, I think I will."

The good old aristocracy, Nic thought, with an inner smile. The rules had been drummed into them for generations. *Don't show your feelings, keep it all chained up inside, and under no circumstances be impolite.*

"This room hasn't changed at all," she said, gazing about her in surprise.

"Nothing has changed, as you'd know if you visited more often."

She flared up like a firework. "How could I visit you after what you did?" she burst out, her voice shaking, rising to her feet. "And now I am glad I didn't. I thought after last time you had learned your lesson but you haven't. You haven't changed at—at—"

"Mother, sit down. Please."

Her knees gave way and she sank heavily into her chair. Nic reached to take her hand, but she immediately stiffened and turned her face away, refusing to speak or look at him until he moved away. With a weary sigh Nic did so, sitting down opposite her and watching her profile.

"Why have you come to see me, Mother? What do you want?"

"I *don't* want to hear any excuses," she said in a low, wavering voice. "Not this time. This time, Dominic, you will do what is right. This time, you will marry Miss Monteith."

Nic stood up and poured himself a drink. He took his time. The clink of the glass against the decanter, the gurgle of the liquid, the first sip, and the lingering taste on his tongue. He allowed himself to get over the shock of his mother's words and the strange tingling joy that had filled him when she spoke them.

"Miss Monteith is a beautiful young woman from a respectable and wealthy family. She can have her pick of husbands, Mother. I am definitely not a suitable candidate."

She stared at him with narrowed eyes. "You have ruined her, Dominic, that makes you a very suitable candidate."

"I can't marry her. Surely you can see that?

The whole thing is complicated enough without making it worse."

"You're young, titled, and wealthy. Your blood-line goes back to the Norman conquest and you have a fine estate. What else could a woman want when she marries, especially when her own family are so much less distinguished than yours? I don't pretend I didn't hope for better . . . the daughter of a duke, perhaps, or even minor royalty. "

"Mother . . ."

"You think the past will be a stumbling block, Dominic, but you wouldn't be the first man with a past to marry and make a new beginning."

"The Monteiths will refuse permission. How can it be otherwise?"

"The benefits will outweigh the difficulties where her family are concerned. They would be very foolish indeed if they denied you permission to marry because of a long-ago scandal."

"You make it sound inconsequential, Mother," he groaned, shaking his head. "Olivia doesn't know. What if she finds out? What if she couldn't forgive me? I can't take the risk."

She looked at him, her dark eyes compelling. "What risk, Dominic? I don't understand you. She will be gaining a fine name and a title, and a grand home. You will have a beautiful wife on your arm, and in time an heir. Why should that be a risk? What does it matter if she finds out, or what she thinks? You will have your roles to play in public, and I'm sure she will play hers no matter how she might feel behind closed doors. That is part of the marriage contract, and Miss Monteith has been brought up to keep her true feelings well hidden."

"I agree that would be so if this was one of those cold and soulless marriages. A mating of convenience. But that's not what I want. You loved my father. You often said yours was a love match. Why should I have anything less?"

Now when she looked at him she was really looking at him, properly, for the first time since his father died, and Nic wondered what she saw to make her mouth curl into a smile.

"Dominic, happiness in marriage is elusive. Who knows, you may find it. I did, and for that I consider myself more fortunate than many of my peers. But if you're waiting for a love match, then you're more of a fool than I thought you. People of our class and position cannot expect to marry for love. Imagine the chaos if we did? Every second duchess would be a parlor maid!"

Nic laughed. "And every second duke would be a groom. You are speaking of lust, Mother, not love."

She waved her hand impatiently, as if the conversation was beginning to tire her. "Dominic, you know what you must do. What your father would tell you to do, if he were here. Marry Miss Monteith."

She was right, of course she was. He would have to marry Olivia Monteith; even a rake accepted when something was inevitable. But the strange thing was, despite all his protests . . .

Nic didn't mind at all.

Chapter 18

When Olivia arrived home she fell into her bed and slept through the night deeply and dreamlessly. She woke the next morning to find Estelle's smiling face bending over her, the maid eager to hear all the details of her adventure.

"The ball, miss. Please tell me what was it like. Abbot has spoken of it but he never tells me the things I really want to know. What are the women like? Are they very beautiful?"

Olivia stretched and yawned. "Yes, well, most of them. I can understand why gentlemen want to go and look at them. I can understand why Nic wants to go."

Estelle tilted her head to the side. "You're not jealous, miss? I think, if it was me, I'd be jealous."

Olivia smiled. "No, I'm not jealous, Estelle."

How could she be jealous, after the way Nic had made love to her? He had shown her with every touch of his fingers and every brush of his lips that she was important and desirable to him. No, Olivia definitely wasn't jealous.

"I'm glad everything went as you hoped," Estelle said.

"Thank you for your help, Estelle," Olivia replied. "I am very grateful for your kindness."

"Well." Estelle gave her a glance that was almost shamefaced, but Olivia was too weary to notice. "I'm just glad it all went well for you, miss. You must love Lord Lacey very much."

Olivia closed her eyes, unable to stop smiling. "I think I do love him very much."

"And if you love someone," Estelle's voice went on, "you accept them as they are. Even if they've made mistakes, or done something . . . well, something you feel is wrong. Don't you, miss?"

"Yes. I suppose so." A puzzled crease appeared between Olivia's brows. "Estelle, is there something the matter?"

Estelle hesitated, as if she might speak, and then smiled and shook her head instead. "Goodness me, no, nothing is the matter. You're tired, miss. I'll let you sleep a little longer."

Olivia sensed there was more to her maid's behavior, but she was happy to let her thoughts drift. The joy of being with Nic was like a warm glow inside her and she couldn't, she wouldn't, believe it meant nothing to him. They could make a life together, be happy together. No matter what he'd done, or the secrets he might be keeping from her, she trusted him. She wanted him.

And she was quite certain he wanted her, too.

* * *

Theodore Garsed tucked his napkin into his dressing gown and surveyed breakfast. All his favorites, and cooked to perfection. What would he do without his chef? Life would be so dull, barely worth living. There was one good thing about being a gentleman of leisure, he could make certain he was never denied all the good things in life.

Besides, he needed to restore himself after his brother Alphonse's arrival last night. Theodore didn't like to admit it, even to himself, but there was something unsettling about Alphonse. When they were children he'd been able to ignore it, pretend his brother would grow out of it. The thing was, Alphonse was always very attached to him, and, awful as it sounded, sometimes his brother's affection for him made him uneasy. There were times when Alphonse's efforts to please him took on a particularly bizarre quality—for instance, when Alphonse had shot and killed the bird that Theodore complained had woken him at dawn when he was longing for sleep. He still recalled Alphonse tossing the limp body on the breakfast table, smiling and so pleased with himself.

Theodore looked down with a frown and realized he'd finished most of his meal without even tasting it. He reached for some ripe, juicy figs, determined to savor them, when one of his servants interrupted to inform him Mrs. Henderson was there to see him.

Mrs. Henderson was a genteel widow whose husband had died in debt, and now she scraped by as best she could, living in rooms above the haberdashery. Her daughter, Laura, was an attractive girl, and despite her financial problems, Mrs. Henderson had managed to have her taught the niceties of ladylike behavior. Theodore admired Laura, and at one time had even toyed with the idea that she might make him a good wife, but that was before he made the acquaintance of Olivia Monteith.

Unfortunately, he realized now, he'd allowed his interest in Laura Henderson to become too marked, and Mrs. Henderson's hopes were raised. Even when he turned his sights to Olivia, she still hadn't given up on making a match between Theodore and her daughter.

So when he was told she was there to see him, Theodore's immediate thought was that she had come to read him one of Laura's letters—the girl was currently staying with a cousin in Somerset. He wished he wasn't so gentlemanly—if he was a cad like Lacey, he'd tell Mrs. Henderson he had no interest in her daughter's gushing letters and ask her to stop calling on him. But Theodore knew he was too polite to do that, and his hope was that, once he was married to Olivia, Mrs. Henderson would finally give up.

"Very well, show her in," Theodore said. "If she will call at such an ungodly hour, then she can watch me finish my breakfast."

"May I bring another plate and cup, sir?"

"No, you may not. Oh, all right. But only a cup. She will not share my toast."

Moments later Mrs. Henderson came in, smiling, her cheeks aglow. "Mr. Garsed, it is so good to see you," she twittered. "But then you are always good."

The compliment soothed Theodore somewhat and he answered more mildly than he'd meant to. "You wanted to see me, ma'am?"

"Yes, I did." Belatedly Mrs. Henderson schooled her face into a troubled expression, but her small dark eyes were as bright as a raven's. "Some dreadful news has been passed on to me, Mr. Garsed, and I just knew I must bring it to you straightaway. You are always so good in these difficult situations. You always know what to do."

Theodore wondered what on earth she was talking about. "Dreadful news? I hope your daughter is well, Mrs. Henderson?"

"Yes, oh yes, Laura is perfectly well, sir. No, this isn't about Laura."

Theodore swallowed a sigh. "You'd better tell me then, Mrs. Henderson."

She leaned toward him, and he noticed with unease that her fingers were clenched on her reticule like a bird's claws on its perch. "My friend Mrs. Brown has been unwell, sir, and because of her ill health her sister, Miss Dorrington, the vicar's housekeeper, has come to stay with her. Last night Mrs. Brown was particularly unwell, and she slept poorly. Well, as you know, she lives in the house at the far end of the village, and after Miss Dorrington had settled her, she happened to hear a commotion outside, and went to look out of the window." Mrs. Henderson took a breath. "And when she looked out, what do you think she saw, sir?"

"I have no idea, Mrs. Henderson, please enlighten me."

"Something most peculiar!"

"Did she indeed?" Theodore did his best to stifle a yawn, hoping she'd get to the point soon.

"Yes, Mr. Garsed, she saw a woman climbing into a coach."

"What is so peculiar about that, Mrs. Henderson?"

"The coach had been waiting at the side of the road for some time, just sitting there. Eventually two people came out of the park—Castle Lacey's park—and it was the woman who climbed into the coach before it drove away. Miss Dorrington cannot swear to it, sir, but she is nearly certain the two people she saw were Miss Monteith and Lord Lacey."

Theodore put down his cup with a clatter. "How—how odd," he managed. Olivia climbing into a coach in the middle of the night? And he happened to know that Olivia had returned last night from her visit to her friend in London. There was something wrong. He wished Mrs. Henderson would go away so that he could work it out.

"I thought I should bring it straight to you," Mrs. Henderson said, her beady eyes fixed on his face. "It seemed the sensible thing to do. I know you are a friend of Miss Monteith's."

"Yes, it was the sensible thing to do, Mrs. Henderson, thank you. I wonder if you wouldn't mind keeping this to yourself until I discover the exact circumstances?" And he gave the woman a hard look.

"Of course, Mr. Garsed." She fluttered her hands. "Although I must say I was surprised to hear of Miss Monteith behaving in such a reckless manner. My own Laura would never—"

"Yes, yes. I would be grateful if you'd tell Miss Dorrington to keep this to herself, too. Just until I discover what it means. I'm sure there must be a misunderstanding."

"I'm sure there must be," but she wore such a smug expression that Theodore knew she was wishing for the opposite. He could only hope the woman held her tongue long enough for him to discover the facts; he didn't expect her to keep such a juicy piece of gossip to herself beyond today.

What on earth was Olivia thinking? It must be a misunderstanding. A simple mistake that would be soon sorted out, and then they would all laugh about it.

But as Theodore sat before the remains of his repast, his appetite quite gone, he was unable to decide on any innocent explanations that would account for what he had just heard about his future wife. Despite himself, his thoughts returned to the day he'd left Lord Lacey hurt in the woods, and he remembered how he'd secretly hoped that would be the end of the matter.

If there was something between Olivia and Wicked Nic . . . would he still want to marry her? Theodore knew that he did. If he saved her from a possible scandal, wouldn't that make her the more grateful to him? He pictured the tears in her eyes, the trembling smile, as she realized he'd restored her honor. Her cool beauty would crumble in that moment of emotion, and she would weep. And he would be privy to that, he and no one else.

Of course I will marry you, she'd gasp. *Oh, Theodore, I've always loved you, only I've been so blinded by that bad, bad man.*

The vision shimmered, and quite suddenly another image replaced it in his head. Olivia in Nic's arms, the two of them engrossed in each other, totally ignoring Theodore, while he stood alone on a windswept hilltop. Then it began to rain, ruining his neck cloth and his new jacket and his carefully brushed hair.

"Theodore? Whatever is the matter?"

Alphonse was standing before him, his eyes narrowed, the muscles in his jaw bunching, looking ready to strike down whoever had upset his elder brother.

If Theodore hadn't been laboring under a severe shock he wouldn't have said anything, but before he could consider the consequences the whole story came spilling out, tainted with bitterness and his sense of injustice. "It is perhaps unworthy of a man like me, but I find myself wishing that Nic Lacey would have another accident, and that this time he wouldn't recover from it . . ."

Alphonse smiled. "Poor Theo," he said, reaching to help himself to a fig. "Just as well I'm here, eh?"

Chapter 19

At half past ten that same morning Olivia discovered just how serious was her predicament. Miss Dorrington, who was staying with her sister in a cottage at the far end of the village, came to call on her mother, but Olivia thought nothing of it until Estelle sought her out and informed her that the two women had been closeted in the downstairs sitting room for well over the usual half hour, and she was worried.

"You're worried? But Miss Dorrington is a harmless old gossip."

"I took their tea in, miss, and Mrs. Monteith was as white as a sheet. I don't know what that old biddy is saying to her, but it isn't good."

"Very well, I'll go and see for myself. Thank you, Estelle."

But Olivia had only just reached the landing when the sitting room door opened and her mother, accompanied by her visitor, came out into the hall, their voices too low to be heard. As Olivia descended the stairs her mother turned, and

Olivia was startled by her bloodless face. Estelle was right, something was very wrong.

Miss Dorrington also turned and looked up at Olivia, and at once her narrow features tightened and she pursed her lips. "Miss Monteith," she said, as if she begrudged speaking the words. She reached for Mrs. Monteith's hand. "Good-bye, my dear." And with the briefest of nods to Olivia, she was gone.

"Mama, what is it?" Olivia cried. "Please, Mama, what is wrong?"

She hadn't seen her mother look like that in a very long time—not since Sarah died—and it shocked her very much.

"Olivia," she whispered, then shook her head as if she couldn't bring herself to speak aloud whatever it was she'd learned from her visitor.

"Mother, that dreadful woman is always gossiping about something or other. You know what she's like. I can see she's upset you—"

The door knocker rattled before she could finish.

Mrs. Monteith jumped, eyes wide, and put a hand to her breast as if to keep her heart from escaping. The servant who had only just let Miss Dorrington out, hurried to open the door again.

Theodore Garsed strode into the hall as if he owned it.

"Mrs. Monteith!" he cried, all smiles. "And Miss Monteith! I am doubly blessed."

Olivia gritted her teeth. His jovial tones were out of place in this emotion-charged moment, but he didn't seem to notice his hosts were not over-joyed to see him.

"Mr. Garsed, what a pleasant surprise," Olivia lied politely.

"I thought I would take a stroll in the fresh air. Nothing like a brisk stroll to focus the mind. And I wanted to share my news—my brother, Alphonse, has arrived!"

"Indeed, Mr. Garsed." Olivia didn't have a clue what he was talking about; she wished he would leave.

But Theodore had no intention of leaving. He turned to her mother, taking her hand in his own, gazing down into her eyes as if he were a vicar offering comfort to the bereaved. It was very odd, and Olivia didn't know what to make of it. "Was that Miss Dorrington I saw leaving just now?"

"Yes, it was," Olivia answered when it seemed her mother couldn't.

Theodore nodded as if he understood every-thing, which annoyed her even more. "I was afraid it might be. I do abhor gossip. And yet, un-fortunately, it is so often true."

Mrs. Monteith swallowed and gave a little moan.

"Actually, I have come to you on a quest, dear madam."

"A quest, Mr. Garsed?" Olivia knew she sounded bewildered but she couldn't help it.

"A quest for my own particular Holy Grail," he said, still looking into Mrs. Monteith's eyes, his words heavy with meaning.

"Are you telling us you're a knight of the Round Table, Mr. Garsed?" Olivia said irritably, very unlike her usual calm and polite self.

"I believe, at heart, that's what I am," he replied seriously. "A knight on a white charger, and a rescuer of maidens in distress."

Mrs. Monteith finally seemed to have an inkling of what he was talking about. "Oh, Mr. Garsed," she gasped, and to Olivia's dismay, tears filled her mother's eyes.

"Mr. Garsed, I don't mean to be rude," Olivia began firmly, "but I think you should—"

And then it happened. Again. The door knocker sounded.

"For heaven's sake," she began, as the servant rushed to answer the door, "I really think we have had enough visitors this morning . . ."

And then a frisson ran through her, as she heard Nic Lacey's deep voice. Her throat dried up and she could only stare as he stepped inside, the door closing behind him. Nic was not the sort of man to make a casual visit, and his appearance this morning was certainly anything but casual.

The perfectly tailored jacket and trousers, the shirt beautifully white and starched, an elegant brown waistcoat with yellow buttons. The cane he carried could have been a fashionable affectation, but Olivia knew he still needed it to help him walk. He looked everything that was handsome and dashing, but as he drew closer the shadows under his eyes and the creases about his mouth made her wonder if he had slept much after she left him last night.

"Mrs. Monteith. Miss Monteith." He bowed elegantly before them.

"Lord Lacey," Mrs. Monteith mouthed, her eyes wild.

"What are you doing here, Lacey?" Mr. Garsed's jolly mood had evaporated at the sight of the other man, and now his face was flushed a dull red. "I wonder you have the gall to set foot in this house!"

Nic gave Theodore a bored look. "At least I am dressed for calling on ladies," he mocked. "Where on earth did you get that waistcoat, Theodore? The church jumble?"

"How dare you!"

Their animosity seemed all out of proportion, and Olivia stepped between them, holding out her hands to stop them from coming to blows. "Please, gentlemen," she said coldly. "If you must fight over who has the most fashionable waistcoat, then do so outside."

Theodore cleared his throat. "I'm sorry, Miss Monteith, but this man should not be here. I don't want to upset you, but . . . well, the rumors . . . the gossip. I meant to keep silent, because I really don't believe for a moment it can be true. But now, with this man being here, I can't help but wonder—"

"Lord Lacey has as much right to call here as you," Olivia cut him short, feeling cross. "I don't know what this is all about but I wish someone would explain it to me."

"Olivia," her mother hissed, catching her arm. "I must . . . I really must talk to you. Now!"

"But we have guests, Mama . . ."

"Now, Olivia."

Confused, bewildered, Olivia allowed her mother to tug her toward the same downstairs sitting room where she had lately been locked away with Miss Dorrington.

Miss Dorrington, who was staying with her sister, Mrs. Brown, who lived in a cottage on the far side of the village, close to where last night Olivia had climbed aboard the hired coach with Nic and Abbot's help . . .

Olivia's steps slowed, and stopped. Her breathing quickened. Belatedly, it came to her. Miss Dorrington, Mrs. Brown, her mother's white face, the two men and their odd behavior . . . this was about her. Her reputation was compromised. And if Miss Dorrington knew about last night, then it wouldn't be long before everyone else in Bassingthorpe knew, too.

Olivia turned from her mother's urgings and faced the two men, trying hard to gather her usual air of calm about her. But she felt shocked and numb, and it was made worse when Theodore couldn't seem to meet her eyes.

Nic had no trouble, and she watched his mouth curl faintly at the corners. "I see by your expression that you have some inkling why I am here, Miss Monteith." He limped forward and took her hand in his, gazing down at her pale, slim fingers between his masculine ones, as if they could tell him what to say. "I would go down on my knees, but if I did I doubt I could rise again."

"Lord Lacey, I don't want . . . You mustn't . . ." she stammered desperately. No, no, she didn't want him to propose. Not like this. Not because he had to. It was all wrong . . .

"Lord Lacey!" her mother shrieked faintly.

"Lacey, you have no right!" Theodore blustered. "I was here first."

But Nic wasn't about to be stopped by anyone.

"Miss Monteith. Olivia. Will you do me the honor of being my wife?"

Desperately Olivia searched his eyes, but they were dark and unreadable, and she couldn't begin to tell what he was thinking. Part of her wanted so much to say yes. This was what she had planned toward—making Nic her husband was her goal. She'd sworn to hunt him, and hunt him she had, and now he was hers.

Only he hadn't come here of his own will, and knowing he'd been coerced into a marriage he didn't want was like a dagger in her heart. She wanted him, yes, but not at any cost, not like this.

"Lady Lacey . . ." she began, her voice trailing off.

But, unlike her, he knew what she was thinking. "My mother is agreeable to the marriage. In fact it was she who suggested I make my feelings known to you as soon as possible."

What was he really saying? Olivia asked herself feverishly. That Lady Lacey had given him an ultimatum? Marry or else? Olivia snatched her hand away as if his fingers were burning hot. "No. I—I cannot marry you."

He looked nonplussed, and then a frown snapped his brows together. "You said you wanted to marry me, Miss Monteith. Do I now understand that you are refusing me?"

"Miss Monteith has every right to refuse you," Theodore interrupted, looking like he wanted to cheer. "Don't you dare try and bully her, Lacey."

"Keep out of this," Nic said between his teeth.

"I will not. I have come to speak and I am determined to do so, although this wasn't how I hoped . . . Well, never mind." Theodore turned to Olivia. "Will you marry me, Miss Monteith? Will you consent to be my wife?" He beamed at her, relieved to have spoken the words at last.

Mrs. Monteith turned her head stiffly, from one gentleman to the other, and back again. "Two proposals," she said in a trembling voice. "Goodness gracious me, Olivia. Two marriage proposals before luncheon. If I may advise you—"

But Olivia had no intention of hearing any more advice. "Mr. Garsed, you do me a great honor, but I must refuse," she said, ignoring her mother's soft groan of disappointment. "I have no intention of marrying anyone at the present time."

"You were seen," Nic said impatiently. "It's all over the village. You have no choice but to marry one of us." He glanced disparagingly at Theodore, then back at Olivia. "And I am thinking that it had better be me."

"You!" Theodore roared. "Why you? She'd do better with a snake! I can make Olivia happy. You will destroy her. You've already destroyed her reputation. A man like you and an innocent like her . . . why, the prospect is nauseating."

"That's probably the rich food your chef is serving you. Change to plainer fare and you'll feel better."

Theodore looked as if he might explode.

"I'm not marrying either of you!" Olivia burst out. "Please, both of you, just go away!"

Her mother caught her arm, but Olivia wrenched away and dashed up the stairs. She wanted the sanctuary of her room. She wanted peace and quiet and time to think.

Behind her Theodore had the final word. "Now do you see what you've done, Lacey?"

Chapter 20

Nic didn't know what he'd expected, but it wasn't this total rejection. Once again Olivia had surprised him. He realized he'd grown used to her strength of character and total belief in her own sense of purpose where he was concerned, and to see her reduced to feminine hysterics was rather a shock. He would have liked nothing better than to follow her up the stairs and persuade her to his point of view—and he knew he could—but he doubted he'd get more than two steps before Theodore would be screaming at him for daring to further sully the name of his beloved.

"My daughter needs time to consider her—her feelings," Mrs. Monteith said, looking as if she'd sustained a shock, as indeed she had. "I'm sure you will be patient. There is a great deal for her to consider."

Her blue eyes, so like Olivia's, met Nic's and slipped away again. But it was long enough for him to read a myriad of emotions in them—pain and regret and fear. He'd warned his mother that the past would interfere in any proposal he made, and clearly it was so.

"Miss Monteith has made her feelings for you very plain, Lacey," Theodore interrupted, his jowls quivering in outrage. "You should leave."

"I don't think she was overjoyed by your proposal, either, Theodore," Nic said with quiet scorn. "Perhaps it was the thought of marrying you that sent her sobbing to her bed."

He shouldn't have said it, but Nic couldn't seem to help himself. Theodore was the ideal person on whom to vent his feelings.

"You cad," Theodore blustered. "Get out before I throw you out."

Nic raised an eyebrow. "Do you think you can?"

The two men eyed each other like dogs fighting for a bone, the one coolly dangerous and the other red-faced and panting with rage.

"Oh please, stop it!" Mrs. Monteith's voice rose shrilly. "I want both of you to leave. Hasn't enough damage been done? I—I must go and comfort my daughter."

Theodore shot Nic a look of triumph.

"After you, Theodore." Nic limped to the door and stood waiting there.

"I want to stay and help comfort Miss Monteith," Theodore said stubbornly.

Mrs. Monteith threw up her hands in despair and hurried up the stairs, leaving them to it.

"Come, Theodore, admit defeat," Nic said with a wicked smile. "Miss Monteith doesn't want either of us to comfort her today."

Theodore stared at him. They were about the same height, and although Nic was broad-shouldered and slim-hipped, Theodore's bulk made him seem the more dangerous. And now there was a depth of feeling in his eyes that surprised Nic.

Theodore hated him.

The other man strode from the house, and Nic followed him outside. Lady Lacey would be expecting success and he would have to tell her he'd failed. At least for now. He admitted that this was not the outcome he'd imagined when Abbot helped him dress earlier. Olivia had wanted to marry him, so he'd assumed she would agree with alacrity.

There was her family to consider, and the awkwardness of past scandals, as well as the impending scandal. But Nic fully expected to soften the blow with his title and position. "Lady Lacey" had such a nice ring to it, and he was certain the Monteiths would come around soon enough, and put practical considerations ahead of old memories. Now that he'd been rejected, he wondered how long it would take Mrs. Monteith to persuade her daughter she had no option but to marry. Someone.

Nic used his cane to strike the heads off a couple of flowers in the border along the drive, and felt a mixture of shame and satisfaction that he'd let his temper show. What was wrong with him? He'd never wanted to marry Olivia—he'd fought against it from the moment she turned up at his door and let her hopes be known. He should be relieved she'd said no. He should be glad Theodore was willing to make her his wife, scandal and all.

But the thing was, he wasn't glad.

"You don't want to marry Olivia."

Nic looked up and saw that Theodore had stopped in front of him, and he looked as if he'd worked himself up for something.

"I said—"

"I heard you. I take it you do want to marry her?"

"Yes. I do."

"Well then, may the best man win." Nic stepped around him.

Theodore hurried after him. "You know you don't want her, Lacey. You're only going after her because of bloody-mindedness. You're bad for her. Let her go. In fact, why don't you go away? Once you're gone she'll see me, waiting, willing to step in, and she'll marry me."

"You don't rate yourself very highly, do you, Theodore?" Nic mocked softly.

"I know I don't have the gloss you do," Theodore snapped. "Your reputation makes you attractive to women, God knows why. But I will stand by her and adore her." He took a breath. "Well, what do you say? Will you step aside?"

"I'd like to oblige," Nic said, "but I can't."

"Why?"

"Because despite what you think of me, Theodore, I want her, too." Nic held out his hand. "Shall we wish each other luck?"

For a moment he thought the other man was going to refuse him, and then Theodore clasped his hand, squeezing it tightly. He gave a strange little laugh. "Why not?" he said, his eyes wild. "May the best man win, Lacey."

"Olivia, please . . . ?"

The frustration in her mother's voice was growing and Olivia knew she should explain—try to explain—but she already knew her mother would never understand. She took a deep breath and made the attempt.

"It is true, Mama. I was at Castle Lacey last night. I was with Nic. But I was there because I wanted to be there, not because he forced me in any way."

"Olivia, I don't know how you could have been so selfish. So irresponsible and—and foolhardy. Your sister . . ." But whatever she was going to say about Sarah was never said. She shook her head. "All these years we've tried to keep you safe from . . . from men like Lord Lacey, and now you tell me you threw yourself at him! I can hardly bring myself to believe it. Ruined, that's what you are! *Ruined* . . ."

That stung. "I do not see wanting to live my own life in my own way as selfish, Mama, and if I am ruined it is entirely my own fault."

"You have a duty to your father and me . . ." An agonized sob caught her voice. "You cannot live your life your own way, you silly girl. Your sister said exactly those words to me, exactly those words, before she . . . she died. I will not let it happen to you. You will marry Mr. Garsed and be safe. Do you hear me, you silly girl? You will be safe."

Olivia felt the tears begin to trickle down her cheeks. "But, Mama, I don't want to be safe."

"No, Olivia. I won't listen to such nonsense. You will do as you are told."

Olivia knew that in the past women were expected to deny themselves their own happiness, to sacrifice themselves for the sake of their families, but she had hoped that with Victoria on the throne things might change. Olivia could feel her heart aching at the idea that she should be tied down and forced to go through life like an automaton, to lock her feelings away from the light of day, and playact her way through it. And that was exactly what would happen to her if she obeyed her mother and married Theodore Garsed.

Then why, oh why, had she refused Nic's offer?

"Mama, you don't understand, you don't want to understand," she cried. "I was with Nic because I want to marry him. I want to live my life with him."

"But, Olivia, you refused him!"

"Yes, I did, didn't I?" She choked on a laugh.

Her mother stared at her as if she were insane.

"I'm sorry, Mama. I know I have disappointed you."

Mrs. Monteith waited, and Olivia knew she was waiting for her to admit to her mistake, submit to her parents' wishes, but Olivia couldn't bring herself to that. Despite what had happened she did not intend to change the course by which she'd already chosen to steer her life.

Mrs. Monteith stood up, her back stiff, her eyes bleak—there was no sympathy or understanding in her face. "I will leave you to consider your future, Olivia, but be warned, I won't allow you to ruin your life, or ours. Mr. Garsed loves you and he wants to marry you, despite this—this shameful episode with Lord Lacey. You must see that marrying him is the best, the only, solution."

The door closed behind her, and Olivia fell back onto her bed and closed her eyes. Her head ached, her throat ached, and she wondered what on earth she was going to do. She needed time to think and plan, to discover why some stubborn worm had entered her brain and was preventing her from taking her happiness in both hands and running with it. Did she really expect Nic to be madly in love with her, just because she felt that way about him?

Perhaps she was hoping for too much from her rake.

When Nic called at the gatehouse on the way home, Lady Lacey kept him waiting only a moment. She looked as weary as he felt, and Nic wondered whether she had slept last night after they parted. He had tossed and turned all night, painful memories and wild thoughts filling his head and preventing him from closing his eyes for more than a few minutes at a time.

"Dominic?" A smile trembled at the corners of her lips before it faded away at the sight of his face. Nine years without speaking and she could read him like a book.

"She turned me down, Mother," he said, tapping the cane against his leg, trying not to sound as if he cared. "She turned down Garsed, too, so I can take comfort in that."

"Garsed?"

"Yes, Theodore Garsed. A fool with more money than sense, but a fool the Monteiths prefer to me. He was there, too, offering her the protection of his name to save her from disgrace. She turned us both down. I won't go into detail, it was all rather humiliating."

"She turned you down?" she gasped. "But the girl is ruined. What does she expect to do if she doesn't marry you?"

"Miss Monteith is a strong-minded woman."

"No matter how strong-minded she is, she cannot restore a reputation that has been lost. Only marrying you can do that." Lady Lacey's haughty tones rose, as if she could hardly believe what she was hearing. "I will speak to her and insist on her doing as she ought."

"No, Mother. I am grateful, but I will deal with Miss Monteith in my own way." Nic glanced at the decanter but resisted helping himself to a swig of brandy. Brandy wasn't going to help what was wrong with him.

"You must try again," Lady Lacey insisted. "I want you to try again, Dominic."

"And if she will still not have me—"

"She will have you and be grateful that a Lacey would condescend to marry a village girl."

Nic's mouth twitched.

Lady Lacey caught his eye, and waved her hand dismissively. "Yes, she has beauty and education, and that is some compensation for her lack of good family. And she will give you healthy children. Castle Lacey needs an heir and it is past time you provided one. Here is your chance to redeem yourself. If your father were here—" But she stopped and looked away, unable to go on.

"I will make her marry me," Nic promised, to fill the silence. "If I have to drag her to the altar, then I will marry her. I give you my word, Mother."

Lady Lacey straightened her shoulders and lifted her chin, her proud face calm, once more masking any emotion. "I am glad to hear it, Dominic."

He hesitated beside her, and then bent to brush his lips against the top of her graying hair. She stiffened, and he thought she would withdraw, but then she reached up and patted his cheek.

"You will come for supper tonight, Dominic. We will discuss this again." She gave the invitation— more like an order—as if it were something they did every night.

Nic wondered if he should point out to her that he hadn't had supper with her since 1828, but decided against it. They were talking again, and it was best not to question it.

He smiled. "Yes, thank you, Mother, I will come to supper."

Chapter 21

Olivia sat on the swing in the garden, disconsolate, in disgrace. She'd loved this swing as a child. She could remember Sarah pushing her, laughing when Olivia squealed, and cuddling her when she fell off. Now here she was, a grown woman, seeking consolation from a thing of rope and wood.

She'd made her decision.

When she really thought about it there'd only ever been one decision all along. Nic Lacey. She would accept him. She hadn't told her mother yet, and she didn't look forward to doing so. This would make her even more upset and angry, and it was possible she might never talk to her daughter again. Olivia knew her parents wanted to protect her, but it wasn't her fault that Sarah had died, and there was nothing she could do to change that. And they couldn't live her life for her, nor did she want them to.

She felt better now that the choice was made, as if her fate was set. No going back now. She had always wanted live her life to the full rather than

make do with second best, and now she would.
Nic Lacey would be her life. Moody and difficult,
charismatic and wild, and so sweet, he was and
always had been the man for her.

Memories of their moments together made her
smile dreamily. In fact she was so caught up in
some particularly heart-stopping parts of those
memories, she didn't hear the footsteps approaching her across the lawn until she was no longer
alone.

"Miss Monteith, you are looking good enough
to eat."

Olivia started and turned her head. Nic was
standing behind her and to the side, smiling, his
dark eyes watchful. She wondered if he could read
her heated thoughts and instantly set her face into
a polite and chilly mask.

"I'm not sure if that is a compliment, Lord
Lacey."

"Oh, it is, believe me."

"How did you know I was here?"

"Estelle told me. She saw me approaching the
door and saved me from another meeting with
your mother."

Olivia looked away, swinging idly. "You can't
blame her for being angry and upset. I have
caused a great scandal in Bassingthorpe, probably
the worst scandal the village has ever seen."

Nic didn't answer her, but she didn't notice his
silence.

"I've never been notorious before," she went

on. "It isn't very pleasant. I can understand why women go off and live in seclusion."

"Yes, I can see you hiding yourself away in a small cottage on a windswept coast, wearing a veil and standing mysteriously on the cliff top." He sounded sarcastic, and she turned her head and narrowed her eyes at him.

"Why have you come, Nic?"

"You know why."

She tightened her grip on the sides of the swing. "If you've come to ask me again if I'll marry you, then yes, I will."

He snorted. "You don't sound very happy about it."

"I . . . It's just that this isn't how I envisaged it would be. I feel as if I've forced you to make a decision rather than coming around to it on your own. I've always known we would be a perfect match, but you didn't. Now you might never discover it. You might feel resentful."

He came up close behind her and she tilted her head back toward him. "Very resentful," he murmured, and bent to kiss her lips.

He tasted wonderful and she felt her body grow warm and languorous, eager for more of his kisses. But Nic was already putting distance between them. She watched him through her lashes as he moved around to stand in front of her.

"You told me you wanted to live your life in your own way. I accept that. I won't demand an accounting for your spending and I won't ask where you've been and with whom. As my wife you will have that freedom."

His expression was intent, watchful, and she wondered what he expected her to say. Olivia knew he was being very generous. Such a life as he described would be free indeed in comparison with that of most married women, and yet . . . Was she very ungrateful? Or just perverse? She must be, because she would have preferred him to tell her he wanted her at his side, under his eye, for the next twenty years, and that he would become unbearably jealous if she even looked at another man.

That he was offering to allow her to go where and with whom she pleased meant she could hardly object if he allowed himself the same freedom.

Olivia smiled her polite smile. "Thank you, Nic."

"There's just one thing," he added quietly. "My mother has informed me I must provide her with a grandson and myself with an heir."

"Your mother . . . ?"

"Yes, she is speaking to me again."

"Well, that is a good thing, isn't it?"

"Yes, it is a good thing." He stretched out his hand toward her, and when she clasped his fingers, helped her down from the swing. "I mention the heir because I do have one stipulation, Olivia. Any child you provide must be mine. Unquestionably mine. Other than that, you can live, and do, as you wish."

Again Olivia felt that ache in her heart. *No, no, that's not what I want. I want you, only you, and I want you to want me.* But of course she said nothing of the sort. Who would have thought the freedom she'd longed for could feel like a small, dark prison cell?

"Of course. I agree." She smiled, her calm mask firmly in place.

There was no hint of triumph in his smile. "Then come. We will return to your house and I will speak with your father."

Olivia slipped her hand into his arm. She knew she wanted to be with Nic, whatever happened, whatever the future held. She'd always wanted to be with him. And she still believed that she could win him to her, bind his heart to hers, no matter how unlikely it seemed to everyone else.

Nic was with her father for more than an hour, and when he'd gone, Mr. Monteith seemed rather bemused by the whole matter. "Lord Lacey was very generous," he admitted. "I won't bother your head with the details, Olivia, but he made no argument with anything I suggested. I must say I was surprised. I thought a man like that would drive a harder bargain."

Mrs. Monteith wasn't happy. "You should have refused him. You know his reputation. He can never make Olivia happy. I can hardly bear to think of it."

They exchanged a meaningful look.

"Well, she has accepted him," her husband

said, "and in the circumstances, I think marriage is the best solution. A scandal like this will not go away, and despite his reputation, Lord Lacey is a good catch. A very good catch. I expect my credit in London will rise tenfold when they hear Lacey is to be my son-in-law. And in time the past difficulties will all be forgotten, you'll see."

Mrs. Monteith looked at him as if he were insane. ' "Past difficulties,' " she repeated in a shaky voice. "Is that what you call them? How can you talk about—about 'credit' and 'good catches' when we are selling our daughter to the man who—"

"Mrs. Monteith, remember what you're saying," he said sharply, glancing at Olivia.

She swallowed, shook her head. "He will take her away from us."

"Don't be foolish. Castle Lacey is his home and it will be Olivia's home, too. I'm sure, with Olivia's steadying influence . . ." He paused, perhaps recalling that Olivia had been anything but steady recently. "With Olivia's influence, Lord Lacey will set aside his wild ways and take up the reins of his estate, instead of traveling half the year and leaving the running of it to others. His father was a good master and a canny landlord, who spread his profits into investments rather than wasting it on his back, as so many of the upper classes tend to do. I'm sure his son will be just as good, or even better."

Olivia hid her smile. Her father was a businessman through and through, with little time for the wastefulness of those of the gentry who believed show was everything. He had raised his family from a comfortable position to a wealthy one, and he was scornful of those who were too idle or thought themselves too grand to see the mercantile opportunities awaiting them. His one vanity was his position as a self-made man, and the respect it brought him from his peers.

His wife wasn't as easily convinced. "You know there are objections, Mr. Monteith. You are choosing not to see them for reasons of your own. Well, I can't pretend everything has ended well. I am not so pragmatic as you."

And she burst into tears and left the room.

Olivia and her father were alone in the study. Mr. Monteith rearranged his papers, embarrassed at the display of emotion. "Your mother will come to accept the inevitable," he assured her gruffly. "It is just that she had her heart set on Mr. Garsed."

"I'm sorry to disappoint, Father."

He looked up at her under his shaggy brows, his eyes keen and intelligent. "I expect you will do the Laceys proud. I admit that if I have a weakness it is to see my daughter with a title. Lady Lacey. Yes, I will enjoy boasting about you to my business colleagues."

Olivia smiled. "I'm glad to be able to oblige."

"There's something I should tell you about your sister, Sarah," he began hesitantly, then stopped. "Or perhaps it is best to let matters lie sleeping?"

"Sarah, Father?"

He met her gaze and then looked away. "Perhaps another time, my dear."

Olivia waited, in case he changed his mind, but

he said no more, evidently distracted by something he saw in the papers on his desk. He sat down, frowning, and picked up his pen. Olivia left the room quietly and closed the door.

There was one more thing to do and she didn't look forward to it. She'd received two proposals of marriage, and Theodore deserved to be told the outcome before news leaked out.

Theodore took a mouthful of the mousse à la Garsed, his chef's latest dish. The rich, creamy dessert seemed to stick in his throat but he forced it down, and forced a smile. "Delicious," he managed, beaming. "You have outdone yourself this time, François!"

Satisfied, the chef returned to his domain. Theodore put his spoon down. He felt ill, his stomach was churning with emotion. It was all Lacey's fault.

Olivia had come to see him after he'd proposed, and he'd known as soon as he'd seen her face that she was going to marry Lacey. Theodore had put on a sad but brave face, his manner disappointed but understanding, while inside he was boiling with jealousy and rage.

"The scandal is nothing to me," he'd assured her. "I want to marry you, Miss Monteith. Please, I beg you will not marry Lord Lacey because you believe he is the only one who will have you now."

Olivia seemed so touched by his words, there were tears in her eyes, and her soft pink lips trembled as she strove to reply. He'd never loved her more, and his heart ached.

"I have accepted Lord Lacey, Mr. Garsed. I'm sorry to cause you pain, and I will always remember your kindness and generosity. But it is all arranged."

Theodore thought he said the right things, he hardly remembered what it was, and she said her good-byes.

"I don't know how you can eat that pap," Alphonse drawled from his position by the fire.

Theodore had forgotten he was there, but now he glanced over at his brother. With his swarthy good looks he was very like his Italian mother, Theodore's father's second wife. Theodore could remember seeing his new half brother for the first time and finding something rather repellent in the mewling bundle, but as time went on he'd learned to accept and even grow fond of Alphonse. There was a bond of blood between them.

"If the woman doesn't want you, Theo, then she is a fool. Do you really want to marry a fool?" Alphonse was holding up his glass of claret to the light, watching intently as the color changed.

"You don't understand," Theodore retorted. "Olivia Monteith would have been the perfect wife. She would have given my table and my home an elegance it lacks. Why, she's almost as interested in François's creations as I am!"

Alphonse smiled.

"What is it?" Theodore said hastily. "Have I said something to amuse you?"

"Not at all, brother." Alphonse set down his glass. "I am very fond of you, Theo. You do know that?"

"Alphonse, I don't want you doing anything awkward," Theodore began uneasily, then he put a hand to his stomach and grimaced.

"I can see you have one of your stomachaches, brother. I think you should go to bed. You'll feel much better in the morning."

Theodore sighed. "I hope you're right."

"Of course I'm right. I always have your best interests at heart. You know that, don't you, Theodore?"

Theodore rose to his feet, paused at the door and looked back. Alphonse was watching him expectantly. "Thank you, Alphonse." He said the words his brother was waiting to hear.

"My pleasure, brother. My pleasure."

Alphonse waited until he heard Theodore's door close, and then he went to find paper and pen and ink in the desk in the library. When he was at school Alphonse had forged a letter of credit from their father to the bank, and no one had ever found out. The money had got him— and Theodore—through a difficult time. There had been other situations in which he'd helped his brother—the dancer who tried to blackmail Theodore and whom Alphonse had dealt with—rather too enthusiastically, some would say.

He'd always looked after Theodore and he always would.

Alphonse began to compose the notes that would draw their prey into the web.

Originally, he'd planned to send one note only,

to Nic Lacey—he'd found Lacey's handwriting on a polite note of refusal to one of Theodore's soirees—but as he carefully copied Lacey's writing, Alphonse decided it would be a good idea to have Olivia there, too. She could witness her lover's death. That should ensure she never strayed from Theodore again.

Alphonse's jaw tightened. Theodore was far too much of a gentleman to stand up for himself. He preferred to suffer in silence. Well, Alphonse would make certain he didn't suffer for long. If Theodore wanted a fairy-tale ending with the woman he loved, then he'd have one, and everyone would believe it a horrible accident that Lacey had died. A poacher's bullet going astray . . . or even a gamekeeper's.

Wilson, the Lacey's gamekeeper, is a most unpleasant fellow, far too zealous for his own good. Alphonse could hear Theodore's voice in his head from earlier in the day, when Alphonse had expressed the intention of going for a stroll. *Don't go into the woods, brother, whatever you do. He's just as likely to shoot you and ask questions later.*

Theodore heard all the village gossip—people tended to tell him things—they trusted him. But people also tended to take advantage of his kind nature, and Alphonse was there to see that didn't happen.

"Tomorrow everything will be settled," he murmured to himself, "Nic Lacey will be dead and his *molto caro* will fall into Theodore's arms."

Chapter 22

Nic swung his leg over the saddle, grimacing at the familiar twinge. The note had come last evening. *Meet me in the woods by the pagan stone at two o'clock. I need to talk. Olivia.* His future bride was impatient to see him alone, he thought, with a smile. Well, he was not adverse to some sensual gratification. From what he knew about marriage, which was little enough, the bride was usually kept well away from the groom until the actual ceremony. This would heighten his desire nicely, but the fact was he'd tasted her once, and it was becoming difficult to deny himself.

Perhaps Olivia felt the same?

She was a sensual creature. He was looking forward to tutoring her, but the interesting thing was Olivia had things to teach him. It was quite an admission for a rake. Nic might know a great deal about technique, the coolheaded ways of increasing pleasure, but Olivia was warm and passionate, and she was ruled by feelings. He found that fresh and fascinating. The shifting expressions on her face as he touched her, the way she arched beneath him, and her eagerness to share her enjoyment with him.

Nic smiled again as he kicked his horse into a gallop and rode across the park. He and Olivia could spend many long hours in each other's company and never grow bored. For a man who'd been more or less forced into making this marriage proposal, he was very cheerful, very cheerful indeed.

Olivia made her way through the densely growing trees, feeling the damp chill creeping through her clothing and into her flesh. She'd never liked this part of the Lacey estate. It was said in the village that these woods were the only remnant of an ancient forest, and the stone that stood in the clearing in the center was all that was left from the days of the pagan Britons, before they were swept away to the west by the incoming tides of settlers.

She remembered coming there as a child and being scared silly by the tales she'd been told of ghosts and monsters lurking in the trees, waiting to pounce on her and gobble her up. Well, she told herself, she was grown up now and she knew there was nothing to fear. Besides, Nic would be waiting there for her.

The thought of Nic warmed her, although it didn't calm her. Her heart began to beat more quickly and her breath to shorten. She'd been longing to see him, but it seemed that since they'd announced their forthcoming wedding there was so much to be done—seeing dressmakers and cloth merchants; arranging for shoes, bonnets, flowers, invitations . . . The wedding was small and was to be held in the village church, but still the arrangements were endless. As soon as she finished one thing, her mother found her another to do. She was quite certain Mrs. Monteith was doing her best to keep Olivia busy so that she could keep Nic and Olivia apart.

Meet me at the pagan stone in the woods at two o'clock. I need to see you. Lacey.

Well, Olivia told herself, she needed to see Nic, too. She needed the reassurance of his smile and his strong arms. She glanced down at the heavy engagement ring he'd presented her with last week, when he and Lady Lacey had come to dine with the Monteiths. It had been an awkward affair, with Nic's mother struggling with her disdain for a family she considered so much lower than her own, and Olivia's mother clearly unconvinced Nic was the right man for her daughter. And then her father had insulted Lady Lacey by asking her how much she paid her estate manager.

Olivia and Nic were the only ones who seemed at all happy, and when he had presented her with the ring, he'd made a pretty little speech about it being a token of his affection. Lady Lacey informed them that the ring had been in the Lacey family for generations and had been worn by every new bride. Then Mrs. Monteith had shuddered and said that emeralds were unlucky. All the same, when Nic slid it onto

Olivia's finger, it fit perfectly, as if it was meant to be worn by her.

Olivia made her way deeper into the woods, ignoring the warning call of a bird far above her and the niggling doubt that if Nic wanted to see her then surely he would pick somewhere more pleasant than this. Unless . . . had he something so secret to tell her that he dared not take the risk they might be overheard?

No, that was just plain silly. If he wanted to tell her something confidential, he would ask her to visit him and sit her down in his library. No one would overhear them there.

Estelle, who'd accompanied her as far as Mother Eggin's cottage, told her that she thought a man like Lord Lacey probably had a great many secrets, but it wasn't likely he'd share any of them with Olivia.

Mother Eggin's cottage was on the Lacey estate, the old woman having been a servant in the castle at one time, and been granted the right to live there. Mrs. Monteith often visited her with a basket of food or other necessaries, and Olivia had taken over the task today. Of course her real reason was so that she could meet Nic, but Estelle would remain at the cottage and wait for her return. Mother Eggin, who was ninety years old at least, would be no trouble; she habitually slept through the visits of her neighbors.

"Gentlemen don't think their private matters are anyone's business but their own," Estelle had carried on, sounding as if she was quoting Abbot.

"Just be glad he's marrying you, miss, and forget about the others. You don't want to be like that Bluebeard's wife, do you, and discover something awful?"

"I don't think Nic has any other wives hidden in the cellars," Olivia had said, smiling.

But Estelle wasn't about to be diverted from her warning. "You never know, miss. Just as well I'll be there with you. Me and Abbot will protect you."

The bird in the treetops called again, bringing Olivia back to her lonely trek through the woods. She wished Estelle was with her now, and Abbot, too. But most of all she wished for Nic.

Alphonse settled himself in the undergrowth. He was wearing an overcoat and an old cap that he could pull down low over his brow. He was trying to look like a poacher, or some other kind of desperate character, just in case anybody saw him. Although he'd taken very good care that no one did. The gun was his own property, and he was a rather good shot, if he did say so himself. It was just one of his many accomplishments.

Theodore was still suffering, and still in bed. Alphonse had left him sipping peppermint tea and complaining about a headache. Well, if Theodore wouldn't do anything to make his dreams come true, then his brother would.

Nic dismounted, leaving his horse tethered at the edge of the thick wood, and began to make his way along the narrow, overgrown path. He didn't come there often—there was something alienating about this place. He knew of the rumors of pagan rites and witches' covens meeting in secret around the old stone, but he'd never seen any sign of it, and he had trouble imagining the good folk of Bassingthorpe cavorting naked under the full moon.

Olivia must know of the rumors, too, and he wasn't sure why she'd chosen this place. Any proper young lady would surely avoid the pagan stone and the clearing, but Olivia wasn't your conventional proper young lady. There was a wild streak in her, a willingness to fly in the face of convention. He remembered that when he'd suggested he might pretend to be his wicked Lacey ancestor while she pretended to be a beautiful peasant girl, she'd not only agreed, she'd reveled in it.

Had Olivia brought him there for more playacting? Nic could be the pagan prince and Olivia the willing sacrifice, or perhaps she was the pagan goddess and he the innocent plowman who'd stumbled into her web.

Nic grinned. He was more than ready, whatever she wanted to do. Devil take it, he could hardly wait. The rake was entirely enthralled by Miss Monteith. Not that he'd tell her that, not yet anyway. There would be plenty of time to tell each other their secrets, and he certainly was in no hurry to share Jonah with her.

Not that he was ashamed of the boy, but a

secret like that . . . Olivia might leave him. Not physically, he knew she wouldn't do that; their social positions made leaving impossible. As Lady Lacey, she'd stay and play her part, standing by his side in public and smiling her calm and beautiful smile, even producing the heir he required. But beneath the brittle surface he would have lost her, she'd have taken her heart and her mind somewhere else, leaving him with nothing but an empty shell.

Nic cursed softly under his breath and quickened his steps.

Olivia saw the clearing ahead of her, with the pagan stone in its center. It was actually three stones—two upright pillars with another flatter stone forming a lintel across the top—giving the impression of a roughly hewn table. The honey-colored stones glowed eerily, as if from a fire burning within them, although Olivia knew it was simply the light filtering through the leaves above. She had the impression of something very old and very powerful, standing as it did in the center of the clearing, in the center of the wood.

Softly, because it felt as if noise was forbidden here, she walked forward. No birds sang now. She might have been the only living thing in the woods . . . if it were not for the sensation that she was not alone. Olivia had a strong urge to glance over her shoulder, just in case there was something there, but she stifled it, telling herself not to be silly.

Nic would arrive soon.

Olivia made up her mind she'd ask him if they could go somewhere else and talk—the place where the stepping stones crossed the stream would be much more comfortable. Soft grass and the ripple of the water and sunbeams shining down on them as they lay in each other's arms. Sheer bliss.

A rustle at the far edge of the clearing distracted her. "Nic?" She listened intently but the sound didn't come again, and she could see nothing but shadows among the trees. With a sigh she stood restlessly by the stone and prepared to wait.

Alphonse heard Olivia's call and knew she was in place. Good. He settled his gun against his shoulder, sighting along the barrel. Nic would be coming along the path in a moment, all unsuspecting and full of his victory. Let him enjoy it while he could, Alphonse didn't begrudge him a few more moments of triumph, because very soon Lacey would be gone and Theodore could take what was rightfully his.

Footsteps.

He watched intently from his hiding place as a figure approached, at first just a dark shape moving between the tree trunks, and then growing clearer as it drew closer. Lacey's head was bowed, and he was limping slightly—Theodore had said something about him being lame. Alphonse knew the exact spot where he was going to pull the trigger. There was a dip in the path and then a fallen log. To get to the clearing, Lacey would have to climb over the log, and that would make him the perfect target.

Alphonse's finger waited on the trigger and he took a breath, clenching his teeth. One moment more and it would all be over.

Lacey reached the fallen log and stopped. Alphonse could see him deciding how best to climb over it with the burden of his lame leg. Finally he sat down and swung his leg over, and in that moment he was astride the log and facing Alphonse.

His finger tightened on the trigger.

The moment had come.

Alphonse heard her before he saw her. Olivia, running along the path from the clearing. She flung herself into Lacey's arms, causing him to lose his balance.

Alphonse barely managed to lift the gun barrel in time, sending the bullet plowing harmlessly into the trees. The crack of the shot was deafening.

Olivia screamed. Lacey leaped over the log with her still in his arms, tumbling her down onto the ground and out of sight. Cursing under his breath, Alphonse did the only thing he could. Ran. He crashed through the undergrowth, his heart pounding, not daring to slow down or turn and see if he was being pursued.

He'd almost shot Olivia. He'd almost killed his brother's future wife!

This was Lacey's fault, Alphonse thought furiously. Theodore was right, the man deserved to die.

The horse was tethered on the far side of the woods, and when Alphonse reached it, he crouched over to catch his breath. It was difficult to hear with his heart thumping, but after a moment he was certain there was no one following him. He was safe. Now all he had to do was calmly ride his horse home again and pretend to be annoyed that the friend he'd set out to visit wasn't at home.

Alphonse tore off his cap and shrugged off the overcoat, bundling both out of sight into his saddlebag. Did this mean he'd have to think up another plan? If all had gone as expected it would be over by now, and he'd be preparing to bask in Theodore's gratitude.

He wouldn't be able to use the forged notes again, and any arranged meeting would be looked on with suspicion. That meant he'd be hard-pressed to eliminate Lacey before the wedding.

But then it occurred to him that if Olivia Monteith was married, and then widowed, she'd stand to inherit the castle and the estate and all the Lacey wealth. As her second husband, Theodore would have the benefit of that; everything that was once Lord Lacey's would become his.

Alphonse's face split into a grin. Theodore would be twice as wealthy, and he'd certainly reward his brother. And this plan was bound to be even better than the last one.

Chapter 23

Nic lifted his head, listening. The sounds of running feet and a body crashing through the undergrowth had faded, and now the usual silence lay over the woods. Whoever had fired the shot had made his escape.

"Are you hurt?" came a whisper. He felt Olivia touching his face, her fingers trembling as they brushed against his skin.

"No." He rolled off her and gave her a humorless smile. "I'm sorry I jumped on you."

She sat up, pushing her hair out of her eyes, looking around. "Who was it?"

"I don't know."

"Could it have been Wilson, your gamekeeper?" she said, no doubt remembering the night the fool had threatened to shoot them.

"No. If it was, he'd have come to make sure we were unharmed. Whoever fired that shot didn't want to be seen and he certainly didn't want to be caught."

Nic climbed to his feet, and reached down to help her up.

She was disheveled, a leaf in her hair, and a streak of earth across her sleeve. The thought that she'd been in danger made him furiously angry, and although there was nothing he could do about it just now, he was coldly determined to discover who'd been trespassing on his land. And when he did, he promised himself he'd punish them, personally.

"Nic, why did you want to meet here?"

Olivia was on her way back toward the clearing where the stone stood. She paused to shake out her skirts and brush them down, and Nic frowned and reached into his jacket pocket, pulling out the folded note.

"Didn't you send this to me?"

"Send what?" She turned, and he opened the note and read it aloud to her. There was a silence while she stared at him in bewilderment. "But you sent the same thing to me! Well, almost the same." She took the paper and read it herself, then peered more closely at the penmanship. "I didn't write this. It is very like, but . . . I *know* I didn't write it."

"And I certainly didn't write telling you to meet me here," Nic said quietly.

Olivia shivered and he slipped his arm around her, pulling her close. "Do you think someone brought us here on purpose?"

"It would seem so."

"But why? The scandal is already common knowledge, and we have announced our marriage."

"I don't think it was to cause a scandal, Olivia."
He looked down into her eyes. "Someone was
trying to frighten us."

"Or harm us?" she said.

"They missed, remember. At such close range,
they must have missed on purpose."

"Oh Nic . . ."

"I know I'm not a popular man," he said dryly,
"but I can't see why anyone would want to shoot
at me. The only virgin I've ruined lately is you."
His mouth curled into a smile. "You don't think
your mother—"

"No, I do not! Nic, this is no laughing matter."

He kissed her lips, just a brush of his to hers. "I
know it's not. Forgive me, my sweet."

She turned away again, shoulders stiff with
disapproval, and walked across the clearing to
halt by the pagan stone. Nic followed more slowly,
watching the sway of her hips, enjoying the muted
glow of her hair in the gloom.

"I often wondered what went on here," he said,
and paced around the stones, allowing his hand
to trail across the smooth, worn surface of the
lintel stone. "Fertility rites? What do you think,
Olivia? Did our village ancestors dance naked
under the stars, taking their pleasure where they
fell?"

Her eyes widened. "You mean . . . ?"

"An orgy? Yes, why not? They'd be masked,
of course, to intensify the excitement and the
mystery."

"Yes," she said wryly, "I can see if you lived in

a village you'd prefer not to know who you were lying with, in case it was your butcher or your baker."

"Or the vicar."

She looked shocked, and Nic chuckled.

"Do you think they made sacrifices on this stone?" she went on, recovering.

"No. I think the only sacrifices here were ones of the flesh. A willing maiden laid out for the master to enjoy."

She shivered, but he didn't think it was from fear.

"Here," he said, and moved around to stand beside her. "Climb up."

Olivia hesitated, her eyelashes shielding her eyes. She licked her lips, like a wild animal in danger, and he felt himself grow hard. He clasped his hands about her waist before she could protest, and lifted her onto the stone. She leaned against him, and he rested his cheek against the softness of her breasts, breathing in her scent.

"What if *he* comes back?"

"Why should he? He's done what he set out to do."

He clasped her hip, pressing her rounded flesh through her skirts and petticoats, and then slid his hand down her thigh. She lifted his face to hers and began to kiss him, slowly, taking her time, enjoying herself. Nic delved beneath her skirts, working his way toward his goal.

He could sense the tension in her, the excitement, as he drew closer. And then his fingers slid inside and Olivia gasped, a slave to her body's demands and Nic's clever fingers, as he began stroking her slick flesh. She groaned against his mouth.

"Nic," she whispered. "Would it be wrong of me to admit that I want you?"

He grinned. "Very wrong indeed," he teased, retaking her mouth with his. He tasted her passion, felt her need for him as she wrapped her arms about his neck and her legs around his waist, pulling him closer against her.

He thought about taking her now, him standing up, but he'd already decided to continue with the fantasy of the willing sacrifice, and he didn't want to spoil it for either of them.

"Imagine it's nighttime," he began, his breathing ragged against her throat, "with the sky full of stars. The master stands over you, masked. He is touching you, just like this . . ." She gasped. "There are others here, and they want to touch you, too, but he won't allow it. You belong to him and only him."

She reached down to where his cock strained inside his trousers, rubbing her hand against him. "And he belongs to me," she whispered, and he heard her smile.

Nic laid her down, arranging her on the stone—it was strangely warm—and then climbed up with her, straddling her as he unbuttoned his trousers. She watched, eyes half closed, waiting to see what he would do. Nic knew he needed to be inside her. The danger they'd been in, the possibility of death, was pushing him to take her now.

When he positioned himself above her, she slid her thigh along his, eager to have him inside her, but perversely he held back, if only to prove to himself that he could.

Slowly he unhooked her bodice, licking her pale skin as he uncovered her lush curves, and then fastening upon her nipples, giving each of them equal time. She arched against him, her eyes closed, her face flushed. He wondered if she was there, in their fantasy, in the star-filled night. Nic reached down to stroke her again, teasing her with promises of fulfillment, and then taking his fingers away.

"Nic, please," she whimpered.

"Master," he reminded her.

"Master, please," she cried, not ashamed to throw herself into their game. "Make me yours. Now. While the moon is full and—and the stars are watching."

Nic laughed. He couldn't remember laughing before at such a point in lovemaking—he'd always been too focused on control—but now he was filled with joy. Olivia reached up and touched his lean cheek, her eyes bright and understanding.

"Take me, master," she said, and smiled.

He entered her with one deep thrust. She cried out with sheer delight. He groaned, moving hard, willing himself to hold on, to make it last, but it was too late. He was already shuddering with the beginnings of his ecstasy, just as she reached her own peak, her muscles squeezing him and prolonging his pleasure.

It was perfect.

They stayed a moment, enjoying the afterglow, until the chill of the air began to seep in through their flesh, and he remembered how vulnerable they were to prying eyes. Nic swung himself down from the stone, lifting Olivia with him.

"I will never be nervous in this place again," she said, straightening her clothing. "There are only good memories here now."

He met her gaze, suddenly serious. "Don't mention what happened here to anyone."

Olivia bit her lip, eyes alight with laughter.

"No, minx, I don't mean *this*," he waved his hand at the stone. "I meant the gunshot, the trespasser. Say nothing. I will try and discover his identity myself, and it would be better to avoid any more scandal."

Olivia agreed and, with a long, parting kiss, he left her at the edge of the woods to make her way back to Mother Eggin's cottage. Nic stood for a time, watching over her. There was a mystery here, he thought. If it wasn't an accident, then someone wished them ill. He knew he had enemies, but he wouldn't have thought they were the kind to do something like this.

Was it a coincidence? The notes forged by one person, a scandal-monger, and the shot fired by someone else entirely. Some lunatic who thought he was shooting rabbits, and had frightened himself as much as them. Nic decided he'd instruct

Wilson to take on an apprentice, just to be certain, though he doubted such a man would be back. Still, he made a mental note to watch out for any of the villagers who couldn't meet his eyes next time they came face-to-face.

Chapter 24

Bassingthorpe Church bells were ringing. Their sound was sweet and slightly off-key, just as it had been for hundreds of years. Lord Lacey and his new bride stood on the porch, smiling and receiving congratulations from their families and guests and well-wishers. Olivia looked more beautiful than ever in her deep cream silk dress and matching cream slippers, her fair hair fastened up with flowers and pearls, while the ribbons sewn upon her skirt fluttered in the gentle breeze. Her wicked husband wore midnight blue, with a white satin waistcoat, and he looked darkly handsome enough for any woman.

Yes, Estelle thought, they made a fine couple.

She slipped her hand into Abbot's. At her warm touch, he glanced down at her and returned her smile. They'd been married in Bassingthorpe Church, too, although their ceremony had been a great deal less extravagant and well attended than this one. Nevertheless, Estelle was now Mrs. Abbot and was moving to live at Castle Lacey, where she would be Olivia's personal maid.

Until her pregnancy became too obvious.

Estelle was determined to keep it a secret as long as she could, but she was comforted by the thought that Lord Lacey was unlikely to be traveling abroad and taking Abbot with him when he was so recently married. Of course, there was the honeymoon and a few weeks to spend in London, but Estelle and Abbot would be accompanying them for that. It would be their honeymoon, too—in a way.

"Everything has worked out perfectly," she said.

He squeezed her fingers. "Yes, it has. Lord Lacey, who swore he would never marry, is married to a proper lady like Miss Olivia, and he and Lady Lacey are speaking again after all these years." His voice took on a sarcastic edge. "It's quite like a fairy-tale ending."

Estelle pinched his sleeve. "You sound as if you don't believe it'll last."

"No," he said, with a sigh. "I don't see how it can. There are too many possibilities for disaster, my dear. You don't know the Laceys like I do."

But Estelle refused to be downhearted. "I may not know the Laceys, but I do know Miss Olivia," she said firmly. "She won't allow any disasters. You wait and see."

Abbot knew when to give in. "I'm sure you're right, Estelle."

Estelle had spied Theodore Garsed and his brother, and nudged Abbot as the man approached the Laceys. He had such a benevolent look on his face, as if he was truly overjoyed for them. How strange, thought Estelle, when everyone knew he'd wanted Olivia for himself.

When she mentioned this to Abbot, he shrugged and suggested that perhaps Mr. Garsed was a genuinely good man, who wished for the best for the woman he'd loved. But Abbot was such a simpleton when it came to human nature that Estelle didn't believe it for a moment.

Mr. Garsed wasn't a good man, she decided, after she'd observed him when he thought no one else was watching. But he was a very good actor.

Theodore showed his teeth, saying all the right things. He was edgy and anxious. Alphonse had told him what he'd done—his brother could never keep anything to himself. The worst of it was Alphonse seemed to think Theodore would be pleased with him! Thankfully there'd been no repercussions; it hadn't even been mentioned to him by anyone in the village, which was a fair indication that Nic and Olivia hadn't spoken of it to anyone else. He was hoping they'd pushed it from their minds.

"Do you want me to stop, then?" Alphonse had mocked, eyes narrowed. "They do make a lovely couple."

"Of course I want you to stop! Alphonse, for God's sake, you can't do something like this. I—I understand you want to help, but this isn't the way to do it. If you're caught you'll be hanged. You do know that, don't you?"

"Then I won't be caught, brother."

"You may have misjudged Lacey," Mr. Monteith said to his wife. "He has behaved very gentlemanly."

"If he hadn't caused this scandal by ruining our daughter in the first place—" his wife hissed, a bitter droop to her mouth.

"Shush, you will be heard . . ."

She looked unrepentant, but he noticed she glanced about her to see if anyone was standing close enough to have caught any of her outburst. Mr. Monteith knew that in his world of business, appearance was everything, and the merest hint of scandal could cause one to be ostracized by customers and friends alike.

"I can't forget what happened to Sarah," his wife said in a bleak tone. "We should have spoken of it to Olivia and then this would never have happened."

"Sarah is in the past," he said, a trifle impatiently. "We agreed it was best."

"You agreed!"

"You know what would have happened if there was the slightest whisper of Sarah and—and her behavior. The business was going through a difficult time. We would have lost everything. We promised we would not speak of this again, my dear."

She nodded, her head drooping. "I'm sorry. It was just seeing Olivia. It reminded me." She turned to stare at him a little wildly as another thought occurred to her. "And how can you be sure this won't end badly? Olivia is such a sweet, innocent girl. He will hurt her. Before long she'll be regretting marrying him. Mr. Garsed is such a good man. Oh, Mr. Monteith, I know Sarah wouldn't listen to me, but I do so wish Olivia had!"

"Hush, my dear." With a sigh, Mr. Monteith held her close. Across the churchyard his gaze rested on his remaining daughter and her new husband. Was his wife right? Was this marriage a disaster in the making? And yet Nic Lacey, elegant, aristocratic, was keeping a close eye on Olivia, and there was something in his manner that spoke of more than mere convenience. Mr. Monteith decided he wouldn't be at all surprised if this turned out to be a love match after all.

The house in which the Laceys spent the first days and nights of their honeymoon was owned by friends of Nic's, who were away in Scotland. The house, which stood on the Thames, up from Richmond, was empty apart from a small army of servants, so Nic and Olivia were more or less left to their own devices.

At first the house appeared huge and unfriendly, and Olivia hadn't known what to expect on their first night, but the intimate dinner in the dining room was close to perfect. The servants delivered the dishes like shadows, vanishing again and leaving the couple alone. Olivia was tired—from their wedding and from soothing her mother, who persisted in believing her daughter was now lost to her forever, and then from their journey here. It wasn't long before she was blinking sleepily over her meal, while Nic leaned back in his chair, watching her over the rim of his glass.

"Tired, minx?"

"Yes." She smiled at him, or tried to.

"No regrets?"

" 'Tis a little early yet, m'lord."

He gave a low laugh. "Ever the cautious Olivia."

"I would say I have been very incautious, my lord. Wildly incautious, in fact. Have you forgotten how incautious I can be?"

He laughed aloud this time and rose to his feet, coming around to pull back her chair. As she straightened her skirts he strolled toward the door, pausing to stretch. She watched him raise his arms above his head, his body arching gracefully, the muscles of buttocks and thighs tightening, and suddenly she was no longer tired. He glanced at her over his shoulder, his dark eyes glowing in the candlelight, his mouth curled in a smile that promised much.

"Coming to bed, Olivia?" he said in a voice that dripped like honey. "This is our first night as husband and wife. Remember?"

"How could I forget?"

His dark eyes gleamed. "I wonder if it will feel different. Do you think it will? Now that our union has been sanctioned by God and man."

Olivia considered it, and then she smiled. "Why don't we find out?"

Nic held out his hand.

A tremor began in her belly, spreading outward, making her flesh tingle and burn. Her fingers clung to his, and slowly, purposefully, he drew her into his arms. He ran his hand down her back and curled it about her waist. When his mouth closed on hers it was warm and rough, but she liked that. It showed her he wasn't as controlled as he liked to pretend, that he cared about her, that she unsettled him in a way he wasn't used to.

He cupped her face, running his fingers up into her hair, enjoying the silky texture. Nic began to take out her hairpins, one by one, tossing them aside all over the floor. Olivia protested, but he only smiled. Her hair tumbled down about her shoulders, and he gathered it to him, pressing his face to the soft, scented strands.

Olivia pulled apart the knot of his neck cloth, opening it so that she could touch her mouth to the hollow of his throat. She curled her fingers about the muscular column of his neck, and felt his hands slide into the dip of her waist, down to cup her bottom. Suddenly he brought her hips hard against him, so that she could feel just how ready for her he was.

That familiar languorous pleasure spread through her veins and muscles, making her skin feel as if it didn't quite belong to her. Her breasts ached and tightened at the tips, and the flesh between her legs grew achy and swollen. The promise of pleasure was so exquisite she couldn't have turned back if she tried.

With her hand in his, Nic led her up the grand curving staircase, pausing every few steps so that he could kiss her. It took them a long time to reach the landing. Once there, he leaned her against the balustrade, and while she arched dizzyingly over the hall below, bent to lap at her breasts, easing down her bodice so that he could suck at the peaks.

By the time he drew her safely back into his arms she was trembling and gasping. He drew up her skirts as she clung to him, his hands running over her stockings and stroking her bare thighs, before reaching around to clasp the soft cheeks of her bottom. His mouth was open against her breasts and she moaned, pulling his head down to her.

They stumbled around the corner into the wide corridor, and he pressed her against the wall, lifting her in his arms so that the only way she could keep her balance was for her legs to clasp his hips and her hands to cling to his shoulders. Between her thighs she could feel his body hard against her softness, sending teasing shivers of pleasure through her as he rotated his hips.

She kissed his face, warm butterfly kisses, before she reached his mouth. He groaned, and lifting her away from the wall, carried her through the bedchamber door and into their room. They fell upon the bed, and a moment later he was inside her.

"Don't wait," she gasped, moving against him.

Nic had no intention of waiting. He thrust deeply, once, twice, and she shattered. A moment later he cried out hoarsely, as he reached his own climax.

They lay, panting, and then Nic threw back his head and howled like a wolf. Olivia, gasping, laughing, tried to cover his mouth with her hands, but he rolled over, taking her with him. When he stopped she was lying on top of him, rumpled and flushed, with her eyes dancing.

"They can hear you in the servants' rooms."

"Good."

"Don't you care?"

"You're Lady Lacey now. Lady Lacey doesn't care what the servants think. Lady Lacey is above such things."

She smiled, but her eyes were serious. "I don't think I can ever be that arrogant, Nic. I wasn't brought up to be Lady Lacey."

"In time it will come as naturally to you as being Miss Monteith."

Perhaps so, but Olivia couldn't see herself ever becoming like Nic's mother, nor would she want to. She would be the chatelaine of Castle Lacey, but she would do it her own way.

"What are you thinking?"

She ran her fingertip over his lips, smiling. "I'm thinking that we've been married for one day."

"So we have." He caught her finger between his teeth, biting gently.

"And I'm wondering if we will still feel like this in a year. Two years. Twenty years."

He released her, turning on his side and gently sliding her off him and into the bed beside him. She propped her head on her hand and watched him. Already she could see the change her words had caused in him, and it worried her. He was uneasy at the thought of all those years with her, with one woman, and he couldn't hide it.

"I can't make promises," he said quietly. "I've seen too many unhappy marriages to do that."

"Was that the reason you didn't want to get married?" Olivia asked him, settling down against the pillows.

Nic shrugged. "Probably. Even people you believe are destined never to stray can surprise you. Disappoint you."

He was talking about someone in particular, and Olivia wondered who it was. She was tempted to ask, but she knew he wouldn't tell her. Nic was the keeper of his own secrets.

She was watching him with that clear blue gaze, like a child seeking knowledge. Nic found her openness disconcerting. His own life was very different, and now he had the added burden of protecting his wife from truths that would hurt her.

He didn't want her hurt.

His leg was aching and he longed to rub it, but she would see and be concerned. He'd feel like a cripple, and Nic didn't want that. He wanted her to see him as the strong one. Carefully, surreptitiously, he stretched his thigh muscle, trying to ease it without her noticing.

But of course she did.

"Your leg is hurting you," she said matter-of-factly. "What do you usually do to help?"

Nic heard himself laugh, and was surprised he could. "Do you always say exactly what you're thinking, Olivia?"

"Yes, nearly always." She moved gracefully onto her knees and edged down toward his leg. Gently she reached out and rested her hand upon him, glancing back at his face and raising a quizzical eyebrow.

"I rub it," he admitted, the words grudging.

"Like this?" She curled her fingers, kneading at his hard flesh. The scar on his thigh from the injury was long and thin, barely noticeable for something so serious, and she worked along it. He lay back, watching her. Her face was taut with concentration, and she stopped to tuck her hair out of the way. He wondered if she even remembered she was half naked, her breasts jiggling as she moved, the sheen of her skin like soft gold in the candlelight.

Nic thought about reaching out and touching her, but then he realized the ache in his leg was gradually diminishing, his muscles relaxing. Her touch soothed him in other ways, too, ways he didn't understand yet. He closed his eyes—just for a moment, he told himself.

Her soft fingers continued to press and knead, and he felt a twinge of desire at the thought of them creeping along his thigh and closing on his shaft. Again he was tempted to reach out, but again he stopped himself. There would be plenty of time to make love to his wife. Years. And this time the thought made him smile.

Still smiling, Nic slipped into dreamless, painless sleep.

Chapter 25

Olivia rose quietly from the bed, slipping her shawl about her naked body, her toes curling on the cold floor. It was early morning and the mist was rising from the river, drifting like smoke over the lawn toward the house. She stood at the window, enjoying the view.

Nic had slept well last night, only waking once. They'd made love quickly, silently, and she could not help but wonder if he even knew who she was. At least she did until he kissed her mouth, sleepily, and said, "Sweet Olivia. Olivia Lacey." Then, with a chuckle, he'd gone back to sleep.

Now she stood, lost in thought, not hearing him come up behind her until his arms slid around her waist, making her start, and she felt his warm, naked body pressed against hers. He reached inside her shawl and cupped her breasts, fingering her nipples until they were as hard as his cock, jutting against her rounded bottom.

"I thought you were asleep," she said breathlessly, trying to turn in his arms so that she could see him.

He held her where she was, against the sill. "How can I sleep with you standing in front of the light so that I can see every beautiful curve of your body."

"I didn't realize—"

"I know you didn't. That's part of your charm, Olivia. You didn't realize, you never do. I find that kind of innocence very erotic."

His fingers stroked the under curve of her breasts, then slid down over her ribs to the gentle swell of her stomach, and farther, to the curls between her thighs. As he probed the opening, teasing the bud, he felt her legs tremble.

"Nic," she gasped.

Olivia realized she could see their reflection in the old glass, wavy and smudged about the edges. Her body looked like alabaster, the shawl a red blur, and behind it his bigger form. His hand moved, touching her, slipping his fingers inside her. Her thighs fell open and she leaned back against him, watching as he bent and began to lap at the side of her neck. Seeing what he was doing increased the pleasure, and she groaned.

He squeezed her gently, rolling the bud, pushing her to the edge. When he knew she was about to reach her peak, he withdrew his hand and, clasping her hips, eased her back so that she could bend over with her hands still gripping the sill for support.

Olivia felt vulnerable, her body open to him, and yet she was excited, too. Nic's hand rested on her lower spine, and then he eased her thighs apart, and she felt his shaft against the slick flesh between them. He held her hips firmly and began to ease himself inside her, a little at a time.

In this position he seemed able to enter her farther than before. He filled her completely. The heat of his chest seemed to scald her back, his hair abrading her, while he thrust with increasing rhythm deep into her body.

He reached around to cup her breasts, and then his fingers slid into the cleft within her curls and began to tease the sensitive bud once more. A ripple of pleasure sped through her and she lifted her head, crying out, her knuckles white as she clung to the sill. Beyond the window the mist was leaving as the sun brightened.

Nic waited until her breath had steadied and then he began to move again. Olivia realized he wasn't done. A moment later she was glad of it. Her body began to ready itself for more pleasure, and she pushed back against him, eager for Nic to have his peak, too.

He kissed her nape, licking the salt from her skin, and she felt his hips shift slightly. Before she knew it, she was crying out, unable to stop herself, as he touched some spot deep inside her. He'd done this before, she remembered, and it seemed he'd committed that particular place to memory. He didn't even hesitate as he pressed again, harder and deeper, and this time she screamed. She couldn't help it. A pleasure so violent gripped her she would have fallen if he hadn't been holding her. As her body clenched and spasmed, Nic was pushed over the edge into his own completion.

The two of them staggered back to the bed and fell upon the mattress, bodies trembling and chests heaving, and slept until the sun was high in the sky.

Estelle pressed her ear to the door but there was no sound, so she made her way down again to Abbot, waiting in the downstairs servants' parlor. He looked up at her entrance.

"They're still asleep?"

"Yes."

"Lord Lacey is a very sensual man, my dear, and it seems he has found a perfect mate in his wife. Leave them to sleep and enjoy their time together. Once we reach London, things will be different."

"You mean they will have to rise before noon?" Estelle said dryly.

"Are you bored already?" Abbot pulled her down onto his lap.

"Of course not." She settled herself comfortably, smiling up at him. "I want to see London and all the sights—the Tower and Hyde Park. Do you think we will have time to visit them, Abbot?"

Abbot pursed his lips. "Hmm, perhaps. You will have much to do, Estelle. There will be dinners and balls and visits to the opera and the theater. Now that Lord Lacey is respectably married he will want to show off his new wife to London society."

"So you don't think he will go back to his old ways?"

Abbot tucked her head beneath his chin, wrapping his arms about her plump body. "I hope not, for Lady Lacey's sake. I think he will do his utmost to be the gentleman he was brought up to be."

"And what of the other one?" Estelle asked quietly. "The woman and the child you told me about?"

Abbot gave her a squeeze. "Shhh. That is a secret, remember. And it's none of our business."

Estelle huffed out an impatient breath, but she let him have his way. She loved him, despite his old-fashioned manners and his failure to understand the ways of the world. Or perhaps she loved him because of it.

The Lacey town house was in Mayfair, and Olivia soon found it was very different from the informality of the Monteith house in Bassingthorpe. When she complained that there were servants everywhere and the housekeeper's favorite phrase was "Lady Lacey, we have a certain way of doing things here," Nic laughed at her.

"You'll win her over," he reassured her.

The last time she'd been in London was with her parents, and although they'd visited the theater and gone shopping, their tastes and outlook were very different from that of the Laceys. Nic seemed to expect the best of everything, and his name was enough to ensure that he got it, too.

He also seemed determined to take her everywhere.

The first night they went to the ballet and drank champagne in their box, while Olivia was ogled by swells from the stalls and Nic sat possessively close. The next day they rode through Hyde Park and visited the exclusive shops along Bond Street. Then Nic took her to an establishment tucked away nearby, which he said catered to the best-dressed women in London.

Olivia found the shop small and dingy, and it was only when they were shown upstairs that her impressions changed. Here the room was decorated lavishly, with small chairs with spindly legs and brocade-covered sofas, and mirrors. A great many mirrors. The heavy golden curtain at one end of the room was lifted aside and a middle-aged woman in a plain gown, which contrasted starkly with the decor, came to greet them.

"Lord Lacey!" The proprietress seemed to know him well. Her eyes were tired, as if she never had quite enough sleep, and as they fixed on Olivia, her mouth widened into a smile that wasn't quite genuine. "Ah, you have brought me your latest companion. What is it you are looking for, my lord? Something elegant and yet revealing for your nights in Paris?"

Olivia realized then that she'd been mistaken for a demimondaine. Such an error hadn't concerned her when she attended the demimonde ball, but today it did. Today it reminded her of all the other women Nic had known in his life.

"Nic, please," she murmured, leaning close, "let us go."

"Nonsense, my love." Nic frowned. "We've only just arrived. Madam Esmeralda has made a mistake, that is all. Esmeralda, this lady is my wife, Lady Lacey."

"Your wife . . . ?" The proprietress gasped. She steadied herself with one hand against a chair back, and then made a dainty curtsy. "Lady Lacey, I do apologize."

Nic ignored the awkwardness. "Madam Esmeralda, I have brought her here to you because you are the best modiste in London."

Esmeralda gave an uncomfortable laugh. "You are too kind, my lord."

Olivia, too, was uncomfortable. She could see now that this was not the sort of dressmaker that the respectable ladies of London patronized. The gaudy furnishings, the opulent mirrors, all bespoke a certain type of clientele. Her fingers tightened on Nic's arm, trying to gain his attention, but again he pretended not to notice.

"I want my wife to shine, Esmeralda," he said, making himself comfortable on a bloodred sofa. "I want all of London to see her shine brighter than the duchesses and the countesses, and all the rest. This is important to me."

Esmeralda looked as if she'd swallowed an egg, whole. "Yes, of course, Lord Lacey," she said, but it was an effort. She began a slow walk about Olivia, inspecting her figure and her coloring, making notes in a little book that was fastened about her neck with a narrow black ribbon. Olivia knew she should walk out, that was what her mother would do, and certainly what Nic's mother would have done, but for some reason she stayed.

Perhaps it was the dark shadows under Esmeralda's eyes, or Nic's pride in her and the fact that he wanted to share it with such important people as duchesses and countesses . . .

Madam Esmeralda had finished her inspection. "Your wife is very beautiful, Lord Lacey, but hers is the beauty of the moon. If you will permit me, I will make her shine like the sun."

Nic unfolded his lean body from the sofa, smiling his pleasure at her words. "Come to my house in Mayfair when you have something to show me, Esmeralda."

"I will, my lord." She curtsied again, a little lower this time, as if to ensure the sale. "My lady."

Olivia was glad to leave, hurrying down the dim stairs and through the shop, and out into the daylight. Their carriage was waiting farther down the narrow street, a group of urchins gathered around it, hoping for a generous toff to provide them with a few coppers.

"I don't know if I want to shine like the sun," Olivia said in a chilly voice, as Nic helped her up. "And I don't like your friend Esmeralda."

He gave her a lazy smile. "Esmeralda is the best modiste in London. Why would I not take you to the best?"

Olivia reached into her reticule and took out a

handful of pennies, giving one to each child, and a smile to go with it. Nic watched her indulgently, and when the ragged crew had vanished back into the streets where they'd come, he helped her into the carriage.

They turned into the busier thoroughfare, moving slowly as the traffic grew heavier. Olivia smoothed a truant lock of hair back under her bonnet, wondering if Nic was really so obtuse or if he was just pretending, and was it for his own amusement or her embarrassment?

"Obviously you've taken other women to her. Your mistresses."

His dark eyes gleamed. "Are you jealous, Olivia?"

Of course she was jealous—she was sick with jealousy! But it occurred to Olivia that it might not be wise to show him how jealous of him she had become. A man like Nic, used to his freedom, might feel suffocated by such an emotion.

"No, Nic, I am not jealous," she said at last, with an indifferent shrug, and turned away. When she glanced at him again, he was resting back in his seat, still watching her, his eyes hooded. His gloved hand rested on his injured leg, his fingers kneading it without him seeming to notice.

Olivia opened her mouth to ask him if he was in pain, and closed it again. He would be irritated with her if she showed she'd noticed his leg was hurting. She'd had a victory the night she touched him and he allowed her to soothe him to sleep, but since then he'd refused to let her repeat it.

"I don't need an angel of mercy," he'd mocked, catching her hand in his, placing it on his groin instead. He'd used her fingers to make himself hard.

Remembering it now, Olivia felt herself blush. Some of the things they did together were intensely erotic. But Nic was a man who lived by his senses, a rake who had known many women, and would never be content with a prim and proper wife. It was just as well, Olivia thought, that she wasn't one.

Chapter 26

Abbot brushed Nic's jacket with the clothing brush, frowning as he worked on a particularly difficult speck of lint. When he was done he stepped back, surveying his master from all sides, before he was satisfied Nic was looking his best.

Nic knew there was something bothering his manservant, but there was no use quizzing the fellow. Abbot would tell him in his own time.

"No need to wait up for me tonight," he said, picking up his gloves and hat. "I intend taking my wife to supper after the opera, and we may be very late."

Abbot said nothing, merely nodding his head as he selected a cane and presented it to Nic. Nic, who had been intending to leave it behind, sighed and snatched it impatiently from his hands.

"My lord," Abbot said, meeting his eyes in the looking glass, "there is something I want to broach with you, if you will permit."

Nic raised his eyebrows. "When have you ever needed my permission, Abbot? Broach away."

"My lord, it has come to my attention that you took your wife to Madam Esmeralda's today."

"I did."

"You took your wife, Lady Lacey, to the same modiste you use for your mistresses."

Nic turned and faced him. "She is the best, that is all that concerned me."

Abbot's expression grew pained.

"You think it was the wrong thing to do?" Nic asked, irritably tugging at his waistcoat. "Abbot, as you are well aware, the nuances of polite society do not interest me . . ."

"They may not interest you, my lord, but your wife needs to be protected from your past. Surely you can see how inappropriate it is for you to ask such a woman to dress your wife?"

Nic sighed. "When you put it like that, I suppose I can. I didn't think she'd mind. And Esmeralda is brilliant."

"Brilliant or not, she is dressmaker to the demi-monde and everyone knows it. Your wife risks being cut by the very people you want her to impress."

Nic knew Abbot was right; he was always right. Devil take it, he'd have to smooth things over with Olivia. He remembered how she'd tried to tell him in the coach but he'd been more interested in whether she was jealous. For some reason, he was spending a great deal of time mulling over whether she would remain with him once the initial gloss wore off. He'd attracted her in the first place because she thought him dangerous and wicked, but as time went on such attractions might begin to pale.

And what of his infirmity? What beautiful woman wanted a limping husband at her side?

In the carriage outside Esmeralda's she'd sounded jealous of the other women, but when he sought to clarify her feelings, she'd shrugged it off. She was like a beautiful fish in a pond, continually slipping out of his grasp. It was odd, because he'd been sure he knew her, and now . . .

Now he wasn't sure that he knew her at all.

It was interval, and they had been served with champagne. The opera was a grand affair, the private boxes full of the rich and privileged, while the gallery and stalls were crammed with rowdy men and women, and even children. Olivia settled back, aware that she was on show, but enjoying herself too much to care. Besides, there were so many people to look at—even the young queen was there.

"Have you been presented to Her Majesty, Queen Victoria?" Nic said, watching her in the light of the grand chandelier.

"No, Nic, I haven't," she replied, with a smile. "I am not the presentable type."

Nic smiled back. "You are now. Do you want to be presented, Lady Lacey?"

Was he teasing her? Olivia wasn't sure. He reached forward and took her hand, the one wearing the Lacey ring, and lifted it to his lips.

"As my wife, you have far more privileges than Miss Monteith ever did."

"I doubt the queen will care what I call myself."

Nic sighed and leaned back again, dropping her hand. "Any other woman would be thrilled by my offer, but not Olivia. She doesn't feel the slightest inclination to meet the queen. She prefers driving around the streets of London, handing out pennies to ragged children."

"I like children," she retorted, staring straight ahead.

"Good. Let's make one."

She turned to stare at him, finally shocked out of her calm reserve, and he laughed.

"Oh, Olivia, your face. I'm sorry, I couldn't resist."

She supposed she would let him see her righteous indignation or refuse to speak at all, but Nic didn't respond to either. So she let herself relax, reaching up to play with the lace on her bodice, and said, "Here, Nic? I don't think the queen would approve, do you?"

He smiled, and then he laughed, and then he shook his head.

But Olivia's eyes had turned serious, that clear blue look that seemed to pierce his soul. "Do you really want a child? An heir? Or is it your mother who wants one?"

Nic glanced down, his fingers twisting on his cane. "The Laceys have lived at Castle Lacey for generations. It'd be a shame to end it now."

"Do you want to be a father, Nic?" she said softly.

He didn't answer her, and a moment later the next act began. Olivia turned back to the stage and pretended to watch the singers, but it took a long time for her heart to slow its beating and the butterflies in her stomach to stop fluttering.

As they made their way to supper in their private room, Nic wondered how Olivia had managed to turn the tables on him, and why he'd let her. He could almost think she knew about Jonah, but he was certain she didn't. If Olivia knew she wouldn't scruple to tell him.

"Oh," Olivia said, her face lighting up as they sat down, and she saw the strawberries and cream. "You remembered."

"Your favorite," Nic replied. "You told me when we feasted in my bedchamber, the day after I brought you back from the ball."

And we made love before and afterward, and it seemed like time stopped for those brief, exquisite moments.

But he didn't say that.

Olivia lifted one of the ripe, juicy fruits between her finger and thumb, and bit into it. The pink syrup ran down her chin and she dabbed at it with her napkin, smiling at Nic like one of the urchins she loved so much.

"Wonderful," she sighed.

Nic helped himself to the next strawberry, popping it into his mouth whole. The juice oozed from the corners of his mouth, and Olivia laughed as he tried to catch the trickles with his tongue. She reached across the table to him and used her finger.

"What will Abbot say if you stain that neck cloth?" she teased, and sucked the strawberry juice from her fingertip.

Nic's eyes went hot.

Olivia felt her body begin to heat up in response. Slowly, she slipped her finger from her mouth and licked it with her tongue. He followed her movement. She reached for another strawberry, biting into it, and he leaned over the table, taking the remaining part of the fruit in his own mouth, so that for a moment they were face-to-face. And then he severed the strawberry in half and his mouth closed on hers.

The sweetness of the fruit, the warmth of his lips, were somehow all the more delicious. Olivia found herself arching across the table, following his mouth. As he moved back, she moved forward, and suddenly he'd grasped her about the waist, and she was sprawled across the table and the strawberries and cream, her arms about his neck.

"Nic," she gasped.

He ran his hand across her décolletage, and then chose a strawberry. The next moment he'd slipped the ripe fruit down into her cleavage. Olivia's eyes widened as she watched him settle it comfortably between her breasts, then he smiled and began to try to tease it out with his tongue.

The sensation made her toes curl.

The strawberry slid farther down between her breasts, lodging there, and Nic pushed down her bodice, finding first one nipple and then the other. Olivia arched against him, lying half across the table, her fingers in his hair. He ran his tongue over the swell of her breasts, lapping at the strawberry juice.

But Olivia wanted to be more than Nic's dessert.

She reached up, clinging to his neck, and he lifted her into his arms and sank back into his chair with her cradled in his lap. She tried to catch her breath, but her stays were tight beneath her evening dress. He seemed to understand her difficulty, and ran his hand down over her waist, splaying his fingers.

"Will I take it off?" he said.

"What if someone comes in?" She glanced anxiously at the door.

"No one will come in, my sweet. They know better than to come into one of these rooms without making a great deal of noise."

Olivia's desire began to fade, leaching out of her like water from a wrung-out rag. "You've been here before?" she asked carefully.

"Yes."

"With other women."

"Of course."

She went still, and then she pushed herself to her feet, turning her back as she dealt with her bodice and the sticky juice smeared across her chest. The napkin, dipped in a glass of drinking water that had somehow survived her tumble on

the table, helped to remove most traces of her debauchery, and when she was finished, she turned
to face him. He was still reclining lazily in his
chair, but there was something watchful in his
face that belied his easy manner.

"You're jealous," he said, but it was a question
rather than a statement.

"No. I don't think so. Not in the way you
mean."

He waved an impatient hand. "Then what?"

Olivia sighed. "I don't want to be another one of
your women, Nic."

He looked into her eyes. "You're not."

"Perhaps. At least, not yet. But I'm afraid that
before long I will be. Just another in a long line of
companions you hire for a year and then set free.
Like—like caged birds."

"Don't be ridiculous!" Nic stood up and he
looked angry, his hair untidy from her fingers, a
swath of it hanging over his eyes, his lean cheeks
flushed. "You're my wife. I don't hire you, and I'm
hardly likely to set you free, as you call it. That
won't happen."

"How do I know? You bring me here and I feel
as if—as if—"

As if I am no more special than the others.

And Olivia knew with heavy certainty that she
wanted to feel special when she was with Nic.

Nic knew he'd done something wrong again.

A moment ago Olivia had been writhing in his
arms, a woman in the throes of undeniable pas-

sion, and the next moment she was looking at him as if he were a stranger.

He wanted to please her, and he'd thought this was the way to do it. Now he didn't know what to do. Apologize? Or give up on understanding her altogether?

"I want to go home," she said, in a voice that trembled on the verge of tears.

Nic groaned. Not tears. Women's tears were the invention of the devil, designed to force men to grovel in an effort to make them stop. He'd have to apologize then . . .

"Olivia, please, if I've done something wrong, forgive me. I only wanted to make you happy. I didn't intend to upset you."

She stopped at the door and turned to look at him.

"Yes, I have brought other women here, but I can't even remember their faces let alone their names. I wanted to bring you because I knew you loved strawberries and I knew we would have some privacy. When I'm with you I have trouble behaving myself, you know that. I don't want to cause another scandal, so I thought—"

She was smiling. Devil take it, she was smiling! Nic wondered what part of the rambling sentences he'd just spoken had made her smile. And then he decided he didn't care, as long as she was happy again.

"Come home, Nic," she said huskily, holding out her hand. "We can be private there, and I can even ask for strawberries to be served in our bed-chamber, if you like."

"Aren't you worried the housekeeper will tell you that isn't the way things are done?" he teased, moving toward her, and clasping her fingers firmly, possessively, in his.

"Do you know, I think I am getting braver where the housekeeper is concerned, because I don't care. Whose house is it, anyway?"

He bent to kiss her lips, keeping her a moment longer, before he opened the door onto the world outside.

"I do, you know," he said in a low, quiet voice.

Olivia gave him a puzzled look. "You do what?"

"I do want a child."

Tears filled her eyes but she said nothing, wiping them away with her fingers. Nic wondered at himself, that he could make this woman cry and smile, that his actions were capable of controlling her emotions. It should have felt like a burden, something to avoid, but it wasn't.

He'd avoided engaging himself emotionally with women because he didn't want to make any connections with them other than the physical, but it was different with Olivia. With her, he couldn't live without the emotional ties.

Nic was surprised at how much he'd changed, and it was she who had changed him.

Chapter 27

The following day Olivia went to a meeting of the Husband Hunters Club. Being in London, it was too good an opportunity for her to miss seeing her friends, and they gathered at Marissa's house. The last time they'd seen each other was at the wedding, and there had been little time to talk. Now there was so much to talk about that the time flew. Each of them had scandalous tales to tell, as they'd set about hunting down the husbands of their choice. There were some surprises, too. Not everyone was enamored with the same man that she'd carefully written down in the book the night of Miss Debenham's Finishing School ball, although some, like Olivia, had not swerved from their choice.

"Is it exciting to be married to Wicked Nic?" Tina asked her.

"I imagine there is rarely a dull moment," Marissa added dryly.

"Lady Lacey," sighed Eugenie. "How romantic."

"I hope you are going to use some of the Lacey wealth for the benefit of the poor," Averil added.

Olivia beamed at them all. "Yes, to all," she said.

When she arrived home her head was still in a whirl, and she felt far more like her old self, as if she'd wrested some of Nic's power over her back into her own hands.

Estelle was waiting.

"My lady," she said, her round face looking unusually disapproving. "There's a person to see you. A Madam Esmeralda. I told her you weren't interested in her wares any longer, but she's insisted on waiting and speaking to you for herself."

"Madam Esmeralda?"

Olivia's heart sank. She'd hoped that was over with. Nic had excused himself to her before the opera last night, saying he wasn't used to worrying about what other people thought of his actions. It was part of his Lacey arrogance, she thought, with an inner smile. He'd shown it again over the strawberries-and-cream supper.

Olivia had believed he was seeing her as no different from the other women he'd known over the years, when in fact he was simply used to doing exactly as he wished. He was a lord, an aristocrat born and bred; that was why he acted as he did. Nic didn't consider it necessary to consider other people's feelings, but once he understood why she was upset he'd been keen to make amends.

"Will I have her thrown out onto the street?" Estelle interrupted her thoughts, a glint in her eyes at the thought of such excitement.

"Goodness me, no," Olivia said. "I will see her, Estelle."

"But, my lady . . ."

"Thank you, Estelle."

Madam Esmeralda leaped to her feet at the sound of the door opening, and Olivia could see she was pale, the shadows under her eyes darker than ever. "Lady Lacey, how do you do?" she said, and curtsied.

"Madam Esmeralda." Olivia could see that she had brought several bolts of cloth with her, as well as something wrapped up in protective coverings and laid out on the sofa under the window.

"I have something to show you, my lady," she said quickly, before Olivia could draw breath. "If you will permit me." And she was already hurrying over to the sofa and reverently peeling back the outer coverings on the object.

Reluctantly, Olivia came to stand by her, wanting to stop her but at the same time not wanting to crush the woman's hopes. But, as the dress was revealed to her, she found herself watching, fascinated, until eventually she was held spellbound by its beauty.

Esmeralda said reverently, "The finest silk. And see the pearls sewn into the fabric? In the light of a ballroom you will truly shine, my lady."

Olivia had never seen any dress so beautiful. It was the softest, palest pink, and the glowing pearls made her think of a summer dawn. Nic had said that Madam Esmeralda was the best modiste in London, and he was right. Olivia knew she'd allowed her jealousy and her prejudices and the opinions of others sway her. She should be more like Nic—if she wanted something badly enough, she should go ahead and do it anyway.

"Thank you, Esmeralda," she whispered. "This is truly a masterpiece. I only hope I can do it justice."

Esmeralda bowed her head, accepting the compliment with a little smile.

Olivia took a breath, deciding to be honest. "I'm uncertain whether I should avail myself of your services. You know why, I think?"

"Yes, I know why," Esmeralda said with a touch of bitterness. "I am known as a modiste who only works with the demimonde. But I have been waiting for a chance like this, my lady. You will set my dresses off to perfection, and you have the confidence to shrug off any ill-natured remarks that may be made. Other women will see what I have done for you, and they will come to me. A trickle at first, but soon a flood."

"You are very certain they will overlook your past clientele, madam."

"I am." Esmeralda reached out to touch the dress lovingly with her fingertips. "No woman, no matter how grand she thinks she is, can resist looking better than her peers."

Olivia smiled. "Very true. You have more to show me? I believe that if I am to make a splash, I will need more than one dress to do so."

Esmeralda hesitated, one hand clenched at her waist, the other resting on the arm of a chair. "Do you mean you intend to employ me as your modiste, my lady?"

"I do indeed."

She toppled, only just catching herself from falling. Dismayed, Olivia hurried to support her, feeling the other woman's boniness beneath her plain gray dress.

"Madam, please sit down. I will ring for tea, or . . . or a restorative. Brandy?"

Esmeralda shook her head. "No, but thank you, Lady Lacey. I have been working day and night since you visited me, and I am tired. That is all, merely tired. So much depended upon this meeting."

Olivia frowned, reading the other woman's face. "Perhaps you are not so successful as you pretend, Madam Esmeralda."

Esmeralda gave a wry smile. "No, I am not. There have been problems with a certain lady— and I use the term loosely—with a vicious tongue. She claims I made her ridiculous and now she has set out to destroy me by driving away my customers. I have very few left, and if she has her way, soon I will have none."

Olivia pushed Esmeralda gently down into her chair, and then seated herself opposite, after ringing the bell for tea. "Who is this person?" And, when the modiste hesitated, plainly loath to make her situation worse by gossiping: "Never fear, I know very few people in London, and I would not repeat what you tell me anyway."

"It is the Earl of Marchmont's mistress, Mrs.

Cathcart. The earl dotes on her and she is very spoiled. If you go into London society you will see her, because although she may be a fallen woman, she is related to so many respectable families she receives most of their invitations."

"A dangerous enemy indeed," Olivia said thoughtfully. "I wonder if she will be at the ball tomorrow night."

"The Querrols' ball?" Esmeralda's eyes sparkled suddenly, and Olivia realized the modiste was not nearly as old as she had thought—it was her tired eyes and careworn face that made her seem so. "Yes, she will be there. I believe she is wearing yellow . . ."

"Then I will wear your masterpiece."

At once Esmeralda jumped up and hurried over to a bag beside the bolts of cloth. She produced a tape measure. "I don't think it will require a great deal of altering, but anything that does need doing can be done very quickly, I promise you."

"Of course."

The next few moments were taken up with measurements and then the dress was taken upstairs and Olivia tried it on. Estelle, when she arrived to help, seemed more breathless than usual, and her eyes widened at the sight of Olivia. "Lady Lacey, you look like a fairy princess," she gasped.

Olivia thought herself rather too tall for a fairy princess, but the dress certainly suited her and she did feel somewhat ethereal. Would Nic be impressed? She hoped so. This dress was perfect for romance, perfect for love.

And therein lay the problem, because Olivia was in love with her husband, and she had no idea whether he was in love with her.

"My lady?"

Estelle and Esmeralda were looking at her curiously, and Olivia shook herself out of endless musings over Nic.

"Madam Esmeralda wants to know whether you'd like her to complete any more dresses for your stay in London," Estelle explained.

Olivia turned again to her reflection in the mirror. "Yes, that is an excellent idea."

Esmeralda beamed.

"And I hope you will get some sleep in between stitches, madam. You will be no good to me, and all your new customers, if you faint."

"I have several good seamstresses I can call upon, my lady."

It would be nice to be admired, even envied, by the cream of London society, Olivia thought, when she was alone again. But that wasn't as important to her as the expression in Nic's eyes when he saw her.

"I love him," she whispered.

Speaking the words aloud released a storm of emotion inside her, and she trembled. She loved Wicked Nic Lacey. But how could she say those words to him, when she was so conscious of making him feel hemmed in and trapped by a marriage he had never wanted? Although he seemed happy enough now, well for most of the time, it was very early days. She must tread carefully.

But knowing that didn't stop Olivia from wishing that when she looked into his eyes tomorrow night, she'd see his love for her, and her world would be complete.

"I love you, Nic," she said again, enjoying hearing the words spoken aloud.

Because who knew when she would be brave enough to say them to his face?

Chapter 28

Nic couldn't keep his eyes off her. When she appeared at the head of the stairs, ready to leave for the ball, he had simply stood and watched her descend. She was beautiful, with her cool English looks—her golden hair and blue eyes and creamy complexion. And yet she was so much more than her appearance. Beneath her calm smile lay a warm and passionate woman who believed in living life her own way, who was honest and kind, and who refused to take second best.

As she reached the last few steps, she held out her gloved hands toward him, and he moved forward in his own elegant evening wear to grasp her fingers.

"Olivia, you look exquisite. You quite take my breath away."

Her smile made her eyes sparkle, and the pearls sewn into her dress and woven into her hair softly glowed.

"You were right," she said. "Esmeralda *is* the best modiste in London." She glanced away, in that manner she had when there was something bothering her. "I hope everyone else will think so, too, when they see this dress."

"It was thoughtless of me to take you to see her, Olivia. For an intelligent man I can be very dimwitted."

"You apologized to me," she reminded him quietly, squeezing his hands, "and there is nothing more to be said. I have decided to make Esmeralda my modiste after all. I like her."

Nic laughed. "You like her? So that is all that is required for Lady Lacey to employ someone?"

"Not just that, but it helps."

Bundled up in her fur cloak, Olivia climbed into the coach, and Nic settled opposite her.

"Do you know Mrs. Cathcart? Will she be there this evening," Olivia began, meaning to explain to Nic about Esmeralda's difficulties and Mrs. Cathcart's part in them, but when she looked up from fussing with the folds of her dress, she saw that something in his face had changed.

"Why do you want to know about Miriam Cathcart?" he asked evenly, his eyes watchful.

But the change in him had made her wary. "It is a simple enough question, Nic. Will she be there this evening?"

"I don't know Mrs. Cathcart's movements, but I would imagine so," he said with studied indifference. "She is asked everywhere despite her reputation."

"She is the Earl of Marchmont's mistress, is that so?"

"She has been mistress to so many men I've lost count."

The comment was malicious, and Nic was not a malicious man. And then it occurred to Olivia that he had been one of this woman's lovers. Of course, it made sense. Miriam Cathcart was someone who lived by her beauty and her wits, the sort of woman Nic would be drawn to. He had probably financed her, taken her to Esmeralda's to be fitted out in the latest fashions, kissed her, held her . . .

The image shouldn't have hurt—she'd told herself Nic's past was nothing to her—she'd come to terms with it. But it did hurt, it hurt a great deal.

Olivia wished she could shrug or laugh off this revelation. She wished she had more trust and confidence in their relationship, but she couldn't tell herself the past was gone and forgotten. Because if he'd been Miriam Cathcart's lover once, then why not again?

Olivia looked away, hoping he could not read her thoughts in her face. Where was her direct honesty? But her pride wouldn't allow him to see that she loved him and was terrified of losing him, so how could she ask him for the truth? How could she bear for him to feel sorry for her? What if he began making love to her because he was being kind to her, rather than because he wanted to?

She'd rather leave now and never see him again.

After a time she found the courage to glance back at him, but Nic was staring off into the distance, his face pensive. She didn't know what he was thinking about but she had a good idea. Olivia looked down at her beautiful dress and felt sad. This was meant to be a night of triumph for her and instead it was turning into a night of despair.

They reached the Querrols' house in Belgravia to find the square choked with vehicles and guests waiting to be admitted. It seemed that anybody who was anybody in London society was there and eager to be seen. There was no option but to join the throng and wait their turn.

Nic looked out over the richly jeweled and fashionably dressed members of the society from which he had considered him outcast. Not because of any decision by them—his birth would always give him an entrée—but because he himself had wished it so. He'd stood in the shadows for a long time, and now he could finally step out into the light and take his rightful place among the aristocracy of England. It was the role he'd been brought up to play.

Before the tragedy, his father had often spoken to him about what was expected of a man in his shoes, usually when he was scolding him for his wild ways. As a young man, Nic knew he'd pushed boundaries, seeking pleasure and adventure wherever he could find it. In the year before his father's death he had begun to turn his back on such youthful indiscretions, but with his father dead and the scandal turning his mother from him, he'd saturated himself in the role of Wicked Nic Lacey.

He remembered feeling betrayed and angry, and wanting to lose himself in every debauchery available to him. And soon it had become habit. Nic hadn't planned to lock his feelings off from the world, but now he could see that was what he'd done. It had taken Olivia to open that door and set him free.

He'd turned another page in the book of his life. He was married, and with Olivia by his side, he could begin to repair the damage of the last nine years. He could take his place among his peers and strive to be a good landlord and master, just as his father was, just as he hoped his own son would be.

The Laceys would go on, just as they'd always done.

Why did she ask me about Miriam Cathcart?

The question popped into his mind, tearing a hole in the hopes and dreams he'd begun to build. Miriam Cathcart was the sister of his school friend, and he'd believed himself in love with her, for a short while. But she had used him, just as she used everyone. She'd turned a callow youth into a cynical man, and he'd sworn never to allow himself to feel like that again.

Olivia was the first woman since Miriam who meant something to him. She'd slipped by the guard he'd placed around his heart, and despite his sworn declaration that he would never fall in love again, she'd won his heart before he'd even realized it.

I love her.

The acknowledgment didn't shock him. Perhaps he'd known it since the moment his mother insisted he marry Olivia and he'd been only too glad to submit. He'd sworn never to love again and never to marry. But here he was, married. Nic had spent years carefully avoiding being involved with anyone, protecting his heart, and now he'd fallen in love with his wife.

"Lord Lacey!" The interruption was welcome.

He bowed, greeting his acquaintance, and introduced Olivia. She was her usual calm and beautiful self, and Nic was amazed as always how chilly she seemed, how emotionless, when he knew only too well the burning passion inside her. He watched as his acquaintance's gaze lingered on her appreciatively.

He told himself he wasn't jealous. Olivia had never shown the slightest preference for anyone other than him, and he knew he satisfied her. It might be arrogance, but it wasn't jealousy that worried him. If anything were to drive her away, then it was more likely to be something he had done in the past.

He groaned softly.

"Nic?" Olivia was watching him worriedly, her fingers tightening on his arm. "Are you all right?"

Nic forced a smile. "Everything is perfect,

my dear. Did I tell you how beautiful you are tonight?"

She returned his smile, although her eyes remained anxious. "Several times, but you can tell me again. Your leg . . . ?"

"Yes, I have two of them. Your point is?"

His voice was curt and she took the hint, falling silent and looking away. He was sorry then, thinking himself a moody bastard, knowing he'd hurt her when she was only showing her concern for him. But he didn't want her pity. Bad enough that he was a cripple, without his beautiful wife drawing attention to it.

They moved forward again, climbing the final step, and this time they reached the front door and stepped inside the entrance hall. A great dome arched above them, colorfully painted with fat, cavorting cupids and smug-looking nymphs. The ballroom was at the far end of the hall, music and chatter growing louder the closer they came.

A servant was helping remove the guests' coats, cloaks, wraps, and other outer garments, while another was serving champagne from a tray as they waited. Finally they reached the ballroom, and a bewigged servant in knee breeches announced them to the crush below. It was a moment to savor. The rising murmur as everyone turned to look, a tribute to both his wife's beauty and the dress Esmeralda had made her, and to Nic's reputation. He'd heard they were calling them the rake and the angel. Well, let them.

"Lacey, a pleasure," drawled Querrol. "And

Lady Lacey?" He raised his monocle, ogling Olivia as she spoke to his wife. "My, you have fallen on your feet, haven't you, Lacey? I heard you'd married a country bumpkin."

"Olivia's family live in the village of Bassingthorpe, but they are not bumpkins, Querrol."

"Will we be seeing you at any more demimonde balls, Lacey? I can't believe you'll still be blinded by married bliss by the time the next one comes around. All mares ride the same on a dark night, as you've said yourself often enough."

Nic shrugged indifferently. "Sometimes it helps to change the saddle, but I expect you're right."

He was sorry for it as soon as he'd said it—it felt like a betrayal of his newfound happiness—but Querrol was such a rumormonger, it was better to play the familiar game. And then Olivia appeared at his side, as calm and serene as ever, accepting Querrol's compliments and saying all the right things.

Nic presumed she hadn't heard his less than flattering comment, but as they moved away she disillusioned him.

"Is that how you see me, Nic? A mare?" Her voice was quiet and low.

"You weren't meant to hear that," he replied, equally subdued. "I'm sorry that you did."

"Why are you sorry? Because it's true?"

"No, it isn't true!"

His raised tones caused a momentary ripple in the crowd around them, as though someone had dropped a stone into a pond.

"Should I believe you?" she said, her blue eyes clear and bright.

Now was the time to tell her he loved her. "Olivia—" But as Nic drew her closer, bending his head to do so, they were interrupted in the worst possible way.

"Nic, how delightful. It has been an absolute age."

He looked up, only just biting back a curse, as he met the calculating gaze of Miriam Cathcart. Her face was harder than he remembered, but she had the same big brown eyes and high cheekbones. She was wearing yellow, a sunbeam among the whites and pinks so prevalent this season, but neither she nor her dress was nearly as gorgeous as Olivia.

"Miriam. The pleasure is mine. May I introduce my wife, Olivia? Olivia, this is Mrs. Cathcart, an old friend of an old friend."

Olivia did not hesitate. She really was amazing at slipping on her polite mask; he'd never have known what she was feeling if he didn't know her so well, and understand her better than he understood any other human being. And what was she feeling? Nic knew that she was feeling hurt and betrayed and vulnerable, and it was all his fault.

"What a splendid dress, Lady Lacey," Miriam declared, her avaricious gaze lingering. "May I ask who made it for you? I thought I knew the names of all the best modistes in London . . ."

"Madam Esmeralda made it. I was so pleased that I have ordered several more."

Miriam stared at her a moment, and then gave a titter, lifting her fan to hide her mouth. "Oh, Lady Lacey," she said, full of malice, "I'm surprised your husband hasn't told you." And she gave Nic a sideways glance for good measure. "Madam Esmeralda is a dressmaker to the demimonde. No respectable woman will go to her. If I were you, I would cancel your order immediately."

Olivia's calm smile didn't even falter, as Nic couldn't help but wonder if she had been preparing for this moment. "Well, now I understand, Mrs. Cathcart," she said.

"Understand what?" Miriam asked.

"Why she knew you," Olivia said.

Nic gave a snort of laughter before he could stop himself, and received a glittering look from Miriam Cathcart and a bland one from Olivia. But Olivia hadn't finished with her yet.

"Besides, I'm not interested in Esmeralda's past. She is a marvelous dressmaker, and that is all I care about. I am fussy when it comes to my clothing, Mrs. Cathcart. It is most annoying to find you are wearing a poorly sewn garment at the very moment when you want to look your best." She smiled, but as she turned away, her gaze slid over Miriam's yellow dress in a meaningful way.

Miriam went an unpleasant shade of red. "Well!" she huffed. "You should explain to your wife who I am," she informed Nic angrily. "From what I've heard about the circumstances of your marriage, she has no right to set herself higher than me."

Nic's smile faded. "Why not, Miriam? My wife is worth a hundred of you."

"You didn't think that once," she pouted.

"I was a child then, Miriam," he said wearily. "Now I'm a man."

"Then perhaps we should have supper together." She let her gaze slide down over his tall, lean body, her brown eyes inviting. "You can show me how much of a man you are."

Nic smiled. "I don't think so, Miriam. Whatever we had is long past. Good-bye."

And he walked away, following Olivia.

Chapter 29

O livia was shaking inside. A storm of emotion she struggled to hide behind her serene exterior. The confrontation with Miriam Cathcart had been worse than she'd thought it would be, but then she hadn't bargained on Nic having been the woman's lover. On the other hand, it was pleasing when Lady Querrol asked for the name of her dressmaker, and had shown none of Mrs. Cathcart's bias when Olivia spoke Esmeralda's name. Several other women, hearing of Lady Querrol's interest, had followed her lead and also asked Olivia. For Esmeralda's sake, Olivia hoped she had found her some new clients among the cream of London society.

Meanwhile, her inner storm raged on.

How could Nic spend his time and his kisses on a woman like Miriam Cathcart? She was truly awful. Attractive, yes, but with a sly, destructive manner that spoke of many hearts broken and many lives ruined.

"Olivia . . ."

Nic stopped her progress effectively by slipping

his arm about her waist and turning her about. Breathless, she pressed her palms to his chest, to keep some space between them as they stood surrounded by the moving river of guests.

"Will you dance with me?"

Surprised, she looked up into his face. He was smiling his self-mocking smile, as though preparing himself for rejection. Surely no one ever rejected Nic? Olivia's fingers crept to his cheek, stroking his skin. He turned his face and kissed the hollow of her palm, before folding her fingers over and holding them in his.

"Will you? Dance with me, Olivia? It would make the night complete."

She nodded, a lump in her throat. "Yes. I will dance with you, Nic."

For a time, she simply enjoyed the feel of him moving with her, his strong arms about her, the touch of his hands, the dark gleam of his eyes, his masculine scent and charismatic presence. He seemed to draw every other woman's gaze toward him without even trying or being aware of it, and there was something very attractive about being with a man like that.

"I thought you'd be angry with me," she said, meeting his eyes and holding them.

"Why would I be angry with you? Because you said what you thought? Olivia, I enjoyed every moment of it."

"But she was your lover once, wasn't she?" After the words left her mouth, Olivia wondered whether she'd gone too far, especially when Nic allowed some time to elapse before answering her.

"Yes, she was," he said, his voice dropping, this conversation for her alone. "You could call her my first love. I thought my heart was broken, but now I know it was my pride."

"She left you?" Olivia asked curiously.

Nic's gaze lowered to her décolletage, warming her skin as he took in the curves of her breasts and the dark shadow of her cleavage. But Olivia wasn't about to be distracted, and she pinched his hand, where he held hers.

He sighed with mock despair. "She left me for another man. I considered it the worst insult. I was a lord and a Lacey, and he wasn't anything very much at all. It was a terrible blow to my self-worth."

Olivia laughed softly. "I can see you've suffered, Nic. Is that the only time you had your heart broken?"

"Yes. I made sure that the next woman knew our relationship was nothing more than a business contract. No promises, no vows, no ever-afters, just money for services provided."

Olivia already knew that Nic was a good man, and now she understood that his seeming coldness where his mistresses were concerned came not from a lack of heart, but from too much heart. He was protecting himself. It made sense. Such a sensual man would be prone to feeling everything more keenly.

When the dance ended, he didn't let her go,

giving a young fellow in a green jacket a baleful glare as he tried to cut in. The next dance was a waltz—until recently considered shocking because it allowed dance partners to actually clasp each other in their arms. Olivia nestled into Nic's embrace, enjoying every moment, as they did their best to twirl around the cramped ballroom without cannoning into any of the other couples.

He spun her around and Olivia gasped, allowing her head to fall back, while the ceiling with its painted panels spun above her. Nic tightened his grip, and she felt his muscular thighs pressing to hers through the layers of her skirt and petticoats.

"I'm sorry about Miriam Cathcart," he murmured, slowing to let her catch her breath. Olivia rested her head against his shoulder and he nuzzled her hair, his warm breath tickling her ear. "She is nothing to me. And I'm sorry about what I said to Querrol. He was ogling you with his blasted monocle and what I really wanted to do was shove it down his throat."

Olivia glanced up at him from the corners of her eyes, before dropping her lashes to hide her thoughts. "I'll forgive you as long as you don't do it again," she said, a smile in her voice.

"I promise not to do it again," he recited like a schoolboy.

She giggled and lifted her head. She was well aware that he would see in her eyes that she desired him, even here, in the middle of the ballroom.

He did see. His dark eyes flared, his face grew taut, his fingers tightened on hers. "We should leave," he said huskily.

"We've only just arrived."

But she was teasing him. She wanted to leave, too. Her skin was tingling, sensitive to his touch, and she felt flushed and languid. His mouth was close, and she knew she'd like nothing better than to taste him . . .

"Stop it," he groaned softly.

Her lips smiled and she darted the tip of her tongue over them, aware she was increasing the tension, building the passion. "Stop what?" she said innocently.

His hand splayed over her waist, holding her firmly against him, so that they were molded together at the hips and thighs. She felt him growing hard against her, and knew from his wicked smile that he was quite prepared to play her at her own game.

She went deeper into his arms, brushing her breasts against his waistcoat, knowing they couldn't be seen in the crush of couples around them. He dipped his head and nipped her fingers, then sucked them. She felt the warmth between her legs, the trembling in her thighs, and the ache in her breasts. Her hand slid down, delving through the folds of her skirt, and brushed the jut of his shaft.

Olivia wondered at her own daring. She was behaving in a manner she could never have imagined before she met Nic—although perhaps she could have imagined it, and that was why they were so ideally suited.

But she had pushed their game too far, and as soon as the music stopped again, he was hurrying her off the dance floor, zigzagging through the other guests with ease.

"Nic . . . ?" she began, breathless.

The coach was waiting, and he could barely wait to collect their outdoor garments, before he was urging her inside the vehicle and closing the door.

"The long way home!" he ordered the coach-man.

They moved off, heading into the London night.

Nic leaned into her as they rounded a corner, pressing her into the soft leather seats, his mouth almost but not quite touching hers.

"I've been wanting to do this since the moment I saw you at the top of the stairs," he said, his voice low and soft, making her skin tingle. "I want to make love to you at least ten times a day, do you know that? If I had my way you'd never leave the bedchamber."

She looked up at him through her lashes, aware of heavy tension between them, making it diffi-cult to breathe evenly.

He stroked one finger down the side of her face, moving to her mouth and tracing its shape, slowly, intently. And then he began to kiss her.

Olivia felt herself melting. Her arms went around his neck and clung, their lips meeting and melding, her tongue sliding against his. He reached down, brushing aside her skirts and her petticoats. She felt his hand seeking and then he stopped, lifting his head to stare down at her.

"You're naked," he said, with a startled grin.

"I thought it would save time," she replied innocently, knowing she looked anything but innocent.

He bent to press openmouthed kisses across her bosom, edging down her dress so that he could suck at her nipples. Olivia groaned and let her head fall back. A moment later Nic was pushing into her, his shaft filling her, stretching her. They paused, panting, and then he began to move, while Olivia met him with urgent jerks of her hips. When she reached her peak she muffled her cries against his shoulder, while Nic groaned deeply against her throat, resting his chin against her as he sought to catch his breath.

It felt wonderful. It always did.

Olivia reached up to brush the rogue swath of dark hair from his eyes, feeling a wave of love so powerful it made her ache all over again. The words trembled on her lips, but for a moment she held them back, uncertain whether saying them would change things between her and Nic. There was a great deal of vulnerability in not only giving your heart to someone, but in saying it aloud.

"I love you," she whispered.

Nic's dark eyes were hooded as he returned her gaze. "Do you realize what you've done by saying that to me?" he said.

"What have I done?"

"You've made yourself my prisoner for life."

Olivia kissed his mouth, tenderly. "A willing prisoner, Nic."

He rested his brow against hers and sighed. "I love you, too, Olivia. I believed my heart was locked up safe and tight, but you snuck in and stole it before I was even aware of you being there."

She caught his face in her hands, lifting it for more kisses.

"How can I maintain my reputation as Wicked Nic if I'm in love my wife?" he protested half seriously, eagerly returning the kisses. "As a rake I'm a ruined man."

"You'll always be Wicked Nic to me," she teased.

Outside the traffic rumbled and jostled around them, and Nic cursed as he saw they were nearly home. He smoothed her skirts and tucked her breasts out of sight. Sitting back, he cast a narrowed look over her, brushing back a curl here and smoothing a wrinkle there, until he seemed satisfied with her appearance. As for himself, he looked immaculate, and Olivia wondered darkly if that was part of being a rake, the ability to never appear rumpled, as if one has just been making violent love, even if one has.

The coach turned into their square, and he smiled at her. Olivia knew then that her happiness was complete. She was aware that she had the Husband Hunters Club to thank for much of her success—if they hadn't given her the confidence to pursue the man she wanted, she'd probably have ended up married to Theodore Garsed, gazing at Nic from afar, and wishing "if only." Instead she'd gone after what she wanted, and she'd won.

Not that there weren't possible problems and differences looming on the horizon, but right now Olivia was certain in her heart that they could work anything out. They loved each other, and surely that was all that really mattered?

Chapter 30

Abbot had been waiting and delayed Nic in the hall, just inside the front door.

Olivia, halfway up the stairs, and still floating on a cloud, at first didn't realize there was anything wrong. She looked back over her shoulder, where Abbot and Nic stood together, deep in conversation. There was something about the way Nic held his body, still and rigid, as if he had turned to ice, and Abbot's furtive glances in Olivia's direction . . .

Slowly Olivia began to descend the stairs again, intent on discovering exactly what was wrong. Because something was definitely wrong—it was as if she could taste it in the air.

"Nic?" she said, as she reached them. "What is it?"

Abbot bowed to her, his expression tense. "Lady Lacey, I apologize for interrupting your evening. I—"

Nic spoke roughly, cutting him short "No, Abbot."

"Nic, whatever is the matter . . . ?" Olivia

cried, deeply worried now and not troubling to hide it.

He wouldn't look at her. Instead he looked at Abbot, a frowning glance. "Abbot, not a word, do you understand?"

The manservant didn't look happy but he nodded. "Very well, my lord." Abbot turned to her then, and his gaze was sympathetic—as if she had suffered a loss.

"Olivia, I have to go out."

"Nic!"

He did look at her then, and his dark eyes were full of pain. Olivia's panic increased, but he stopped her before she could ask him again what was wrong. Holding her hands tightly in his, he said, "Please, my love, no questions. I will explain everything to you when I get back." He didn't wait for her answer, he just turned and walked away.

Olivia was very afraid now. She stared after Nic, watching him hurry out of the door and down the front steps, back to the coach and horses. A moment later, the vehicle had rumbled away again.

"My lady." Abbot was waiting anxiously by her side.

"What is happening, Abbot?"

He did everything but wring his hands. "My lady, I cannot tell you, you heard Lord Lacey say . . ."

"Oh, very well," she said impatiently. She turned to the stairs but stopped again and looked back at him. "Can't you at least tell me where he has gone, Abbot? Is that betraying your master's orders?"

Abbot hesitated, and then said firmly, "Lord Lacey will explain when he returns."

"I want you to explain to me now. Abbot?" Olivia tapped her shoe, glaring at his profile.

Abbot crumbled, but not the way she'd hoped he would. "My lady, forgive me, but I am only a servant. I do as I am told. How can I do as you wish when Lord Lacey has expressly told me not to?"

Olivia knew she was being unfair, but this was Nic, her husband, and she wanted to know. "Tell me what is happening, Abbot. I will explain to Lord Lacey."

His face was creased as if he was in pain. "I would love to, my lady, believe me, but I have promised to be silent on this matter. Forgive me, please."

It was unfair of her to press him, Olivia knew that. Abbot had his loyalties, too, and his position was dependent on his holding firm to them. She would have to wait for Nic to return and then ask him what on earth could have made him leave her without a word, with a single glance at the wife he had just told he loved with all his heart.

A moment ago Olivia had been so very happy, and now she felt as if there was a stone lodged in her heart.

The coach came to a stop outside the narrow house and Nic climbed out, ordering his driver to return home, and saying that he had no idea how long he would be. As the coach moved away, Nic stood alone in the cobbled street and watched it go. Across the river the fog obscured his view of the city, although he could pick out the occasional church spire. As if to increase his feeling of isolation, bells rang, sounding hollow and forlorn.

Why now? Why did she have to send for him *now*? Just when everything was perfect with Olivia.

He felt suddenly resentful, and remembering the way he'd left Olivia, and the expression on her face, only made him feel worse. But he couldn't explain to her—there was no time. She would have been upset, and rightly so, and he didn't want to face that, not until he was able to tell her the full story, in his own way. Make her understand.

Nic sighed and shifted his weight from his lame leg. Who was he fooling? How the devil was he going to be able to make her understand? She was more likely to walk out and never return, and he wouldn't be the least surprised if she did. He wouldn't blame her if she felt her love for him was a betrayal and a sham, but still he'd have to try. Because Nic knew now that if he lost her he himself would be lost.

He turned toward the narrow house. Better get it over with, he thought wearily. If it was anything like the last time, it would probably take him hours to smooth over the crisis, and the sooner he started, the sooner he could go home to his wife. And he walked up to the front door and rattled the knocker.

A moment later Mildred, the housekeeper, opened the door, her unsmiling face as un-friendly-looking as ever. Appearances could be deceptive—Mildred was a kind and generous woman, and, importantly, Nic trusted her.

"Lord Lacey," she said with obvious relief. "Thank you for coming, sir. I'm so sorry to bother you on such a night. You know I wouldn't have asked if—if—"

"I know, Mildred," he reassured her. "Where is she?"

"She's locked herself in the pantry," she said, showing him inside the house. "There's a key. I keep it myself to stop the kitchen maid from filching. The mistress must have found it, and now she's locked the pantry door from the inside. I've tried talking to her, but she won't listen. She keeps asking for you."

"Of course."

He followed Mildred down the corridor that led past the stairs and into the back part of the house, where the small kitchen, scullery, and laundry were situated. A fire was burning merrily in the hearth, and the table and other surfaces shone, while the floor was spotless. A tray of small cakes was sitting by a tin, ready to be put away when they were cool enough.

Mildred saw him glance at them. Her mouth curled up in a surprisingly sweet smile for such a

dour face. "There're for Master Jonah, sir. His favorite. When he's home I always like to bake him
a treat or two."

Nic smiled back, thinking Jonah was a lucky
boy to have Mildred. "Is he well?"

"Oh yes, bright as a button. And he'd doing very
well at his lessons, sir. Even when he's on holidays
he has his head in a book."

"Ah, an intellectual. My father was the same.
One day I will have to show Jonah the library at
Castle Lacey and—"

Just then there was a loud thumping coming
from behind the pantry door.

"Nic, Nic!" screeched a high-pitched voice. "Is
that you, Nic?"

He and Mildred exchanged a glance. "Lord
Lacey is here now," Mildred called. "Please, do
come out, mistress."

Nic walked over to the pantry. The door was
old and heavy, and looked as if it might once have
belonged to a cellar. He didn't relish the thought
of breaking it down, and hoped it wouldn't come
to that.

"I'm here," he said in a gentle tone, leaning
against the door. "I've had to leave in the middle
of the Querrols' ball, just to come and see you."
The lie was a small one, but he knew she preferred
the dramatic.

"In the middle of a dance?"

"A waltz, yes. I left the lady in the middle of
a spin, and I don't know what happened to her
afterward."

She giggled. Always a good sign if he could make her laugh.

"You're a wicked man, Nic," she said.

"That's my name."

A heartbeat later they heard the key turning in the lock and the click of the latch. Slowly, cautiously, the door opened a crack, and a woman's piqued face loomed out of the shadows.

"Nic," she sighed.

Nic smiled, held out his hand for her to grasp, and prepared to have his patience stretched to its limits.

Olivia had undressed and washed, and now Estelle finished helping her into her nightgown. Nic still hadn't returned.

"I don't want to go to sleep. I want to wait up for Lord Lacey," she said, as Estelle slipped the warming pan beneath the covers of her bed.

Estelle said nothing.

"He promised me that when he came home he'd explain why he rushed off like that."

Estelle said nothing.

Olivia sat upon the stool at her dressing table and watched as her maid moved the warming pan on its long handle back and forth inside the bedding, taking the chill off the sheets. And all the while Estelle was carefully avoiding her eyes.

"Estelle?"

"My lady?"

Olivia decided that Estelle looked plumper than she used to, and there was a dark, unfaded strip of cloth on the side of her uniform, suggesting she'd recently taken the seam out to give herself more room. Both clues meant something, but just now Olivia was more interested in what she saw in Estelle's face.

"You know something, don't you?" Olivia folded her arms and fixed her bright eyes on her maid. "Estelle, I want to know."

"I don't know anything, miss . . . I mean, my lady."

"Estelle."

Estelle sighed and finally turned to face her mistress, her expression a mixture of doubt and concern, with a touch of excitement. "Abbot told me not to tell you, my lady," she protested.

"But you *will* tell me, won't you, Estelle?"

For a moment Olivia thought her maid was going to refuse her, as Abbot had, but then Estelle came and stood beside her at her dressing table, fiddling nervously with her frilly white apron. The swell of her stomach was quite prominent, even with the bulk of her skirt and petticoats, and Olivia knew then that Estelle was with child. There would be time later to discuss that, she told herself.

"Please, Estelle, I need to know. I thought you were my friend. You've helped me before. If it wasn't for you I'd never have become Lady Lacey, and I wouldn't be so happy . . ."

Estelle rushed into speech, almost as if she wanted Olivia to stop. "He's gone to see *her* and the boy, Jonah."

"What do you mean?" It made no sense, and yet in a terrible way—if she was to think the very worst—it did.

"My lady," Estelle murmured, tears in her eyes, "I am so sorry. I didn't know until the night you came home from the ball . . . from Castle Lacey, and then there was the scandal . . . I didn't say anything because I hoped it wouldn't matter. There're many gentlemen with children born on the wrong side of the blanket."

Olivia stood up, trembling as if she were cold. "You're talking in riddles, Estelle. Explain to me what you mean or—or I think I will scream."

"Lady Lacey, do you really want to know?" Estelle said, and it sounded like a warning.

"Yes!" Olivia cried. "Of course I want to know. I need to know." She took a breath, lowering her voice, calming herself. "Tell me, Estelle. You must tell me."

Estelle chewed on her lip. "Abbot will be very cross with me. He swore me to secrecy."

"It is not Abbot's secret to keep," Olivia replied coldly.

Estelle nodded her head. "Lord Lacey has a child, miss, a son. His name is Jonah Lacey."

Nic was a father? Olivia opened her mouth, then closed it again. She didn't know what to say. The first tingling of shock was followed by a wave of confusion, and then a sense of betrayal. She felt as though he'd been unfaithful to her, which she knew was ridiculous in the circumstances. Whatever this woman had meant to Nic, it was in the past, and the child was simply the result of their liaison.

"I have never heard mention of a child at the castle," she said, finding her voice at last.

"Jonah lives here in London, with his mother. Lord Lacey visits them whenever he's here."

"Visits them" had so many connotations. Did it mean Nic was somehow involved with the woman? Was she his mistress? An image of a cozy family entered her mind and refused to go away. She pictured them in a parlor with a crackling fire, laughing, happy. But even as the picture sharpened in detail, tormenting her, there was something unreal about it.

Nic was not that kind of man.

"This woman was a respectable lady," Estelle went on, her voice dropping confidentially. "He ruined her. Then one morning she arrived at Castle Lacey with a babe in her arms, begging for his help. There was an awful to-do when Lord Lacey's parents found out about her and what he'd done."

"I imagine they would be disappointed."

"There's worse to come, miss. Are you sure you want to hear it?"

Olivia had a cowardly urge to stick her fingers in her ears, but it was too late now. She must know the whole truth, no matter how painful. "Yes, Estelle. Go on."

"His father was so angry he dropped down dead. His mother blamed him for his father's death, and I suppose it was his fault, in a way. She never spoke to him again."

It explained a great deal. The scandal her parents knew of but wouldn't share with her, their uncertainty and disappointment when it was clear she'd chosen Nic over Theodore, and Nic's own warnings to her that he was no good. Yes, it was all far clearer now. But there was still one question that demanded an answer.

"Why didn't he marry the woman? Surely that should have been the solution to the scandal? And then none of those dreadful things would have happened."

Estelle shrugged. "I don't know, my lady. Abbot didn't say. Perhaps she wouldn't have him after what he'd done to her, and who could blame her?"

Olivia shook her head resolutely. "No, that doesn't make sense."

Estelle's face grew worried. "You really do love him, don't you, my lady? I'm sorry that I've upset you."

"I'm not upset," she insisted. "At least, I'm trying to think rationally. There are many gentlemen who have children born out of wedlock, and I am not so innocent I don't know that. Why, there was even a girl at Miss Debenham's Finishing School who boasted about being the love child of an Irish duke."

Estelle brightened. "Well then, it isn't so bad after all, miss."

For all her calm acceptance, Olivia found Estelle's story difficult to digest. In fact it was making her feel a little sick. But was it so very bad? Nic had been involved with a woman to the extent that they had a child, and he was still caring for the two of them.

It didn't change what she thought of him. He was at heart a good man. Of course he would care for the woman and child, she wouldn't expect any less of him. And the tragedy of his father's death and his mother's lack of understanding would hurt him terribly. No wonder he spent so little time at Castle Lacey and the rest of his life traveling, with a different companion every year. Once he'd been burned he wouldn't want to risk his heart again.

Olivia was so deep in thought she hardly heard Estelle speaking.

"When the message came tonight, and Abbot told me, I knew I should have warned you before, when I first found out. I blame myself."

Olivia tried to focus, to understand. "The message? I presume it came from this woman who is . . . was Nic's mistress? Is something wrong, is that why he had to go so abruptly, without time for explanations?"

Estelle clasped her hands together and stared at them, as if working up her courage. "Abbot told me that this woman calls herself Mrs. Lacey."

Suddenly Olivia felt cold. "Mrs. Lacey?" she gasped.

"*Mrs.* Lacey. She sent for Lord Lacey tonight and he went to her. You know he did. I don't understand the hold she has over him, unless it's the boy, but there's something odd and I can't help but think it isn't going to make you very happy. My lady, I am so sorry I—"

Olivia had stopped listening. Was it possible that Nic was already married? Estelle had wondered why, if this woman was respectable, Nic hadn't simply married her, and now Olivia found herself wondering, too. Perhaps he had married, then kept it secret. But was it really possible he would do such a dreadful thing, and then marry Olivia and lie to her? No! She didn't believe it. The "Mrs. Lacey" might well be a courtesy title, in which case this woman and Nic must be close— close enough to be assumed to be married.

Tonight she had told Nic she loved him, and he said he loved her. She had believed him, utterly and completely. What had happened since then that she was here alone, doubting him, and he was with another woman? She didn't know. She didn't know anything anymore.

"I think I will go to bed now," she said at last, in a small voice that didn't sound at all like her own.

Estelle seemed relieved. "I think you should sleep, my lady. When Lord Lacey returns he'll explain everything, and . . . and . . ." But her voice trailed off for lack of anything more positive to say, and she hurried back to the bed, fussing about, turning down the covers.

Olivia slid off her wrap and climbed into the bed. She lay back and closed her eyes, and Estelle turned out the lamp and gently closed the door, leaving her alone.

Olivia opened her eyes, staring at the ceiling.

She felt empty, as if her heart had been removed from her chest and her body was just a shell. Nic had betrayed her, he'd lied to her. Olivia had believed in him, trusted him. She'd believed she knew him as well as she knew herself. How could she have been so completely wrong?

The question was: What should she do now?

Outside a vehicle clattered by, hurrying on to its destination. Was Nic already tucked up in bed with his lover, this Mrs. Lacey? Had he completely forgotten the promises he'd made to Olivia? Well, she needed to know, and if Nic wasn't here to tell her, then she'd find out the truth for herself.

Tomorrow she would go and visit this woman who called herself Mrs. Lacey, and see her for herself. She'd call upon her and ask her exactly what was going on, and then she'd make whatever decision she could about the future.

Whether she would stay or whether she would go.

Nic closed the door to Olivia's bedchamber, causing the candle in his hand to flicker wildly. He paused while it steadied. He was tired, beyond tired. Unfortunately, as he'd feared, once she got him to the house, he had the devil of a job getting away again. He'd been bearing this burden alone for far too long, and now he wanted nothing more than to share it with Olivia.

The bedchamber was quiet apart from the crackling of the fire in the hearth. Nic made his way toward the bed. The flaring light of his candle showed him his wife's shape beneath the covers and her fair hair like spun gold upon the pillow.

She was asleep.

He stood, looking down at her calm and beautiful face for a very long time. The sight of her, the memory of her love for him, seeped in and eased his troubled soul. He was tempted to climb into bed beside her and hold her in his arms, but she was sleeping so peacefully.

Tomorrow, Nic told himself, he would tell her the truth. From start to finish. He could only hope she would understand and forgive him, and then they could begin to make their lives together. His decision made, Nic turned and made his way back across the room to the door. Tonight he'd sleep in his own bed and leave Olivia to her own sweet dreams, free of his dark shadows.

Chapter 31

The narrow house was neat and respectable, and it stood on a quiet street in the direction of Hampstead. When Olivia finally worked up the courage to use the knocker, the door opened on a soberly dressed maid with a flat, unsmiling face and unfriendly eyes.

"Can I help you, ma'am?"

"I've come to visit the lady of the house," Olivia said, stepping over the threshold. "Can you fetch her for me, please?"

The maid backed away, allowing Olivia in, but she wasn't happy. "My mistress doesn't see visitors, ma'am."

"She will see me. I am Lady Lacey."

The name acted as a key. The maid's eyes widened, and reluctantly she nodded her head, unwillingly agreeing.

Olivia removed her gloves, curiously looking about her. The entrance to the house was spotlessly clean, and the banisters on the steep staircase shone with polishing. The housekeeper—as she now said she was—showed Olivia into a sitting room and left her there. The furniture was old and well kept but rather too large for such a small room. An Oriental rug added color, as did the flowers in a large Chinese vase. Outside the window was a view of a handkerchief-sized garden, and when Olivia went to the window, she saw a child there, reading. He was perhaps nine or ten, with dark hair, and he kept glancing up at his companion, a young maid, who was evidently there to keep watch on him.

Olivia scrutinized the boy. Dark hair, dark eyes, and a thin, narrow face. He reminded her painfully of Nic, and there was only one person it could be—Nic's son, Jonah.

She hadn't expected to feel such a pain in her heart. Nic's past was nothing to do with here and now, and she wasn't foolish enough to believe he was squeaky clean—normally it would not matter to her. Her heart was warm enough to allow her to forgive him, and even to embrace this boy who was part of him and love him as her own.

Except she was certain now there was more to this than a long-ago affair.

The way Nic had rushed off last night, refusing to explain . . . Whatever was in this house was important to him, and his emotions were as engaged now as they'd been ten years ago.

Olivia had to know, even if it meant the end of her brief happiness.

"Lady Lacey?"

She hadn't heard the door open behind her. The voice was soft and breathy, as if its owner had hurried down the stairs, and as Olivia turned she didn't know what to expect.

A petite woman stood in the doorway, neatly dressed in a blue wool skirt with a waisted jacket of the same color. Her hair was so fair it looked white against the shadows behind her. She was ethereal, ghostlike, her eyes the only things that were really alive. They were bright blue and burning with emotion.

Exactly like Olivia's own eyes, and those of her mother.

Olivia felt the floor beneath her feet begin to rock, and reached out to grasp the windowsill for support. The woman came toward her, but cautiously, as if she wasn't quite sure if Olivia was real. She reached out her hand, her fingers stretched wide, but didn't touch her, allowing them to drop to her side. "Is it Olivia?" she whispered. "My own sweet Olivia?"

"Sarah." There were tears on Olivia's cheeks, but she didn't remember crying them. Her elder sister Sarah was dead. That was what she'd always been told, what she had accepted without question. But here she was, living in London, and very much alive.

"I don't understand." She forced the words through the lump in her throat. "Why did I think you were dead? Why do Mama and Father think you are dead?"

Sarah's mouth twisted into a parody of a smile. "The scandal," she said. "You *know* it is better to be dead than ruined, Olivia."

"What scandal?" Olivia cried, but inside her head an inkling of the truth was beginning to reveal itself, and she didn't like what she was thinking.

Sarah gestured for her to sit down, and arranged herself neatly on the chair opposite. There were dark shadows under her eyes, Olivia noticed. Ten years was a long time, but Sarah still looked a great deal older than she should have. Olivia sat, as the shock receded, thinking it strange that she hadn't hugged her sister and her sister hadn't held her.

"You call yourself Mrs. Lacey," she said. "Why do you do that, Sarah?"

Sarah stared at her a moment, and then gave a delicate shrug. "I feel like Mrs. Lacey."

"I don't—"

"Let me explain, Olivia." The name seemed to please her, and she smiled. "I did not think I would ever see you again. Do you remember when—" But she stopped herself, shaking her head. "No, first I will explain, then we can talk of the past."

"I would like that."

Sarah gathered her thoughts. "I fell in love. I suppose that is the beginning of my story. I fell in love and agreed to allow my lover to keep me."

"But didn't Mama—"

"Mama didn't know until I told her. By then the situation was beyond our parents' control. I left Bassingthorpe. My lover kept me here, in London, and I was happy. By the time I realized he'd tired of me, or had begun to listen to the persuasions of his family and friends, I was with child. He didn't answer my letters, and I was desperate, so I wrote to Mama and she and Father arranged for me to go to Cornwall, to a distant relative, to have the child there."

"Why was I never told this?" Olivia said, torn between anger and sorrow. "I should have known."

"You were a child," Sarah replied matter-of-factly. "You wouldn't have understood. As far as you were concerned I was away at school."

"You wrote to me, I remember," Olivia said, the memories coming back to her. "You told me all about your lessons."

"Yes." Sarah smiled sadly. "I enjoyed making up those stories. I thought of your face when you read them, and I wanted you to smile and believe I was happy."

"But you weren't happy."

"No. I missed my lover."

"Sarah . . ."

"You can't tell your heart who to love, Olivia. I'm sure you know that by now. I decided to come back to Bassingthorpe and throw myself upon his mercy."

"You were the woman with the babe in her arms," Olivia said as the pieces fell in place. "The woman who turned up at Castle Lacey."

"Yes. But he abandoned me. Again."

Responding to the pain in her voice, Olivia reached forward and grasped her sister's hand.

Her skin was cool and dry, and her fingers lay limp in Olivia's. "Oh Sarah."

"My parents abandoned me, too. They decided to say I had died while I was away, to save themselves the embarrassment of a scandal and explanations. Tidy me away, you see. Father couldn't bear to be looked down on by his colleagues, and Mama was embarrassed."

Remembering her mother's woebegone face and her father's reticence, Olivia didn't think it had been quite that easy, but now was not the time to come to their defense.

"Nic bought me this house and I live here. I see him when he comes to London, and he pays my bills and sees that Jonah is cared for as befits a Lacey." She smiled, gazing toward the window, where her son sat in the garden.

"So you're not abandoned after all. Nic *hasn't* abandoned you."

Sarah turned to stare at her, her expression confused. "Dominic. Is he here?"

"No, Sarah. I've come alone."

"My husband will be here soon," Sarah said, her fingers closing tightly on Olivia's, painfully so. "He comes to see me when he can. But it's a secret, so don't tell anyone." She lifted a finger to her lips and gave an exaggerated shhh. "No one must know."

It occurred to Olivia then that her sister wasn't altogether well. She was staring at the window again, humming softly, as if she'd forgotten who Olivia was and what they'd been saying. Olivia wanted to ask more questions, she wanted answers, but it was clear she wasn't going to get any.

"The mistress is tired."

The voice startled her. The sober housekeeper was back, and Olivia wondered if she'd been there all along, outside the door, listening to their conversation.

"You should go now," the woman added, with a meaningful look. "Mrs. Lacey needs to rest."

Olivia stood up, hesitated, and leaned forward to clasp her sister firmly in her arms. Sarah felt small and vulnerable and not at all the big sister Olivia had remembered with love all these years. Sarah hugged her back, smiling, but she appeared puzzled, as if she wondered why this stranger was being so affectionate.

"Good-bye, Sarah," Olivia murmured. "I will come again, and soon."

"Good-bye," Sarah echoed vaguely.

The housekeeper led the way to the front door. "Mrs. Lacey has lucid moments, but they are short. You were lucky."

"What is the matter with her?" Olivia asked, pulling on her gloves.

"The doctors don't know. A disease of the brain, a nervous disorder." She raised her eyebrows as if to say she didn't hold much with the opinions of the medical profession. "She has suffered and now it is telling on her. We keep her as quiet as we can and she wants for nothing."

"And her son, Jonah?"

The housekeeper smiled, and the change to her dour face was quite remarkable. "He goes to school, a good school, but he only boards during the week. He doesn't understand why his mother is sometimes so odd, but he loves her anyway. Lord Lacey takes a great interest in him, and one day he will live at Castle Lacey where he belongs."

Olivia tried not to look surprised. "I'm sure everything will work out as it should," she said neutrally. "Good-bye."

"Good-bye, Lady Lacey."

The door closed behind her, and Olivia was alone on the doorstep.

She'd been lied to. For half of her life she'd believed her sister was dead and it wasn't true. Her parents, Nic, everyone, they had all lied. Anger gripped her, and as she turned through the gate and began to walk away, it began to build. Her cheeks were wet with more tears, and she dashed them away with her gloved fingers.

Nic had seduced her sister and then abandoned her. No wonder her mother had been so distrustful of him. She'd lost one daughter to the Laceys and she didn't want to lose another. Her father, more pragmatic, had accepted the situation and Nic's generous settlement, but her mother . . . Olivia took a shaken breath. They should have told her. If she'd known the truth she'd never have hunted Nic. She'd have despised him for his selfish and callous actions.

But isn't he looking after her now? a voice in her

head reminded her. *She is being cared for, and her son—his son—has everything he might need. If he was such a monster, wouldn't he have refused to do anything to help?*

Olivia accepted the truth of that, but the fact he'd treated Sarah so ill in the beginning—and no, she wouldn't accept his youth as an excuse—told against him. She didn't know if she would be able to forgive him for that. Certainly she could never forgive him for lying to her. He was arrogant, she knew that, but there were numerous times when he could have told her, explained, apologized, but he hadn't. All this time he'd kept his guilty secret.

Nic Lacey had seduced her sister, abandoned her and her child, and now he'd married Olivia, while continuing to keep Sarah hidden away. Olivia wondered how long he'd planned to keep the truth from her. Forever? Or until he had his legal heir and would no longer be bothered if she stayed with him or not?

There was a hackney stand in front of her, with a queue of vehicles waiting for fares. She gave her destination to the driver, climbing aboard like an automaton, and sat back to stare blankly at the passing scenery, going over and over in her head the truth as she now knew it.

And yet, how did she reconcile Sarah's experience of Nic with the man she loved? She had always found Nic to be a basically decent human being, a man to be trusted and relied upon. She had held firmly to that image despite her parents' rejection and Nic's own opposition to her wish to marry him. Why, now, was she discarding it?

Olivia put her head in her hands. She felt betrayed; she felt like a fool. What she needed was to get away from here, go back to Bassingthorpe and try and decide what to do. Not to the Monteith house, she couldn't go there, but Castle Lacey would be empty. She didn't imagine Nic would follow her when he discovered she knew the truth about him.

She would flee to Castle Lacey.

Chapter 32

Nic had found Olivia missing in the morning. No one seemed to know where she'd gone. Perhaps she was cross with him for leaving her last night, but it wasn't in her nature to be vindictive. Still, he searched for her in the few likely places, even at Esmeralda's shop. No one had seen her.

By the time he returned to Mayfair he was worried. As he rounded the corner he saw a coach pulling away from in front of his house—the Lacey coach—and Abbot standing bereft on the footpath. He kicked his horse into a gallop and caught up with it as they reached the busy main thoroughfare, riding alongside in what was a highly dangerous and risky manner.

He could see Olivia inside, her face white, her eyes blazing back at him, and beside her was Estelle, looking equally pale but forlorn. There was a shout of warning, and when he looked up he saw a cart bearing down on him. In that split second he knew he could either hold his line and have an accident, or drop back and live to fight another day. Nic dropped back, ignoring the cursing of the cart driver, and watched his coach disappear.

He knew where they were going. Home to Bassingthorpe. Olivia was leaving him. And there could be only one reason that she would do that.

She knew about Sarah.

Slowly he turned his horse and rode back to the Mayfair house. Abbot was still standing there, his face solemn and his gray eyes suspiciously bright.

"My lord," he said, "I'm sorry but I couldn't stop her. Nothing could have stopped her. As I told you before, she is a very determined young lady." He paused, grimacing. "And now I find my own wife is equally determined."

Nic dismounted, handing the reins to the servant who'd hurried from the house. "How did she find out?" he said bleakly.

Abbot didn't bother to ask what he meant. "Estelle told her where the, eh, household was situated. It seems she went visiting this morning, my lord. As soon as she returned she began to pack. I have never seen a lady gather her luggage together so quickly. It was . . . truly amazing. I tried to stop her but . . . what could I do? I wanted to send word to you, my lord, but I didn't know where you'd gone. When I—I—"

"Yes, yes, Abbot, take a deep breath."

Abbot did. "My apologies, my lord."

"Estelle told her about Sarah. Who told Estelle?" he said, narrowed eyes fixed on his manservant.

"I did, my lord." Abbot's shoulders slumped. "I will leave immediately."

Nic was tempted to take him at his word, but Abbot had been with him a very long time, and frankly he didn't know what he'd do without his craggy-faced manservant. Who would tell him the truth and pull him up when he was acting childishly? Who would have the courage to approach him when he was in one of his bad tempers? Who would comfort him if Olivia refused to have him back? No, Abbot must stay.

"Don't be ridiculous, Abbot," he said. "I need you, you're staying."

Abbot blinked, and then bowed his acquiescence. "Eh, yes, my lord."

"We have to return to Castle Lacey, but first I will visit Jonah and his mother. See to the packing and so on. We'll set off as soon as I get back."

"You can rely on me, my lord."

"I know I can, Abbot. That's why I need you. Thank you."

He remounted his horse and rode off, leaving Abbot staring after his master, openmouthed.

As Olivia had expected, Castle Lacey was empty apart from a skeleton staff of servants. Estelle said little during the journey, but Olivia didn't mind that—she didn't want to talk. She'd tried to sleep but kept waking up suddenly and wondering where she was, and then she'd remember all over again.

She asked herself how she was going to bear it. Because each time she remembered, it hurt a little more. She loved Nic . . . she *had* loved Nic. She'd thought she had everything she wanted—with a single-minded determination she'd pursued her dream. Dominic Lacey loved her and she'd truly believed that, but now she wondered how she could have been so deluded. If he truly loved her, how could he have lied to her about this?

Her parents had lied, too, but somehow she could accept their need for respectability and the success of her father's business. They lived in a world where Sarah's fall from grace would be worse than her death.

Nic's lies were worse.

Eventually the coach reached the castle and started up the long drive, rumbling slowly past the gatehouse. Olivia didn't want to talk with Lady Lacey, she didn't want to talk with anyone, and as soon as they drew to a stop, she rushed inside and up the grand staircase to her rooms, and closed the door.

Most of the second-story east wing rooms were hers, as well as the east tower. Traditionally they always belonged to the bride of the current Lord Lacey, and were elegantly furnished and decorated. Olivia had loved them on first sight, and now she felt her shoulders relax and her breathing slow as she made her way to the narrow stone stairs that led up to the tower room.

The first time Nic had shown her this room they'd spoken about it.

"Many Lady Laceys have sat up here bemoaning their fate, or else watching for their lovers," he'd told her, smiling.

"Why not watching for their husbands? Surely some of these ladies were happily married, Nic?"

He smiled. "A very few, my romantic Olivia."

"Well, if I sit here, I promise you, it will be to watch for you."

"As long as you watch for me, I will come home to you," he'd said, and he'd kissed her.

At the time the words lodged in her heart, warming her. Now, remembering them, tears stung her eyes and she blinked furiously, determined not to weep again. She'd shed enough tears over Wicked Nic; it was time she thought of herself.

The tower room was furnished as a sitting room, and there was a window seat groaning with cushions and bolsters. Olivia sat down, cuddling among them, drawing a warm rug about her. Outside the small glass panes the estate spread out before her, and she could see the rooftops of Bassingthorpe and the blunt tower of the church where she had been married. Her childhood home wasn't visible, the trees of the woods hid it from view, but she knew where it was.

Emotion swelled within her, threatening to burst out, and she clenched her fists to hold it in. Everything she'd believed in was a lie. She felt as if the family portrait she'd been treasuring all these years had suddenly peeled and cracked and now showed a completely different group of people in a foreign world.

Now Olivia remembered her wish to live her life to the full, as if it was the desire of another woman, someone she hardly knew. Well, she'd had her wish. The trouble was, try as she might to regret the days and weeks and months spent with Nic, she couldn't.

He might have torn out her heart, but she loved him still.

Suddenly the emotions she'd been holding in overwhelmed her, and she crumpled against the silken cushions, weeping uncontrollably, her shoulders shaking and her chest heaving. Olivia cried until she was exhausted, and then, at last, she slept.

Estelle had shed a great many tears on the journey home, stifling her sobs in the folds of her wool cloak. She was drained now. She went about her tasks without a word, putting away Lady Lacey's clothing and sorting through the garments needing cleaning.

Olivia was upstairs in the tower room. Estelle had peeped in on her, and seen her mistress curled up on the window seat, asleep, her fingers curled beneath her pale, tearstained cheek. She looked so alone, so lost.

Estelle knew this was all her fault. If she hadn't been so desperate to arrange other people's lives to suit herself, she'd never have pushed Olivia into marrying Lord Lacey. Now everything was such a mess, and she and Abbot were separated again. Estelle could see them spending the rest of their lives in different households while their employers feuded. The old Lady Lacey hadn't spoken to her son for nine years until recently—who was to say the same thing couldn't happen with Olivia and Nic?

When Estelle heard the clatter of horse's hooves approaching, she looked out of the window without much interest. It was only when she recognized Nic hastily dismounting that she understood, with a lurch of her heart, that perhaps all was not lost.

Olivia awoke with a start. She sat up, bleary-eyed, her tangled hair over her face, trying to remember where she was. It came back to her soon enough, and with it the now familiar ache in her chest. She pushed her hair back and stood up. Her dress was creased and crumpled, and even though her appearance suited her current frame of mind, she knew she should change. Perhaps take a hot bath first . . .

Then she heard voices below in her rooms. Olivia went still, listening, as the sounds drifted up the stone steps into the tower. Estelle's high-pitched tones and a deeper, masculine voice. Nic.

He'd followed her!

Her first response was a sense of overwhelming joy, followed by deepest despair. She couldn't see him; she didn't want to. She still hadn't come to terms with the shocking truths she'd discovered. Sarah's pale face and soft voice were in her head, and it would seem like a betrayal of her sister if she were to listen to Nic's excuses.

She whirled around, trying to see a way out, but there was none. As she stood, expecting any moment to be found, she realized the voices were fading. Slowly, cautiously, Olivia began to descend the steps, one hand on the cold wall, her heart thumping like a steam train in motion.

By the time she reached the bottom of the narrow stairs the voices were gone completely, and the rooms below were empty. Hurriedly she ran to the door and peered out. Nothing. Estelle, bless her, must have led Nic away. With luck he'd climb upon his horse and ride off again.

Olivia headed toward the curving staircase and down into the baronial hall, where the walls were covered in savage-looking weapons and the heads of long-dead animals. It wasn't until she paused before the portrait of one of Nic's ancestors that she heard the voices again, this time drawing closer.

She looked about, trying to decide which way to go, but there was nowhere to hide in this vast, open space. Just then Nic appeared through a doorway, coming from the library.

He saw her.

His face lit up, his eyes gleaming, and suddenly she felt like one of the heads on the wall.

Olivia took off at a run, circumnavigating furniture, setting a fern on a plinth wobbling dangerously. When she glanced over her shoulder she could see Nic was behind her, and gaining. Ahead of her was the front door, an openmouthed servant standing by it. Olivia brushed by him and flung the door open, catapulting out into the chilly day, taking the stairs two at a time, and taking off across the gravel drive toward the safety of the gardens.

At least out here there would be plenty of places to hide.

You're a coward, Olivia Lacey, she told herself, but she didn't care. Nic had a way of persuading her to his point of view, and she wanted to sort out her thoughts for herself. She no longer trusted him to tell her the truth, only what was in his own best interests.

"Olivia!" he called out, both anger and desperation in his voice. "Olivia, *please . . .*"

But Olivia ignored him and kept on running.

Chapter 33

Nic had lost her.

He'd seen a glimpse of Olivia in the orangery and after that she'd vanished. He knew she was there, somewhere, but with so many nooks and crannies to hide in, he could search all day and never find her.

Why had she run?

When he'd come upon Estelle, she'd told him Olivia was downstairs somewhere. Now he knew she was lying, drawing him away from his wife so that she had a chance to escape. Was he such a monster that she couldn't even speak to him? He'd hoped for a chance to explain, but it seemed she didn't even want to allow him that much.

In his heart Nic couldn't blame her.

From where she was standing his failure to tell her the truth must look like a terrible betrayal. An unforgivable betrayal.

He tightened his lips and kept going, peering around hedges and under shrubs. Nic wasn't going to give up. He was certain that if he could only speak to her, look into her eyes, he would be able to begin to mend matters between them. Not completely, perhaps, and not immediately, but he could make a beginning.

He loved her. He couldn't live without her. Nothing mattered when it came to that, not his pride or keeping his awful secret or the fact that she might no longer want anything to do with him.

Olivia sat on the edge of the fishpond and trailed her fingers in the water. Nic had probably given up looking for her and was waiting for her inside the house. She knew she'd have to go back eventually; it was ridiculous to keep running away from the inevitable. At some point she would have to listen to what her husband had to say, she just wished it was later, when she'd had a chance to sort out her own feelings and compose her reply.

The clop of horses' hooves and a rumbling of wheels heralded the arrival of a vehicle. Nic had probably ridden ahead of the carriage, and now it had arrived with Abbot and the remaining luggage from the house in Mayfair. At least Estelle would be happy again; she'd been as miserable as Olivia ever since they left London.

Poor Estelle. Olivia felt a niggle of guilt, remembering how happy the maid had been when Olivia married Nic, and she knew that she and Abbot could at last be together. Perhaps Nic would allow Abbot to stay with Olivia? More likely, she thought darkly, he'd refuse to let Abbot go, forcing them to remain apart. At the moment she would believe him capable of any malice.

She left the pond and began making her way down the long walk toward the ruin of the old castle wall. Over by the rose garden she could see a woman in a black dress and bonnet, stooping to inspect the denuded stems. Lady Lacey was about, and Olivia didn't want to run into her and have to explain, so at the end of the walk she turned to her left, quickening her pace as she followed the old wall, intending to return to the house the long way.

Nic stepped around a perennial border and stood in her path. He was still twenty yards away but there was nowhere for her to go apart from back the way she'd come. She glanced behind her. Lady Lacey was strolling up from the rose garden, heading in her direction. Olivia turned back to Nic.

He looked dangerous, and intent on capturing her. His smiling mouth was a hard line, and his dark eyes were narrowed and fixed on hers.

"Olivia, come here," he said, and it was an order.

Olivia had no intention of coming willingly to a treacherous man who had betrayed her and lied to her and made her life a misery. She turned again, this time toward the wall, and looked up at the top of it. There were some flowering vines growing along and through the old stones, and there were plenty of hand and toe holds, for anyone crazy enough to want to climb it.

"Olivia!"

Too late, she thought triumphantly. Nic him-

self had told her about the times he and his
father climbed this wall. If he could do it, then
so could she. She put her hand up and gripped
the age-smoothed corner of one of the blocks
and, dragging her skirts out of the way, stuck her
slipper into a gap between two smaller stones.
She began to haul herself up, concentrating on
getting high enough, so that by the time Nic
reached her, he wouldn't be able to pull her back
down again.

"What the devil . . . Olivia, come down at
once!"

Nic's shout was loud enough to be heard in
Bassingthorpe itself, but again Olivia ignored
him. Her skirts tangled about her legs and she
reached down with one hand to pull them out of
the way, allowing herself free movement as she
climbed. A quick glance at the wall stretching
above her showed she'd made surprisingly good
progress—of course, climbing like this was a dangerous thing to do, but she couldn't think about
that now.

She just wanted to get away from him.

"Olivia, what on earth do you think you're
doing?" It was Lady Lacey, her haughty tones as
rich as plum pudding. "Dominic, get her down at
once."

"I would if I could, Mother," Nic said between
gritted teeth.

Olivia ignored them, searching with her hands
and fingers for the next ledge, stepping up with
her abused slippers. Another step up, another

ledge. It wasn't so difficult, she told herself, and made the mistake of glancing down.

Her head spun dizzily as she saw how far she had now come. Lady Lacey's pale face gazed up at her, fear in her eyes, while Nic was glowering as if he'd like to strangle her. Olivia gulped and pressed her body hard to the wall, wishing she could squeeze inside it. Her fingers and knuckles were already bleeding, but she didn't care. She felt light-headed from the height and the need to escape Nic, but Olivia knew she had no choice but to go on.

Slowly, heart in her mouth, Olivia began to climb once more.

Nic wanted to curse her and stamp about, but he knew that although that might help him to feel better it wouldn't achieve anything. Besides, his mother was there now, and if he remembered rightly she didn't appreciate bad behavior.

But when he saw her begin climbing the wall he thought his heart might stop, so afraid was he she'd fall, but as she climbed higher he saw how nimble and quick she was. Not that she couldn't still fall. He needed to get her down.

"Olivia!" he shouted, looking up at her bright skirts and white petticoats, her legs and arms outstretched as she clung on.

"Why is she doing this?" his mother wailed—he'd never heard her wail before. "She knows you fell from this wall? That was how you broke your leg, Dominic."

"She knows," he said grimly.

"Then why . . . ? I don't understand."

"Olivia!" he roared.

She stopped and glanced down. Her face looked pale but he couldn't really see her expression. She released one hand and tucked her hair out of her eyes. "Please don't distract me," she called down primly.

"Distract you!" he blazed. "What the devil do you think you're doing?"

"I want to see the view," she said blithely. "You said it was magnificent."

For a moment he was speechless. "You're risking your life for the view?" he choked.

"Why not?" she said. "What else should I do? I suppose I could sit and wring my hands."

"Don't be so bloody melodramatic!" he growled.

"You lied to me," she replied, her voice like ice.

"Olivia, please . . ."

She looked away from him, back at the top of the wall, and then began to climb again. Another couple of steps and she clamped one hand over the top, then the other, and soon afterward she'd pulled herself up and was sitting astride the wall, her feet dangling either side. Olivia peered down at him, her bright hair silhouetted against the gray sky.

"Go away, Nic," she called breathlessly. "I have nothing to say to you."

"What does she mean, you lied?" Lady Lacey interrupted.

"Not now, Mother."

"If you won't tell me, Dominic, then go up and get her down."

Nic hadn't climbed since he fell and broke his leg—he hadn't wanted to. Now he looked up, gauging the distance and the hand holds of the route he had once known so well he could have climbed it in his sleep.

The memory of the agony when he'd broken his leg was still sharp, and it was difficult to gather any enthusiasm for what he knew he must do. But this was Olivia, his wife, and he loved her. He didn't want to lose her. Climbing up to be with her was probably the only possibility at this point, and he knew he had to do it.

Nic stripped off his jacket and handed it to his mother. She didn't try and dissuade him, but he could see she was worried. Just before he stepped up to the wall, she caught his arm and forced him to look around at her. Her dark eyes searched his.

"Take care, Dominic," she said.

Nic smiled, and then she let him go and he moved to the wall.

His heart was pounding. His hands were sweating. He took a deep breath and, reaching up, began to climb. At first he felt clumsy and out of tune with his body. His leg ached, and at one point his foot slipped, so that he almost did fall. It took him a moment to find his courage again, and to still the thudding of his heart.

As he climbed farther the old rhythm began to

come back to him, while as if by magic his hands went to the correct holds, and his feet slid into the gaps. A feeling of elation came over Nic as he realized that despite his lame leg he was still more than capable of achieving the top. Perhaps he wasn't a cripple after all.

Before he knew it, he was lifting his head and there was Olivia's solemn face, just above and to the right of him, gazing down into his.

"You were right, the view *is* wonderful," she said evenly. "Worth the climb."

She spoke as if he was a stranger, and a not very interesting one. If he'd felt as if he was in a hopeless situation before, then it was worse now. His chest constricted with loss and misery, but he knew he still had to try.

Nic dragged himself onto the top of the wall beside her and swung his leg over the uneven stones, settling himself nearby. His estate lay all around him, the woods and the park and the garden, the gatehouse, and the castle. He could hear his father's voice in his head, telling him what his future held and what sort of man he needed to be to make a good master.

"The land is what counts. The land is what makes us what we are. We must care for the land and all those who live upon it, under our authority, just as we have for hundreds and hundreds of years."

He spoke aloud, remembering. As a boy he'd found the thought of such responsibility daunting, but his father had assured him that with time, and training, his position would become natural to him.

"My father told me that I could mold myself into the kind of man needed to take charge of the Lacey estate. I was his son and he expected great things from me. I idolized him."

He tipped back his head and looked at the sky, feeling the sting of the wind against his face. It looked like it was going to rain, but as much as he wanted to urge Olivia to climb down with him, he had to tell her the truth. It was his only hope for the future he wanted.

Chapter 34

*T*he woman came to the door carrying the baby in her arms and demanding entry. Nic's mother was visiting friends, and only he and his father were there to receive her. Until that moment Nic had no idea that he was about to have the solid foundation of his world rocked beyond repair.

"My father took her into the library. I could hear them talking, and then she was crying. He was comforting her. After a time I couldn't stand it anymore, so I went in to see what was happening.

"He was holding her in his arms. Gently, tenderly, like a lover. When he saw me he didn't let her go. He held her tighter, cradling her face to his shoulder, and stared at me over her head, as if defying me to stop him."

The memory was very clear, even now, and just as painful. "He arranged for the woman and the child to be looked after and sent them off with Abbot. I didn't know what he said, but later on I found out he'd told Abbot the child was mine, and the woman was someone I'd seduced. I suppose it was safer that way, as far as he was concerned."

"Oh, Nic . . ."

"No. Let me finish. I need to finish, Olivia."

He felt her hand, soft and warm, close over his. He felt her strength and her love, and he bowed his head.

"We had a terrible argument, my father and I. In the library. I shouted at him. I said unforgivable things, but I was so hurt and angry with him. I'd believed him to be perfect and he wasn't. He was begging me not to tell my mother, pleading with me one moment and ordering me the next. At first I refused, but he wore me down, and I suppose I could see the sense in what he said. Why hurt her when it was possible to keep it all a secret? Abbot would never tell, he was completely loyal to the family."

"So you came around to his way of thinking," Olivia said quietly.

"Yes." He looked at her, and her lips trembled into a smile of encouragement. "I left him there in the library. He looked utterly exhausted. I felt as if everything I thought I knew had been turned inside out."

"I felt exactly the same when I saw Sarah."

He turned his hand in hers, grasping her fingers tightly. "I'm sorry. I promised to tell no one the truth. I promised my father I'd let everyone believe Sarah was my lover, and that Jonah was my son. He resembled me anyway."

"You've allowed yourself to be blamed for this, Nic. For a promise to your father ten years ago?"

"For my mother's sake," he corrected her. "It didn't matter that she wouldn't talk to me. Like me, she loved my father beyond reason. If she'd known what he'd done she would have been destroyed. When he died, it was the least I could do to keep my promise to him, and protect his memory."

"You should have told me," she said, and she was angry and upset. "Sarah is my sister and I thought she was dead."

Nic put his palm against her cheek, feeling the tears. As he'd been speaking she'd been crying, mourning for him and his father and her sister.

"I should have told you," he murmured, "but how could I? What would you have done if I had?"

Olivia stared back at him. "I would have asked why I was lied to."

"Of course you would have. And if I'd then gone on to tell you that my father was Jonah's father and not me?"

"I . . . I don't know."

"Could you have kept silent? My mother"—and he glanced down to where she was standing, waiting anxiously, below them. "My mother would find out. I wanted to tell you, Olivia, but I had to be careful."

"But you took the blame, Nic!"

He shrugged, dismissing it, but she wouldn't be stopped.

"It changed you, Nic. You weren't able to live your life as you wanted to."

He grinned. "I've led a very good life, Olivia. A very diverse life."

She shook her head, refusing to be pacified. "You sacrificed yourself to your father's conscience, to save him. He should never have asked that, Nic, and you should never have agreed."

"Olivia," he murmured, inching closer. "I can't change the past, but I don't want it to mean nothing. I will continue to let people believe that I am Jonah's father."

Her eyes filled with tears. "Sarah . . ."

"That was your parents' doing. They wanted to pretend she was dead so there was no scandal attached to them or you. And Sarah has suffered, too. The man she loved died and she was left with a young child. I've done what I can but she hasn't been well. You saw for yourself. Sometimes she gets mixed up about the past and the present."

Olivia had seen for herself. The thought of her sister, alone and suffering, was almost too much to bear. She remembered her own childhood and her mother's desperate attempts to keep her from repeating Sarah's mistakes.

"Did my mother and father know about Sarah and your father?"

"Yes. When they discovered the affair they tried to separate them, and then when Sarah was expecting Jonah they sent her away, but she came back. She loved him, Olivia, and I think, in his way, he loved her. I didn't understand that then, or I couldn't understand it. Now that I've lived myself,

I can understand and forgive, even if I don't want to go down that road myself. Not if you'll stay here with me and be my wife, Olivia. I swear"— and he leaned closer, his dark eyes intent—"I will never look at any woman but you."

Olivia wrapped her arms about him, forgetting their precarious position, and rested her cheek against his shoulder. "Nic, I'm sorry I didn't stay to talk to you. I was so upset when I recognized Sarah, and then to think you'd lied to me . . ."

"My fault."

"No, no . . ."

He turned her face and kissed her, lingering. "Let's go down," he said. "It's starting to rain."

Surprised, Olivia looked up. She'd forgotten where they were, so intent had she been on the conversation. With a shaky nod, she allowed Nic to precede her. As she watched him descend, she wondered if she could do it. The climb up had seemed easy in comparison.

But Nic wouldn't allow her to think too long.

"Come on," he said, waiting. "I'll guide your steps."

Olivia took a deep breath and began to clamber down the wall. Nic caught her heel, moving her foot to the gap in the stones, and slowly they climbed lower, Nic showing her the way.

He remembered when his father died and his mother went into mourning. She refused to speak to him, blaming him for what had happened. One evening, after drinking all day, he'd climbed this wall and fallen, breaking his leg.

He'd never climbed the wall again, until now. Olivia had done that.

And at that moment everything seemed to fall into place. The land, his place in the world, and the woman he loved at his side. He looked at her, her glowing face and brilliant eyes, the warm flush in her cheeks. Olivia was his love and his life.

All these years he'd lived in a kind of limbo, never allowing his heart to be engaged, remaining untouched no matter how sensual the excesses he sought out with the women he met. But then Olivia came into his life, and even though he fought it, arguing with himself that she was better off without him, he wanted her.

Perhaps he'd loved her all along.

When she reached the ground at last she seemed surprised to find herself clasped in Lady Lacey's arms, being scolded all the while.

Nic, laughing, led them toward the castle, a woman on each arm. He was making up some tale about having dared Olivia to climb the wall and saying that he'd never thought she would take him up on it.

"My firebrand wife," he murmured, looking at her lovingly.

Lady Lacey began to scold again. "When you fell and broke your leg I thought you might not survive it," she admitted, trembling. "I thought I would lose my husband and my son. We've been at loggerheads for so long, Nic. I don't want that again. Ever."

Nic patted her hand. "I agree. From now on we'll be a proper family."

The rain grew heavier, and they quickened their steps, hurrying up the terrace to where Abbot and Estelle were waiting to dry them and sit them down before the fire and serve them hot tea.

They felt like a proper family, Nic thought, with a smile. A new beginning for the Laceys. And he was looking forward to it.

Chapter 35

Theodore heard the news as he was sitting down to his supper. A poached egg, cooked to perfection. He'd taken only one mouthful when Mrs. Henderson arrived in a flurry. The servant tried to block the way into the dining room, but she ducked around him, arriving breathless at Theodore's side.

"Mr. Garsed!"

Theodore dropped his fork against his plate and snatched the napkin from out of his waistcoat, where he'd tucked it. "Mrs. Henderson, please . . ."

"Lord and Lady Lacey are back from London already. It is very strange. First Lady Lacey arrived in the coach, and then Lord Lacey galloped up on his horse. I did hear"—and she looked behind her as if expecting to see Nic standing there—"from my friend the cook that Lord Lacey was roaring and ranting all around the castle looking for her, and then he hauled her in from the garden. Cook had to make hot tea and crumpets, and then there was a great deal of fuss about hot water being carried upstairs for a bath for Lady Lacey, and fears that she might have caught a chill."

Theodore had stopped protesting, sitting staring at her, with the napkin still crumpled in his hand.

"I haven't told Mrs. Monteith yet, but dear Mr. Garsed, I fear for her daughter. She should never have married that man."

Theodore stared at her with wide eyes in his pale face. Since Olivia had gone away he'd begun to feel almost his old self again. While she wasn't there he could relax and slip back into his old life again, and now she was back and under threat from Lacey.

And Alphonse! Theodore glanced about him wildly, as if expecting his brother to appear in a puff of smoke. He had to get Mrs. Henderson out of the house before Alphonse heard her news.

When he grimaced and pressed his hand to his paunch, it wasn't entirely pretense. "Mrs. Henderson, I beg you will stop. You are giving me indigestion."

But Mrs. Henderson had no intention of stopping. "Of course, my dear Laura would never have put herself in such a position, where she was forced to marry a man like that."

Theodore stood up. "Mrs. Henderson, I am most unwell. Forgive me, but you will have to leave."

The woman blinked at him. "Oh. Well, if you insist . . ."

"I do. I do insist."

"I wouldn't have bothered you, I'm sure, only Mr. Alphonse, your brother, told me to tell you the news. He was most complimentary of my neighborly feeling," she added, preening herself.

Theodore froze, staring at her. "Alphonse?"

"Yes. As soon as I told him he rushed off, but he said I was to come to you and explain. Well, if you want to be alone I will go now. I don't want to stay anywhere I'm not wanted."

He was rude and she wouldn't soon forgive him, but Theodore didn't care. The pain in his stomach was genuine now, and he wanted to lie down. But Alphonse had gone off to do goodness knew what mad act, and Theodore knew it was up to him to put a stop to it.

Theodore accepted he was not a brave man—he might not even be a very good man—but it was time to stand up for what was right.

His decision made, he rang for a cup of peppermint tea to calm his roiling insides, and hastily scribbled a note to be delivered by hand. When that was finished he sat back and closed his eyes.

Olivia might not love him—in fact he knew very well she didn't—but when she discovered what he had done she would have to admire him. He'd saved lives tonight, and that made him a hero.

Alphonse gripped his gun, moving stealthily through the trees. The castle was ahead, a jumble of dark shapes against the stars, while the gatehouse sat vaguely to his left. He'd already made his plan. A diversion outside was needed, to keep the servants busy, while he crept inside and found Lacey.

One good clear shot and then escape, back into the woods, and home to bed. No one would suspect him—why would they?—and Theodore would have a clear run at the rich widow.

Alphonse smiled to himself at the brilliant simplicity of it.

He had the "diversion" in his pocket—a mixture of gunpowder and other combustibles, wrapped in a cloth. Gathering the ingredients had taken a little time after his conversation with Mrs. Henderson, but one spark and it would make a lovely big bang. He thought he might set it off on the terrace.

All his life Alphonse had felt a sense of isolation, of being different, and perhaps that was why he tried so hard to please his brother. Of course, the money would be very pleasant, too.

With a smile, he left the trees and moved like a shadow toward the castle.

"Stop! You there, stop or I'll stop ye for good!"

The Scots voice was closer than he could have believed. How the hell did Wilson the gamekeeper get behind him without his noticing? Or had Wilson been waiting there? Whatever Wilson wanted, Alphonse wasn't about to be stopped this close to his goal. Slowly he turned, a big friendly smile on his face.

"Don't I know you?" the gamekeeper said.

"I don't believe we've been formally introduced," Alphonse retorted.

"You're the brother of Mr. Garsed," Wilson said. His gun lowered slightly, as if being a gentleman meant Alphonse was unlikely to be a dangerous character.

Fool, Alphonse thought, and swiftly brought his own gun to his shoulder.

"No!"

He heard Wilson's shout, became aware of someone else on the other side of him, and then the explosion. Somewhere in his head it occurred to him that he hadn't been as clever as he'd thought, and then the gunpowder in his pocket ignited and blew up, and he knew no more.

"What'll we do now, Mr. Wilson?"

The eyes of his new apprentice were like saucers. Wilson looked back at what used to be Mr. Garsed's brother. Whatever the gentleman had been carrying had certainly done for him, but he couldn't feel sorry. In those last moments it had been clear to Wilson that the note he'd received was no hoax. Alphonse was planning mischief at the very least, and murder at the very most.

"You remember those shots I told you about, in the woods?"

The lad nodded, his eyes even bigger. Of course he remembered. It was Lord Lacey's close call that had got him this job.

"Did this gentleman fire at Lord Lacey?" the lad asked.

"Aye, I believe he did. Who would have thought it, lad? I'll get the gardener to cover this fine fellow up. I think we'll wait till the morning to tell His Lordship," Wilson said. "No need to spoil his evening, eh, lad."

The boy nodded. "Aye." He swallowed, and Wilson noticed he was turning slightly green.

"Come on, lad," he said gruffly. "I'll fetch ye a dram of my best whiskey. That'll settle your stomach."

And he set off back toward his cottage, the lad following.

Chapter 36

Abbot shivered as he climbed into bed beside
Estelle, drawing her soft, warm body against
his with a happy sigh.

"I thought they'd never retire," he said, as Estelle lifted her face for a kiss. "The dowager Lady
Lacey staying for dinner and not leaving until
near eleven o'clock. Unheard of. And then Lord
Lacey insisting I escort her home."

Estelle giggled. "You are indispensable, my
love."

Abbot secretly agreed.

"I'm so glad everything has worked out for the
best. I would have been so miserable without you.
On the journey home I was blaming myself, Abbot,
for being so selfish as to want to marry you and
be with you, and encouraging Olivia in her wild
ways. But now . . . I think I did a good thing."

"Dear Estelle, you may think you are to blame
but I doubt Lady Lacey needed any encouragement from anyone. As I've said a number of times
already, she is a most determined young lady."

"Do you think they'll argue like that again?"

Estelle asked in a worried voice. "Will we be parted again, Abbot?"

Abbot considered her question. "It is possible, although not likely. But we are talking about the Lacey family, and I have learned not to make any predictions where they are concerned."

"Well, I've a prediction for you, Abbot," Estelle said, grimacing in pain as she took his hand and placed it against her swollen belly. "This will be a very unruly baby."

"Then, my dear," Abbot said with a smile, "he, or she, must take after you."

Nic was brushing his wife's hair. She sat at her dressing table, naked apart from her silk robe, while he stood behind her, drawing the brush slowly through her long, fair locks. The fire crackled behind them, and the only other light was from a candelabra.

"Do you remember when I told you I stopped meeting you at the stepping stones because I was bored?" Nic murmured.

"I remember."

"I wasn't bored."

"I didn't think you were."

He laughed.

Olivia arched her neck, as Nic drew the brush through her hair again, intent on the gleam of her golden hair. She watched him in the looking glass, his trousers low on his slim hips, his naked chest gleaming behind her, the muscles in his shoulders and arms moving beneath his skin.

The telling of secrets had brought them closer, and Olivia knew she would never doubt him again. She would have to speak to her parents, but that was a separate issue. For now she and Nic were at perfect peace with each other.

He set down the brush and lifted her hair in his hands, letting it fall through his fingers. His eyes in the mirror met hers, narrowed and gleaming. Her face was flushed, and she was finding it difficult to breathe. He slid one hand down inside her robe and cupped her breast, caressing her soft flesh, circling her nipple with his finger until it went hard.

Nic opened her robe, tugging it over her shoulders, so that she was naked before the mirror. He began to fondle her again, watching her face reflected in the glass. Seeing him doing something so intimate to her, Olivia discovered, increased her desire. Her head fell back, her hair streaming over her shoulders, and her throat arched. He bent his head and began to kiss her warm skin, working his way down to her breasts, licking at her lush curves.

It was too much. Olivia groaned and turned in his arms, just as he lifted her and carried her to the bed. Nic pushed down his trousers, stripping, as he climbed onto the mattress beside her, pressing his naked body to hers, so that it seemed that every inch of them was joined.

Olivia wound her arms about his neck, kissing his lips, enjoying the wondrous sensation of being with the man she loved. When he slid inside her, he moved slowly, taking his time, and his face was solemn.

He's claiming me, she thought. *He's making certain that I know I'm his, just as he is mine.*

Passion rose within her and she clung to him, moving with him, caught up in the perfect moment. And then it was over.

But as Olivia held him, her body trembling from the aftershocks, listening to the heavy beating of his heart, she knew that wasn't true.

It would never be over between them.

Their story was just beginning.

Next month, don't miss these exciting new love stories only from Avon Books

Desire Untamed by Pamela Palmer
They are called Feral Warriors—an elite band of immortals who can change shape at will. Sworn to rid the world of evil, consumed by sorcery and seduction, their wild natures are primed for release. And Kara MacAllister has just realized she is one of them.

Surrender to the Devil by Lorraine Heath
Frannie Darling wants nothing to do with the men who lust for her. She can take care of herself and feels perfectly safe on her own—safe, that is, until *he* strides into her world, and once again it becomes a very dangerous place indeed.

Four Dukes and a Devil by Cathy Maxwell, Elaine Fox, Jeaniene Frost, Sophia Nash, and Tracy Anne Warren
Fall in love with the unpredictable and irresistible dukes (and one dog named Duke). Join five bestselling and award-winning authors for tales of noble danger and devilish desire.

For the Earl's Pleasure by Anne Mallory
They were once cherished companions, until a scandalous secret tore them apart. Now Valerian Rainewood and Abigail Smart are the fiercest of enemies. But when the earl is viciously attacked, Abigail's distress tells her that something still binds her to the wild Rainewood.